END GAME

THE MAN OF WAX SERIES

END GAME

MAN OF WAX TRILOGY, BOOK 3

ROBERT SWARTWOOD

RMS PRESS

www.robertswartwood.com

For my readers—
Thank you for your support, your enthusiasm,
and, most importantly, your patience

The only thing necessary for the triumph
of evil is for good men to do nothing.

—Edmund Burke

Like most Sunday nights, she can't sleep.

Jennifer thinks maybe an extra tablet of Melatonin might help, but she knows it probably won't. Other sleep aids come to mind—the brand-name ones, the more expensive ones—but she doubts those would help either, even if they could afford them.

There is always a sense of anxiety before a Monday. Because it's when the week starts. Not just her week—and her job is stressful enough, for sure, what with all her clients and her cases—but Casey's and Ben's week too.

Laying out Casey's clothes. Packing Casey's lunch. Making sure her daughter has everything she needs for her day at preschool.

Ben, thankfully, is a bit more self-reliant. He can dress himself (except, well, matching colors isn't exactly his strong suit), and he can make his own meals, though oftentimes when he is given full range of the kitchen those meals don't turn out to be the healthiest. Fact is, there isn't much for her to stress about when it comes to Ben's day, but she knows his job is stressful in its own way, and that makes her worry too.

She may be the bread winner in the family (as a public defender she doesn't make a ton of money, but still more than her husband), but that doesn't mean Ben doesn't contribute too. Every dollar counts. Heck, every *penny* counts, if she's being honest, and there are times—dark times, she supposes, when she's feeling most frustrated and anxious about everything going on, especially when it looks like they might not have enough to pay certain monthly bills—that she will wonder what life would be like had she agreed to marry Jeremy and was still in good standing with her father.

But no—those are selfish thoughts, and Jennifer Anderson does not think of herself as a selfish person. Maybe when she was younger, back when she was into drugs and gallivanting around the city. And then, when things became really dark and she didn't think she could handle it anymore, she tried to kill herself, which, when you think about it, is one of the most selfish things a person can do.

Anyway, that's all in her old life—her past life—and what matters now is her new life, the one where she is married to Ben and they have their wonderful daughter Casey, and even though finances are tight at times, they're still content together, still happy.

Except … are they?

Beside her, Ben is already asleep, snoring softly. As the night wears on, his snores will sometimes grow a bit too loud, and she's talked to him more than once about getting some of those strips to put on his nose, but so far he hasn't followed through.

Who knows, she thinks, maybe that's what he spent so much time looking at on the computer in the den with the door closed earlier tonight.

It's a ridiculous thought, yes, but still one that she wants to believe is true. Because otherwise she has a pretty good idea what it is he was doing. A few times she's checked the web browser to confirm her suspicions, but Ben has done a good job of deleting the history, and that is usually when Jennifer starts to wonder if she's making things up in her head.

The truth is, she has no idea what Ben often does in the den. She's walked in on him twice, just to see if she can catch him in the act, but both times he didn't seem to be doing anything untoward, and when she'd crossed the room to view the computer screen she saw that he had been researching various paints.

Which, come on, seems a bit too convenient.

She thinks most likely it's porn, and if that is the case, then so be it, though she just hopes that it's ... well, *appropriate* porn. Stuff that a man Ben's age is legally allowed to look at and nothing that will get him busted by the feds if for some reason they search the computer.

Even though Ben routinely deletes the browsing history—which, again, she doesn't know he does for certain but suspects—she's pretty sure the authorities could still find everything he's looked at if they were to go through the computer, like digital trace evidence or something along those lines.

Then—and here is a thought that keeps her up most nights—maybe he's chatting with somebody else. A married woman, perhaps, or a young college girl. That instead of looking at porn, he's having an affair.

Yes, it is the thought of a possible affair that keeps her up most nights, Jennifer realizes. It's what causes her anxiety. Not worrying about getting Casey ready for the next day, or about her own clients and cases, but that what she believes she's shared with her husband—a solid, loving relationship—is simply a sham, a thing that isn't—

Jennifer pauses her thoughts, her body stiffening.

Did she just hear a noise downstairs?

She listens carefully, trying to seek out any sounds past

Ben's soft snoring, and without thinking she nudges him, just enough to wake him.

His eyes still closed, he smacks his lips, yawns, and murmurs, "What?"

The tension in her whisper surprises her.

"I think someone's in the house."

Ben's eyes snap open. He stares at her in the dark, and then sits up.

"What do you mean?"

"I thought I heard something downstairs."

Ben is silent for a beat, listening to the quiet house, and then he leans over and grabs his glasses off the bedside table. Gets up from the bed with a muted yawn, sleepily shuffles over to the door, opens it silently.

He stands there, listening again to the quiet house, and then slips out into the hallway.

Jennifer holds her breath, counting the seconds in her head, and almost a minute passes—a minute that feels way, way too long—before the door opens and Ben reappears.

"I didn't see anybody," he murmurs as he crawls back into bed, sets his glasses on the bedside table, and pulls the sheet up over him.

Within seconds, he has started snoring again.

Jennifer lies there quietly, again trying to listen past her husband's heavy breathing to the rest of the house.

Outside, a car passes by the on the street, but that's normal even at this time of night.

Maybe it was just in her head. Her head already cluttered with so much other stuff that it makes sense she's become paranoid.

Maybe taking another Melatonin is a good idea, after all. Maybe two more, just to be safe.

She pushes the sheet off and slips out of bed and goes directly to the bathroom. She pulls the Melatonin out of the cabinet, taps two tablets into her palm, and swallows them. Then she's heading back to bed before she shifts direction and veers out into the hallway.

Their house on Cherry Oak Lane isn't large, not like the mansion she once lived in, but it is comfy enough, and she supposes that in the end that's all that matters.

There are only two bedrooms, and she crosses the hallway to the other bedroom to poke her head into Casey's room.

Her daughter is sound asleep, which is good. Casey sometimes wakes up screaming from nightmares, much like Jen sometimes does. Ben often does his best to try to calm them down, but it isn't always easy.

Jennifer enters the room and moves closer to the bed. She stares down at Casey as she did when her daughter was just a baby in her crib.

Her baby girl. Her one and only.

She leans down and softly kisses Casey on the forehead.

Then leans back—thinking that everything is okay, that she will have a conversation with Ben to find out what exactly it is he does in the den and that they'll work it out, that everything will work out—and she turns away to find someone standing behind her in the dark, a tall man wearing all black.

She opens her mouth to scream just as the man reaches out and places a gloved hand over her mouth—

Jennifer jerked awake.

She was breathing heavily, a light sweat beading her forehead. Like she did most times when awaking from a nightmare —and they seemed to have become more frequent in the past week or so—she sat up to check the bed next to hers.

Casey looked to be sound asleep. The simple sheet covering her body. It wasn't really needed—their captors kept their room at a comfortable 69 degrees—but Jennifer had taught her to always cover as much of her body as she could while they were in their room.

Because even though it was just the two of them, that didn't mean they were alone.

There was at least one camera in the room that Jennifer knew about, though she wouldn't be surprised if there were others. At least the camera in the corner near the door wasn't trying to be stealthy. It wasn't hidden, like any number of other cameras might be. Jennifer was told in the early days that there was no camera in the bathroom, which was just off their room, but she wasn't sure if that was true.

The bathroom was tiny, just a toilet and sink and shower, nothing more. She'd spent countless hours going over every square inch, searching for a hidden camera or microphone, and while she hadn't been able to find any, that didn't mean one didn't exist.

Though ... she was pretty sure none did exist. Because that was where she kept the weapon.

Jennifer slipped out of bed. She took a few steps toward Casey, just to make sure her daughter was okay—the bright lights in the ceiling were off since it was night, but still there were soft halogen bulbs set around the room like nightlights—and then she headed straight for the bathroom, ignoring the ever-growing desire to glance over her shoulder at the camera in the corner of the ceiling.

How many days had they been here? How many months? How many years?

Time no longer seemed to exist in this place. There was no clock, not even on the TV. Their captors allowed them to watch any TV show or movie they requested, but that was it.

She still remembered those awful first days—the not knowing, the constant terror, Casey crying nonstop, and then Jennifer being dragged into another room where a man was waiting with a pair of wire cutters—but since then everything had been different. She still wasn't sure who these people were, or why she and Casey had been taken, other than Ben had somehow been involved.

"This is gonna hurt," the man with the wire cutters said with a smile as the other men held her in place. "This is gonna hurt real bad, but just remember it's not me doing this to do you. It's your husband. He's not following the rules of the game, so we need to teach him that following the rules matter. You get me, darling?"

Somehow the man calling her *darling* infuriated her more than the fact that they planned to cut off one of her fingers. It was such a strange, irrational thought that instantly vanished the moment the man applied pressure to the cutters, and then all Jennifer knew in that moment was a white burst of pain.

But since those crazy first days, things had been different. Jennifer was certain that eventually the same man or another man just like him—a man with soulless eyes, a man who got off on causing others pain—would come for them.

By that point, Jennifer didn't care much for herself—she had always been a bit suicidal, so death over whatever these monsters had planned was certainly welcome—but she would be damned if that meant leaving her daughter behind.

It was probably because Casey was so young that she had been the one who adjusted more easily to their captivity, especially once they got into a routine.

Breakfast in the morning, just like always, and then lunch, and then dinner, with activities sprinkled throughout the day. They were even led outside, down a bright white corridor and up an elevator. They were taken to a courtyard, whose walls were at least ten feet high. The courtyard had a swing set and a picnic table and that was about it. They were told that they could have a few hours out here to get some sun and fresh air before they returned to their room. They were told that screaming was useless—which Jennifer certainly did those first couple of visits—as nobody would hear them.

They saw the same people every day, two men and two women with blank faces. From the start they hadn't provided any names, and Jennifer hadn't asked. The men and women brought them food, took their clothes to wash them, brought back the clothes when they brought more food. They hadn't provided any answers to the countless questions that Jennifer asked the first couple of weeks before she realized it wasn't worth wasting her time anymore.

Everything became a routine. Breakfast, lunch, dinner. Watching TV. Going outside. Going to bed.

It was all so numbingly routine until the day there was an extra spoon with their breakfast of cereal and oatmeal.

Jennifer, without thinking, had palmed the extra spoon and hid it under her pillow. She only realized seconds later that maybe it was a trap. That after all this time—had it been a year yet?—their captors had decided to mix things up. She'd panicked, worried that Casey would somehow be the one to take the punishment, and she had considered returning the spoon but then before she knew it the door opened and one of the blank-faced women returned to take away their trays.

The woman hadn't noticed the missing spoon.

Nobody had, apparently.

Jennifer wasn't sure what to do with the extra spoon at first. She found a spot in the bathroom, just behind the toilet, to hide it.

She didn't say a word to Casey, for fear that her daughter might somehow let it slip.

Late at night, after she had one of her several nightmares, she would get up and pad into the bathroom, and she would take the spoon out from behind its hiding spot, and she would stand at the mirror—which she had determined was not a one-way mirror, or had a camera behind it watching her—and she would spend a few seconds quietly dragging the side of the spoon's end against the underside of the sink, enough to start wearing it down.

She did this every other night for weeks. For months. For over a year. Until the spoon no longer resembled a spoon. At least, not on its one end. The spoon part was still there, but the handle ... well, it had become one of those things that people in prison knew all too well.

A shank.

But what was she going to do with it? Jennifer still didn't know. She still worried that it had been a test and not just a random screwup by someone in the kitchen. That all this time —weeks and months and a year later—their captors had been waiting to see what she would do with the spoon, like this were all some elaborate social experiment run by a group of overeager college students.

And then yesterday, when the blank-faced men came for them and took them to another room—a room they had never been in before—and tied their hands behind their backs and put tape over their mouths and then cloth bags over their heads and sat them in chairs, Jennifer was certain that their time was up and now they were going to be killed.

But all she could hear was a man speaking, and a voice speaking back, and the voice that came through a speaker—like a character in a TV show—sounded familiar. Almost too familiar. And it wasn't until the cloth bags were pulled off their heads and Jennifer found herself staring back into bright lights did the realization hit her that the voice belonged to her husband.

"How about now?" the man who'd been talking said behind them, and everything after that was a blur—being marched back to their room, trying to calm Casey who had started crying, and having absolutely no answers for all the questions Casey asked.

Jennifer had worried that their room had been searched

while they were gone, and it had taken everything she had not to enter the bathroom immediately to check the spot behind the toilet. She only did that later in the night, after another one of her nightmares. Slipping out of bed and padding into the bathroom, leaning down, knowing that the spoon would be gone and then issuing a soft sigh of relief the moment her fingers touched the cold metal.

It was then that Jennifer knew what she'd intended on doing with the shank. Unconsciously, she realized, though maybe she had known all along.

Even now, as she entered the bathroom, reached behind the toilet to make sure the spoon was still there, she acknowledged that the purpose was not to protect herself and her daughter from their captors, but instead to put each of them out of their misery. First Casey, in her sleep, and then Jennifer. The blank-faced men and women would find them in the morning, lying in their beds, their sheets soaked with blood.

Jennifer had once believed killing one's self was the ultimate selfish act, but what about when it was to protect your most loved and cherished thing in the world? She couldn't bear to let these monsters do something to her daughter, and every day that passed that worry became more of a reality, the idea that their captors were just waiting until Casey reached the right age, and then terrible things would happen to her.

No, Jennifer would not allow that to happen. Absolutely not. No way she would ever let that happen.

But then there was the new knowledge that Ben was still alive. That the people who had taken them—their captors—wanted Ben to do something.

Whatever that something was, Jennifer didn't know, but it was clear to her now why she and Casey were still alive.

After all these weeks, after all these months, after all these years, they were still hostages.

And Ben … Ben was out there, still trying to get them back.

Her husband. The man she had given up everything to be with. The man who she had worried near the end no longer loved her.

He was out there somewhere. Trying to find them.

She left the spoon where it was and turned to the sink and washed her hands. She returned to bed, pausing briefly over Casey to watch her sleep before slipping back into her bed.

Jennifer had never been religious, but now she offered up a small prayer.

Dear God, she thought. Please let Ben find us. Please let him save us. Please let us wake up from this nightmare.

PART I

DÉJÀ VU

ONE

That morning—the first day the second game officially started —the ringing of a phone woke me.

It was a distant, somewhat familiar noise that dipped its hand into the dark I'd been floating in and abruptly pulled me out.

A moment passed, that was all, just one single moment that allowed me to reorient myself coming out of the forced stupor, and I shot up in bed, reaching for the gun which I always kept under my pillow.

But there was no gun. Of course there wasn't. This wasn't my room. My room had burned with the rest of the farmhouse. What felt like a hundred years ago, when in reality it probably hadn't even been two days.

The phone on the bedside table kept ringing. I didn't reach for it, not yet. I just sat there on the bed, in a pair of boxers that may or may not have been mine, staring at the TV facing me across the room. It was one of those older TVs, before flat screens became all the rage. It looked somehow familiar, just as did the four-drawer dresser underneath it.

I took a moment to scan the room—what was clearly a

motel room, a very *familiar*-looking motel room—and muttered under my breath.

"You've got to be fucking kidding me."

The phone continued to ring, unabated. Like the TV, it looked as if it came from another generation. A period in time where smartphones and computer tablets and YouTube didn't exist. It was a drab off-white, though maybe its coloring was due to years and years of neglect. Take some soap and water to it, and maybe the color of the phone would be something brighter.

I reached over and picked up the phone and placed it to my ear.

Silence on the other end.

I waited, and it was after another second or two that I realized the person who'd called was waiting for me to speak first. To utter my single-word line.

"Hello?"

"Yes, hello," said the voice on the other end, just as exasperated as the voice had been two years ago. "This is your nine o'clock wake-up call."

I said nothing. Didn't want to contribute the follow-up line, which was to echo the part about a wake-up call. Because two years ago, when I'd woken in a room very similar to this one, I hadn't had any idea where I was or what I was doing there or where my wife and daughter had gone. I had become that metaphorical fish out of water, and I had been so lost, so confused, so scared that I couldn't even think straight.

Now, before the person on the other end could disconnect first, I set the phone back in its cradle.

I looked around the room once more. Besides the familiar old TV and dresser, a wooden table stood in front of the closed curtains overlooking what would be the parking lot. Underneath the curtains, the air conditioner kicked on, and cold air started to push its way through the small, musty room.

I stood up from the bed, my bare feet sinking into the shaggy carpet, and I circled over to the table.

Clothes had been placed on top, each expertly folded. A pair of jeans. A plain black T-shirt. White socks. Black leather belt.

Underneath the table on the carpet was a pair of sneakers.

Just like before, an opened bible was on the table. I squinted down at it. Two years ago, the bible had been opened to the Book of Job. Now, all the pages had been turned so it was open to the very last book.

"A little too on the nose," I said for whatever hidden microphone was in the room. No use trying to search them out; the same with the hidden cameras. I wasn't going to be in the room much longer.

I turned away from the table and started toward the rear of the motel room. The bathroom door was closed, just as it had been two years ago.

I opened the door, reached in, and flicked on the light switch.

The fluorescents in the ceiling buzzed to life. These were even brighter than they had been before. I had to look away, give it a moment for my eyes to adjust. Then I stepped forward onto the cold tiles so I could grab the pair of glasses sitting beside the sink.

Two years ago, the strange pair of glasses I'd found in the bathroom hadn't fit me well—they'd been too heavy and pinched around the nose—but they'd been my prescription and that was all that mattered.

Surprisingly—or maybe unsurprisingly—these glasses fit perfectly. And, of course, they were my prescription.

I stared at myself in the mirror, naked except for the boxer shorts. I imagined all the thousands of people who were right this moment switching over to my POV. Part of me wanted to raise my hand, flip them the bird, but another part just wanted to get this over with.

I turned back around. The bathroom door hadn't closed. It was still partway open, so the back of the door wasn't easily seen.

Leaning forward, I used a finger to nudge the door closed, and the message was there on the back of the door just as I'd anticipated.

Before, I'd believed the message on the door was written in dried blood when it really wasn't. Now I didn't care what the message was written in, though it appeared to be just dark red paint.

Even if it wasn't paint—even if it was blood—I didn't care. All I cared about was the message. Simple but direct.

LET THE GAME CONTINUE

TWO

"We're up."

Carver stirred in the wheelchair at the Kid's voice. He didn't realize he'd been dozing until he opened his eyes, lifted his head, remembered where he was. When he spoke, his mouth tasted sour.

"How long?"

"Just a couple of minutes."

The Kid typed at the computer, then leaned back in his large leather office chair so that Carver and Graham and Bae and Chin could see.

On the screen was the black box with an image inside it. The camera was in the ceiling corner of what appeared to be a motel room. Ben was on the bed, still unconscious or asleep; it was difficult to say, and in the end it was basically the same thing. On the bedside table, the phone began to ring.

Carver stared for a long moment, and then shook his head.

"This has to be some kind of joke, right?"

Nobody answered him, not even the Kid who almost always had a comment to make. They watched as Ben awoke, as he answered the phone and then as he stood up from the bed. They watched as he finally made it to the bathroom, and then the Kid flicked over to the player point of view once Ben put on the glasses and turned around and looked at what was on the back of the bathroom door.

Again, nobody said anything. Carver had to glance back at the three men to make sure they were still there. The space in the Kid's basement was tight, what with the eight computers scattered about on different tables, and he typically only had the two office chairs, so they'd needed to bring down some of the wooden chairs from the kitchen table.

Graham had arrived late last night, after driving all the way from Colorado. He'd stayed at the motel with Carver. Initially Carver had shared that room with Ben, but it had only been for one night. Because then they'd gotten the call from the Kid who had been made aware of the message sent out for Ben, and then they'd learned that Caesar hadn't died in all the chaos at the Fillmore after all, and that—even more incredibly—both Ben's wife and daughter were still alive.

"How about now?" Caesar had said after he'd unveiled Jen and Casey Anderson, both of whom Ben had believed dead all this time, especially after he'd *watched* them tortured and killed in that video they'd been sent a month after Ben first woke up at the Paradise Motel.

Carver had known the instant he saw the woman and girl —maybe even an instant before, once he got the sense of what was about to happen—that Ben would do whatever it took to save his family, even if the chances of beating Caesar's game were slim to none. Caesar clearly had something up his sleeve, but there hadn't been any time to try to guess what it was, because Caesar had set a deadline for Ben if he wanted to save his family, which was to wait behind the Smithsonian National Museum of American History at five p.m., and that when a black SUV pulled up along Constitution Avenue, he was to get in, no questions asked.

The Kid had been the only one to try to talk sense into Ben. Carver had known better, just as Ronny had known better. The same with Drew and Beverly and even the new guy Mason. Bae hadn't said anything either, only wished Ben luck before Ben took one of the cars and headed out. If he drove nonstop, he'd make it to Washington D.C. with maybe an hour to spare. There was no telling if he'd even made it, because Caesar had stipulated that Ben come alone without a cell phone or any other communication device. The only confirmation that Ben had made it was when the Kid had managed to find the new game, and so they had all sat in the basement, quiet, waiting for it to start.

Well, not all of them. The others were standing by, ready to head out at a moment's notice. Ronny and Drew and Mason and Bae's daughter Ho Sook. Chin had wanted to go too, but it was clear that four would be more than enough, and besides, they didn't want to waste all their resources. And so for most of the morning they'd been down here in the basement, the carpet an ugly yellowish orange, the walls fake wood, and just waited while the Kid worked on trying to break the encryption on the three laptops that Ben had managed to bring back from the Coliseum.

Now they watched, silently, as Ben quickly dressed with the clothes that had been left on the table and went to the motel door.

He paused a beat, his hand on the knob, before opening it.

Carver held his breath, certain that it couldn't be true, but then bright sunlight flashed into the room and Ben had stepped out and slowly surveyed the sand-speckled parking lot and the few cars that were parked in the spaces, including a familiar-looking old Dodge.

The Kid mumbled under his breath as he reached for one of the disposable cell phones.

"Jesus fucking Christ."

Carver said, "What are you doing?"

"Texting Ronny the location."

"We don't know it's the same place."

"I guaran-fucking-tee you it's the same place. It's what these assholes do. Tell me I'm wrong."

As much as Carver wanted to, he couldn't tell the Kid he was wrong. Still, better to be cautious.

"At the very least, let's wait until he's on the road. If you're right—and I suspect you are—he'll be on the road pretty soon, and once we get confirmation from one of the highway signs, then we're good to go."

The plan was for Ronny and Drew and Mason and Ho Sook to head out wherever Ben was currently located. There was a chance he might wake up in another country, but they didn't think Caesar would do that. In Carver's gut he knew Caesar would keep the game in the United States. After all, Carver was almost certain that that was where Caesar's whole operation was based. That's why the Inner Circle—which included members from all over the world—had come to New York City to meet.

The Kid kept the phone in his lap and watched the screen. The image was still from Ben's POV as he walked across the parking lot toward the office.

Behind them, Bae shifted on the wooden kitchen chair. He had his cane resting between his legs, just like Graham sitting on the chair next to him. Carver, who suspected he would be stuck in this wheelchair for the foreseeable future, figured they all made for a sore sight.

"I thought"—the old Korean paused, as if searching for the words—"you burned it down."

Carver looked at him. He still wasn't sure what to think of the man. He'd heard from Ben what had happened after what went down at the Beachside Hotel—how Bae and his people had tracked them down and had saved their lives from those crooked cops—and while Bae clearly had the same objective as Carver, Carver still wasn't ready to trust the man one hundred percent. Still …

"That's right."

"So they … rebuilt it?"

"Looks that way."

"Why?"

Carver thought about it, and then sighed as he settled back in the wheelchair and turned his attention once more to the computer screen.

"I think we're about to find out."

THREE

The man behind the counter didn't have a scarred face, not like the man from two years ago, but he did have short hair and bright blue eyes that matched his polo shirt.

His name tag said KEVIN, just like the man who had stood behind the counter two years ago, though I had been certain then that that man's name wasn't Kevin just like this man's name wasn't Kevin.

That man—the one from two years ago—had been killed when Carver and his men returned with me to the Paradise Motel to save my family.

This man, I decided, would die in much the same way. But not today. Not until this was over.

He smiled at me as the bell above the door jingled, announcing my arrival.

"Good morning, sir. What can I help you with?"

I glanced around the small manager's office. It was pretty plain—some generic photographs on the wall showing the beach at sunset, though I couldn't remember if they'd been there last time—but overall it looked to be the same.

"What day is it?"

The man's smile faltered a bit.

"I'm sorry, sir?"

"Cut the bullshit. I get it—this game is just like the last one. I have to admit, the details so far are pretty good. Did you guys build this place overnight, or have you been sitting on it for a while?"

The man just stared back at me, his brow wrinkled in confusion. He did a good job looking at a loss for words.

"Seriously," I said, "let's just cut to the chase. What day is it? What state am I in? Do you have a phone or something for me so I can speak to Simon?"

The man whose name tag said KEVIN shook his head cautiously.

"I'm sorry, sir, but I don't think I understand. Who is Simon?"

I stood silent for a beat, my jaw clenched, my hands balled into fists. The easy move was to grab the man by the throat and drag him across the counter where I would continue to beat the living shit out of him. But that wouldn't get me any closer to saving Jen and Casey. This was a game, one I had played before, so I knew the rules, what was expected of me.

"Okay, fine. I don't know where I am. I just woke up and have no idea how I got here."

Somehow the man's brow wrinkled even more.

"Are you serious? You checked in here last night."

The man stared back at me, waiting for me to say my line, and when I didn't, he reached below the counter and shuffled through some papers until he brought up a credit card receipt.

"This is your name, right? I watched you sign it."

The signature actually looked like mine. Which wasn't very impressive as my signature was basically just a scribble. I'd sometimes joked with Jen that I'd missed my calling as a doctor because practically nobody could read my cursive.

A small calendar sat on the counter by the wall. It was turned to Monday.

I tilted my head at the calendar.

"Is today really Monday?"

Kevin just stared back at me. I had the sense he wasn't looking at me so much as the glasses on my face, at the tiny camera hidden in the frames. Right now thousands of people—maybe hundreds of thousands—were watching him. Many no doubt remembered my original game.

The man cleared his throat, and leaned forward as if to share some tantalizing secret.

"To be honest, you looked pretty out of it when you came in. I—well, I thought you might be drunk or something, but I couldn't smell anything on you. You paid with your credit card and then asked me to give you a nine o'clock wake-up call."

My hands, I realized, were still balled at my sides. I let out a deep breath, and then smiled back at the man.

"Do you know what happened to the last guy who played your part?"

Something flickered in the man's eyes. He knew my meaning but didn't want to appear rattled in front of all the viewers.

I said, "Somebody cut his throat. Carver Ellison cut his throat, to be exact. You know, the guy your boss and all the douche bags in the Inner Circle thought they were going to kill. You weren't there that night, were you?"

Again something flickered in the man's eyes. He wanted to break character, probably wanted to grab me by my neck and pull me over to his side of the counter, but again, he was playing a part, he was just a minor player in this entire drama, and he had several bosses above him that would probably kill him if he didn't do what he was told.

"Sir, are you all right? Do you seriously not remember checking in last night?"

I lifted a finger to the side of my neck, drew it across to the other side.

Just like that, I mouthed.

The man with the name tag KEVIN forced a smile.

"Is there anything else, sir? If you don't mind, I need to get back to my duties."

"Yeah," I said. "Give me the phone or whatever it is this time around so I can communicate with Simon."

The man shook his head, and pointed at the door behind me.

"I don't know any Simon, sir, but maybe she can help you."

I glanced over my shoulder and saw the delivery truck gliding into the parking lot. A bit sooner than anticipated, probably, but that was okay.

The sooner this show got rolling, the better.

FOUR

The delivery truck didn't park right in front of the office but instead in front of Room 6. My room.

The Paradise Motel—just like it had been two years ago—was U-shaped, the bottom part of the U facing toward the ocean, the sides hugging the parking lot. The motel offered only ten rooms.

There were three vehicles parked in the lot, just as before. Besides the rusted and paint-flaked Dodge—what I knew I would be driving soon—there were a pickup truck and van.

Despite the fact I wanted to kill each and every person who worked under Caesar, I had to admire their attention to detail.

I approached the delivery truck as the engine died. The driver was a young woman, just like before, and she wore a blue uniform. There was no company logo on her uniform—I didn't remember there being one before—but like that woman from before, she had a plain but somehow pretty face and was chewing bubblegum.

As she stepped out of the truck, handling a plain brown box, she paused and squinted at me.

"Benjamin Anderson?"

I didn't bother with my line. I just took the box from her hands, stepped past her, and headed toward my room.

"Hey!"

I paused to turn back around.

The woman said, "You need to sign for that."

She looked serious, too, like her job was on the line if she didn't get a signature. She reached into the truck, came back out with a small device.

I let her advance five paces toward me before I said, "Go fuck yourself," turned away, and stepped up onto the walkway to let myself into the room.

I set the box on the table, pushed the bible aside, and started working the packing tape with my fingernail. Last time there hadn't been anything in the motel room to help me open the box—not even a cheap pen I could use to score the clear masking tape—so I didn't bother looking.

I heard the delivery truck's engine start up outside as I dug up enough tape to tear it away and then opened the box.

Like before, the thing was full of white Styrofoam peanuts. I tipped the box over, let the peanuts pour out as well as the items inside.

A leather wallet was one of the items. Last time I'd found only five hundred dollars inside, but this time there was a thousand, all in crisp fifty-dollar bills.

Along with the wallet was an overlarge cell phone. I powered it on as I turned to the third item, which gave me pause for the first time since waking up.

It was a ring case, the kind you typically got from a jewelry store. It made me think about the day Jen and I had gone to the jeweler to pick out an engagement ring. By that point we'd discussed marriage, and I'd even asked her father for his permission, though he had refused. Howard Abele had been a mean son of a bitch, who I eventually learned was part of the Inner Circle, and it was because of him that I'd first woken up in the Paradise Motel two years ago, my wife and daughter nowhere in sight.

Since Jen would forever wear the ring—death do us part, right?—I felt it only fair she get a chance to pick out a ring that she actually wanted to wear. I'd never understood the guys who picked out the rings on their own. What if the girl they were asking to marry them hated the setting or even the style of the diamond?

Jen knew I had bought the ring she liked—nothing crazy expensive, though it had been quite a bit of my meager salary —but she didn't know where or when I would propose. There was excitement there. Anticipation. So when the time did come, she was floored.

Of course, it was only a few years later when she and my daughter were abducted, and then I later received her ring finger—including the engagement and white gold wedding band—from a courier. The monsters who oversaw the games had decided I needed to be taught a lesson, and so they had cut off her finger.

That was how they doled out punishments. Instead of physically hurting you, they tortured those you loved.

I blinked, realized I'd been holding my breath. My hesitation was that I would find another body part in this box. Maybe not Jen's this time, but Casey's. God, she wouldn't have even turned six years old by now.

By that point the cell phone had powered on. I expected a call to come through, a new Simon to welcome me to the game. Only the phone didn't ring or buzz.

I set the ring box aside, picked up the phone, and opened it.

There was only one app on the screen. As far as I could tell, there wasn't even a settings app, or a way to make a phone call.

The app was pink, and titled PEEKABOO.

My thumb hovered over the app, ready to tap it, but I

wasn't sure I wanted to see what would happen when I did. Clearly this phone wasn't meant for me to stay in communication with Simon. That, I realized, was what I would find in the ring box.

I set the phone down, picked up the box again, hefted it in my hand. Wasn't very heavy at all. In fact, it weighed next to nothing.

Feeling my stomach start to churn, I flipped open the box.

No body parts, thank God. Instead, it was a tiny earpiece. A note on the inside lid of the box said TWIST TO TURN ON AND THEN INSERT IN RIGHT EAR.

I did as instructed. Twisted the piece slightly, enough for a minuscule green light to flash, and then I inserted it in my right ear. It fit perfectly.

I closed my eyes, took a deep breath.

"Hello, Simon."

There was a beat of silence, and then a familiar voice answered.

"There will be no Simon this time around, Ben. You've graduated past that."

It was Augustus Caesar.

FIVE

"Before we begin, I really should congratulate you. Typically in life there is no restart. Nobody has ever been put back into the game before. They always lost the first game. Or a few would be pulled out on those rare occasions when your friend Carver happened to get involved. Speaking of which, how is Carver?"

I didn't answer. I stuffed the wallet in my pocket, grabbed the cell phone, and started toward the door.

Augustus said, "Come on, Ben, don't be like that. I'm trying to have a friendly conversation with you."

I opened the door, stepped out onto the walkway. Heard the ocean off behind the motel, the traffic on the highway. Smelled the salt in the air.

"I just want to get this over with."

"As do I, Ben. As do I. Before we do, however, I want you to see something."

"What's that?"

"Your family."

My stomach twisted. My legs suddenly went weak. Still, I managed to remain calm, to not alert Augustus that his words had had any effect.

"Where is my family?"

"They're safe."

"Let me talk to them."

"No, Ben, we're not going to play that game. I know Carver taught you to always ask for proof of life, and while it certainly is good advice, I'm not going to be your errand boy."

I gritted my teeth, tried to control my voice from wavering when I spoke next.

"You said you wanted me to see them."

"And I do, Ben. I do. It's why I'm mentioning this now before you get on the road."

My gaze momentarily settled on the beat-up Dodge parked a few spaces away.

"Where am I headed?"

"Soon, Ben. Very soon. But for now, please do me a favor —do yourself a favor—and go back into your room."

"Why?"

Silence.

I swallowed, thinking maybe the connection had dropped from the earpiece but knowing that the silence on his end was a warning not to question him. I waited a couple of seconds, just standing there, and then I turned and entered Room 6.

After I'd closed the door, after I'd stood there in the cold dimness for several seconds, Augustus spoke again.

"Thank you, Ben. As I'm sure you know, the less you question me, the less we'll be forced to hurt your family."

I figured they were going to hurt my family regardless, but that was beside the point. I didn't want to give them an excuse. Didn't want to push their buttons any more than I already had.

"So what do you want me to do?"

"The phone in your hand," he said. "Turn it back on."

I held up the phone, pressed the home button to wake it from sleep. Again, nothing on the screen except for the single Peekaboo app.

Augustus said, "I mentioned how you were the only person who has ever had the opportunity to play the game again. Obviously our games are not traditionally what most players expect. In many games you get several different lives, several different chances. In this game, you only get one."

I said nothing, staring down at the screen.

"We know you care about your family, Ben. That's why you agreed to go back into the game. It's the thing that drives you —that has been driving you these past two years, except for when we made you believe that we'd killed your family, and then I suppose it was revenge that was driving you. Anyway, we know you love your family and we know that you will do anything for them, and it's that drive that we want to keep going. So the app there on your phone—if you press it, you will see your family."

Before he could say anything else, I tapped the Peekaboo app. The entire screen went blank for a second, and then a picture appeared on the screen.

It was a single room. White walls, linoleum floor. Two beds were in frame. On one was Casey, lying on her side, her knees pulled up to her chest. It looked like she'd been crying. Jen sat on the same bed, right beside her, holding her close, whispering to her.

The camera was in the ceiling, angled in the corner. I couldn't see any door. Couldn't see any windows. Couldn't see anything except my wife and my daughter and the two beds.

"Jesus Christ," I whispered.

Suddenly, on the screen, Jen paused. She sat very still, her hand no longer rubbing Casey's back, and then she tilted her face up toward the camera.

"Hello? Who's there?"

I sucked air in between my teeth, at the sudden knowledge that Jen could hear me. That they *both* could hear me. I opened my mouth, ready to tell them it was me, that I was coming to save them, when the picture disappeared.

"What the fuck?"

I went to tap the Peekaboo app again when Augustus said, "I wouldn't do that if I were you."

I paused, my finger right over the screen.

"Why not?"

"We can't give you several different lives in this game—you only get one, just like everybody else—but we can limit how much interaction you have with your family. After some back and forth, we decided three was a reasonable number."

"What are you talking about?"

"You already accessed the app once. It stays up for ten seconds. You can see your family, and you can speak to them, but again, you only get ten seconds before the app closes. If you want to launch the app again, go right ahead, but then that will be your second time, and after ten seconds, the app will close, and you'll only have one more opportunity to interact with them."

"What happens after the third time I use the app?"

"The entire phone will shut down. You'll no longer have access to your family. Unless, of course, you manage to win the game. Though be honest with me, Ben: just how realistic do you think that is?"

I didn't answer. Just stood there staring down at the phone. My finger right over the Peekaboo app. I wanted nothing more than to tap it again, see my family if even for just another ten seconds, but I knew I needed to have patience. To space out how often I used the app. It would drive me crazy, but like Augustus said, it would also keep me driven.

I wet my lips, cleared my throat.

"How many viewers does this game have right now?"

"The last numbers I saw were one point two million. That's

worldwide. It's the highest viewership we've ever had for a single game. You should feel honored."

"There are that many people in the Inner Circle?"

"Don't worry about the Inner Circle, Ben. Worry about yourself. And your family."

"I can't believe you rebuilt this place."

"Don't feel too special. My people rebuilt it six months ago. Room 6 is the only room that's actually completed. The rest of the rooms are hollow."

"Is that Dodge outside for me?"

"Of course it is. The key is under the seat, just like last time. We've tried our best to replicate everything from your original game. The Dodge even has almost eighty-seven thousand miles on it. Three quarters of a tank of gas. But don't worry, Ben, there is no body, living or dead, in the trunk, though I'm sure you'll check anyway."

"Is there a gun in the glove box?"

I heard the smile in Augustus' voice when he said, "Of course."

"The bible was a nice touch, by the way. The Book of Revelations. Very ominous."

"Thank you."

"The calendar in the manager's office said it was Monday. That true?"

"Sadly, no. We may be powerful, but we're not powerful enough to change the days of the week. The calendar simply replicates what you saw on that first morning of your first game. No, today is Friday. It hasn't even been twenty-four hours since you got into that SUV in Washington. As you remember, you were given a sedative, and once you were knocked out, we flew you here. We didn't want to waste any time. Now, Ben, why don't we get the show on the road?"

I stared down at the phone again, tempted to tap the Peek-aboo app just one more time. But no, not yet.

Slipping the phone into my pocket, I opened the door and stepped back out onto the walkway.

"Which direction am I headed?"

"Come on, Ben. Do you even need to ask? We're starting this game just like your last. Head south."

SIX

Mason sat on the bed, his back against the headboard, and held his wife.

She had been crying for a while now—she'd been crying off and on ever since they arrived in this piece of shit motel—and Mason had felt like a complete failure because he didn't know what to say or do to try to make things right.

Because, well, there was nothing to say or do. Their son was dead. He'd been tortured before he died, tortured like he was nothing, just a piece of meat, and if Mason had been a better father—a better goddamned man—he might have managed to save Anthony before it was too late.

Now, Anthony was buried in the Kid's backyard, like a family fucking pet, and Mason hated it because his son deserved so much more. Anthony deserved an actual funeral. A suit to wear in the casket. Fuck, his son deserved an actual casket, instead of having been wrapped in plastic before being buried in the dirt.

A tear rolled down Mason's cheek. He wiped it away quickly, like he was afraid somebody might see. That was how he'd been conditioned when he was in prison—never let them see you sweat, most definitely never let them see you cry—and he felt ashamed because there was nothing wrong about a father crying over his dead son.

Except that a father should never cry over his dead son. A son should bury his father, not the other way around. Especially after that son had been tortured to death.

Another tear fell down his cheek. Mason instinctively went to wipe this one away too but managed to catch himself.

Fuck it, he thought. Let the tears come.

Gloria shifted on the bed, tilting her face to look up at him. She opened her mouth, meaning to speak, but of course she couldn't. Not without her tongue. The sick bastards had done that to her, just as they'd tortured their boy. They'd cut out her tongue for no other reason than to be cruel. Because they thought it was fun.

"It's okay."

Mason forced a smile because he wasn't sure what else to say to her. He saw the concern in her face. Or was it something else? Gloria was in so much pain it was impossible to say. Beverly had been checking on her every hour, giving her medicine when needed. The girl who worked for the Kid—the one who took care of the Kid's mom—had managed to get some medication. Mason realized he wasn't even certain what drug it was, only that it seemed to help numb the pain. Which was good. The last thing Mason wanted was for his wife to be in pain.

Gloria kept watching him, the concern in her face deepening. Mason didn't know what else to do so he leaned down and kissed her forehead. He wanted to tell her just how much he loved her, but he'd been doing that the past five days, whenever he got the chance, and he worried that by saying it too much it would somehow lose its meaning.

Oh, fuck it.

"I love you."

Gloria's mouth twitched. That was her way of smiling, though he couldn't be sure. At one time he'd known every part of his wife's body—every curve, every freckle—but now her body had become an undiscovered world. It had been bruised and battered so badly he had barely recognized it the one time he'd seen her naked, right before Beverly helped her into the tub to give her a bath. The sight had horrified him, and the knowledge that her body now horrified him made him terribly ashamed of himself.

Eventually, Mason knew, he would come to get used to the sight of his wife's body, and that alone made him want to rage. Not because it was no longer flawless—he would love Gloria no matter what happened to her, no matter how she looked— but because of what had been done to her.

The motherfuckers who did this to her were going to pay more than those motherfuckers back at the Fillmore had paid.

There was a soft knock at the door.

Mason's hand immediately went for the FNX-45 lying on the bedside table. He knew it was probably Ronny or Drew or one of the Koreans, but that didn't mean he wasn't going to be safe.

He slipped off the bed, the pistol in hand, and crossed over to the door. Glanced through the peephole, then opened the door.

Ronny was standing there in jeans and a T-shirt. His left arm was still wrapped because he'd been grazed in the shootout at the Fillmore. He still looked weird without his beard. Of course, Mason had barely known him two weeks, but still the man felt like family to him.

Ronny glanced past Mason at Gloria on the bed before shooting Mason a worried look.

"How is she?"

He whispered the question, though they appeared to be the only ones out on the walkway. There were a few cars in the parking lot, and the housekeeper's cart was outside one of the rooms, but that was it.

Mason slipped the FNX-45 in the waistband of his jeans. He stepped out onto the walkway, softly closing the door behind him. He waited until it clicked shut before speaking, his voice just as low as Ronny's.

"Well?"

Ronny nodded, and gestured at the van down in the parking lot. Mason now saw Drew was in the passenger seat, and it looked like the Korean girl was in the back.

"Just got confirmation from the Kid. Ben's game has already started. It looks like he woke up in the same place he did last time."

"California?"

"Yep. Smith River. He's already been on the road for a half hour. The Kid confirmed his location by the highway signs."

Mason released a deep breath. He'd been expecting this to happen. After all, that was what the plan had been, though there hadn't been much discussion. Once Ben learned his family was still alive, he wasn't going to be talked out of going. Mason didn't blame him.

Still, part of Mason didn't want to leave, not with Gloria in such bad shape. Beverly would look after his wife, so he knew she would be in good hands, but still.

Then again, another part of Mason wanted to make every single person associated with the Inner Circle pay for what they'd done, so he couldn't just stay here and feel bad for himself either.

The plan was to catch up with Ben. The Kid was spending a fortune to use the same pilot he'd used back in Florida to fly them wherever they needed to go. They'd head out to where Ben was, and then follow him. Not too close, as they didn't want to risk being seen by any escorts, but close enough that they could intervene if and when the time came to give Ben backup.

At this point, there was nothing else they *could* do.

The door in the next room opened, and Beverly stepped out. Ronny smiled at her, and she smiled back. Mason was pretty sure they had something going on but didn't know the whole story and right now didn't quite care.

Beverly said, "I'm going to take good care of her."

Mason nodded, suddenly worried another tear might roll down his cheek.

"I know you will. Let me say goodbye."

He went back into the room. The lamp beside the bed was lit, making it easy to see that Gloria had fallen asleep. Still he approached, quietly, and stared down at his wife for a long moment. He thought about waking her but knew he should let her rest, so he leaned down and softly brushed his lips against her forehead.

"I'll be back, baby. I promise."

Mason kept his promises. Which was why he added:

"And I promise I'm gonna make those motherfuckers pay."

SEVEN

"How are we doing, Ben?"

It had just been a little over an hour and a half since I'd left the Paradise Motel before Augustus Caesar's voice spoke again in my ear. I'd been so focused on driving that I'd almost forgotten the earpiece nestled in my ear. Hearing him now surprised me, but I didn't react, knowing that there were probably at least two cameras situated around the Dodge so that viewers could watch me drive because apparently that was what they considered entertainment.

I'd driven through Redwood National Park, had just passed Clam Beach, the Pacific Ocean spread out endlessly on my right, and both my hands were on the steering wheel, tight, like I was strangling the thing.

"Ben, can you hear me?"

I tightened my jaw, took a deep breath.

"Yeah, I can hear you."

"Then I ask that you don't make me repeat myself. Come now, Ben, this isn't your first rodeo. You know the rules. You are, after all, the Man of Wax. What do you think of that name, by the way? Your Simon was the one who came up with it. From what I understand, he was quite intrigued by what happened to you in college. You know, how you watched a young woman being practically beaten to death but didn't do anything to help her."

"Can I help you with something?"

"I just wanted to say I'm impressed with you so far. If I were a betting man, I would have placed money on you checking in on your family an hour ago, and yet so far you've managed to abstain."

Actually, I'd been tempted to grab the phone at least a dozen times so far and hit the Peekaboo app, but I knew I had to be patient, that I needed to stretch those moments out. This game could last for days, and the last thing I wanted to do was lose the chance at seeing my family.

"Ben, I paid you a compliment."

Augustus, it turned out, was going to be just as annoying as Simon, if not maybe more so. At least Simon had been constrained by the rules of the game. He'd liked to talk a lot, but he had people over top of him. Augustus, however, was the big kahuna. Nobody was going to tell him what to do.

"Thank you," I said, my jaw clenched, because I knew if I didn't say it something might happen to my wife and daughter.

"Are you hungry? During the last game you stopped at a McDonald's along this highway. That McDonald's is still there, by the way. They've actually renovated in the past year. They now have the kiosks where you can order without having to interact with staff. That's what our society has come to, of course. The more technologically advanced we become, the more we try to avoid interacting with other people."

"Is that why you want to change the world? Because people prefer to send text messages than to talk on the phone?"

"Of course not, Ben. Don't be silly. The acceleration of technology has nothing to do with it, though I must say that advancement has made it much more possible for us to fulfill our mission."

"How so?"

A soft chuckle on Augustus' end.

"Nice try, Ben."

"Can you at least give me a hint about the Pax Romana?"

"I've already given you a hint, remember?"

Yes, I did. Augustus had asked me what was the greatest gift the Roman Empire had given the world. I'd answered roads, but he'd smiled and shook his head.

Augustus said, "If you're not going to stop for food, then merge onto 299 east coming up."

I saw the sign for the exit and got into the right lane which looped up into an overpass and then became a new highway.

"Do you recognize the area?"

Not really. Most of my time in the previous game I'd spent driving. Much of it had been mindless, or at least as mindless as one can manage when they're scared out of their wits for themselves and their family. I remembered the Paradise Motel very well, because that was where I had woken up, the first level to this godawful madness. But much of the driving that followed was a blur.

"Well, Ben?"

"No, I don't."

Augustus made a soft noise, like he was debating with himself whether or not to believe me, and then he sighed.

"Well, do you remember who you made a call to around this area two years ago?"

Something in the pit of my stomach soured. Despite sitting in the cramped Dodge for almost two hours, I'd managed it so far without much fuss, but now I suddenly felt uncomfortable, like I needed to move around, to stand and stretch my legs, only I couldn't because my sole purpose right now was to drive.

My answer was so quiet it was almost a whisper.

"Yes."

"Marshall Gibson."

Augustus spoke the name as if he was announcing it to all the viewers, though I didn't think the viewers could hear him. With Simon they hadn't been able to, so it was doubtful they could hear Augustus.

"Yes, Marshall."

"A colleague of yours, if painters refer to themselves as colleagues."

I never thought of Marshall as a colleague, at least not in the technical sense. I'd just thought of him as a friend.

"Imagine how his day started out that morning. He probably had breakfast with his wife. Her name was Lydia, yes? He and Lydia had breakfast—I'd like to imagine blueberry pancakes, drenched in maple syrup—and then poor Marshall kissed his wife on the cheek before heading out to whatever job he had that day. His wife, well, she ... what did she do again?"

I closed my eyes briefly, not wanting to think about Marshall and Lydia Gibson and what had become of them because of me. I spoke again, just as quietly.

"She worked as a radiologist assistant."

"Ah yes, a radiologist assistant. Well, Marshall went to work, Lydia went to work, and that should have been that. Eventually they would have returned home from their respective jobs, briefly told each other about their day, made dinner, watched some TV, maybe video chatted with one of their grandchildren. They had three, you know."

I briefly shut my eyes again. Of course I knew. Marshall had talked about his grandchildren all the time. He may have been twenty years older than me, but when we interacted it had been like we were close friends.

"Is there a point to this?"

A brief silence on Augustus' end, and I realized just how stupid it was to ask that question.

"I'm sorry, I didn't mean to—"

Augustus cut me off.

"Of course there's a point to this, Ben. There's always a point to my stories. Otherwise why would I waste my breath?"

I didn't answer. Knew the question was rhetorical, or at least hoped.

When Augustus spoke next, there was a hint of irritation to his voice.

"Anyway, both of them should still be alive today, video chatting with their grandchildren in the early evenings after work, if it wasn't for one simple phone call. Tell me, Ben, what were you thinking that day? You called Marshall just to … what?"

I opened my mouth but shut it. Wasn't sure what to say.

"It's because of you, Ben—because of you Marshall and his wife later died. And I must say, they didn't die peacefully. It's hard enough to set up a car accident to look legit, but even harder to make it so that the driver and passenger die without much pain. Though, to be honest, it wasn't like we cared much about saving them from any pain."

Augustus paused, as if expecting a round of applause or laughter, but in my ear there was just silence while the Dodge's tires hummed along the highway.

"It looks like you're low on gas. There's a gas station coming up. You may recognize it. After all, unlike that McDonald's I mentioned earlier, this place hasn't been renovated."

If it was in fact the same gas station from two years ago, that meant it was the place Simon had made me shoplift a Snickers bar. Such a simple, easy task, yet at the time it had felt like the hardest thing in the world.

"Let me guess," I said. "You want me to steal a candy bar."

"Maybe. Or maybe I'll tell you to do something a bit more extreme."

Again, that sense of dread in the pit of my stomach.

"Such as?"

"Such as I might tell you to take that gun in the glove box and shoot the clerk in his face."

EIGHT

The gas station just off the highway—the same gas station I'd stopped at two years ago—had six gas pumps. Two of those pumps were currently being used. There were four parking spots in front of the gas station, and only one of those spots was occupied.

I parked beside pump 3 and shut off the Dodge. Climbed out of the car and stretched my legs and back and then headed toward the gas station.

I stepped inside, an electronic sensor on the door emitting two dings, and the first thing that hit me was the frigid air. They must have had the A/C on blast. I glanced around the store, noting the candy aisle was positioned in a way that gave the clerk a good view of all those sugary snacks. Great. If I remembered correctly, it had been that way before, but I had managed to do it without much trouble. Of course, the clerk at the time had been focused on customers so I hadn't needed to worry about him watching me.

A woman was standing at the counter, a tall blonde in her mid-twenties who was purchasing an energy drink and a refill of one of those electronic cigarettes. It looked like the gas station had upgraded in the past two years; they now had the ability to let customers pay with their smartphones and smartwatches, which the woman did now, holding her wrist to the credit card reader until there was a loud *beep* and then the clerk asked if she wanted a receipt.

It was then that I noticed the clerk. An old black man, who looked to be in his mid-sixties. He had short gray hair, just like he'd had the last time I saw him, only the gray mustache was gone. Today he was clean-shaven, or at least it looked like he'd shaved in the past day or so. There was maybe a little stubble on his face, but it was hardly noticeable.

The man's name tag, just like it had read two years ago, said FRANK.

As the woman moved away with her items, Augustus whispered in my ear.

"You recognize him, don't you?"

I didn't answer. Because at that moment Frank had shifted his focus away from the exiting customer to the one who had just entered the icebox that was the gas station.

I stepped forward, reaching into my pocket for the leather wallet, extracting one of the fifty-dollar bills and placing it down on the countertop.

"Fifty on pump three, please."

Frank nodded, punched some numbers on his register, and took the fifty-dollar bill. Because it was a large bill, he used one of those special markers to ensure the bill wasn't counterfeit.

"Did you want a receipt?"

I shook my head, momentarily speechless. It was one thing waking up in the Paradise Motel, but the players had been different, the guy playing Kevin behind the check-in counter and then the woman from the delivery truck snapping her bubblegum. But the man standing here was the very same from two years ago—and he wasn't even part of the game. He was just a regular guy, working to make a buck, and for whatever reason he was still working well into retirement.

Maybe some of the viewers watching now through the camera in my glasses recognized him, but most likely they didn't. To them he was just another regular person, somebody disposable, somebody who didn't matter at all. The kind of person they would abduct and use as collateral in one of their games because to them this man didn't contribute anything to society. He was just another cog in the massive machine, helping to keep things running, and he could easily be replaced.

"No, thanks."

I barely managed the words before I turned and headed back outside where the temperature spiked at least twenty degrees.

A car pulled in as I crossed toward the pumps, a new-looking GMC pickup truck. Despite the four empty parking spots, it happened to pick the spot the blonde woman had vacated less than a minute ago.

As I lifted the pump and inserted it in the gas tank, Augustus spoke again.

"Well, Ben? You didn't answer my question."

I made a quick sweep of the area to see if anybody was nearby. It was one thing to talk to myself in the car—those passing by would just assume I was talking on the phone—but as far as anybody standing nearby could see I wasn't on my phone and didn't even have one of those Bluetooth devices in my ear.

"Yes, I recognize him."

"That man has worked at this gas station for almost seven years. He often works a full forty hours a week, sometimes more, though somehow his bosses manage to screw him out of the overtime. Can you believe that?"

I watched the numbers on the pump as they cycled up and

up, feeling for the first time a rumbling in my stomach. Maybe I should have stopped at that McDonald's. I didn't have much of an appetite right now, but there was no telling just how long this day would last, and I could use all the strength I could get.

"Ben, I asked you a question."

"No, I can't believe it."

Why had I just said that? Of course I could believe it. That was the American Dream, after all, right? Work your ass off every day, earn a pittance, get screwed over by your employer, end up in debt and forced to work well into your golden years.

Augustus continued, that smile in his voice.

"Frank's wife works too. She's a year younger than him. She works at a diner not too far away. As I'm sure you know, waitresses don't make much to begin with, and the tips she gets? They're a joke. The two of them have been married for forty-five years. They have two children, both who almost never call them anymore. Frank's wife had some health issues about a decade ago, and they've struggled with debt ever since."

The numbers started to slow down as the price went past forty-eight dollars.

"Is there a point to this?"

"Of course there is, Ben. Everything I tell you has a point. In regards to this particular point … you do know what's in the glove box."

As the numbers hit fifty dollars and the pump kicked off, I placed the pump back on the handle and then screwed the cap on the gas tank. I glanced around again to make sure nobody was nearby.

"I'm not going to kill him."

"You're being selfish, Ben."

"I won't do it."

"Just hear me out. Frank and his wife … they aren't happy with their lives. They're crushed by debt. Every day, they owe more and more money. Their Social Security hasn't kicked in yet, and even when it does, it still won't be enough. Frank has considered contacting his children and asking them for help, but he's too proud of a man to do that."

I glanced toward the gas station, then out at the highway. All I wanted to do was get back on the road. All I wanted to do was save my family.

"Everybody struggles. It doesn't mean I should kill him."

"Doesn't it, though? Frank has life insurance. It's not a lot, but it's just enough that it would pay off all the debt. Think about it, Ben. You would be doing him a favor in many ways. Do you think this is the life he wants? He's miserable. He just wants it to end. But he can't do it himself as that would make his life insurance void."

"After I steal the Snickers, where am I going next?"

Augustus didn't answer for a beat. Maybe he was pissed I was so quickly dismissing him. Maybe he had gotten so wrapped up in the story he was telling he had started to feel bad himself.

It was doubtful—that Augustus could feel bad about anything—but I also didn't want to discount the idea that it was all just bullshit. Simon had done the same thing to me with a man named Phillip Fagerstrom. He'd been at the Hickory View Retirement Home, along with several other residents and staff, many of whom were killed when a bomb exploded. A bomb which I'd left behind because at the time I'd just thought it was a briefcase. I should have known better. But I'd been scared for my family, set on doing whatever it took to save them, and Simon had told me I could kill Phillip instead, which in retrospect would have at least saved many more lives.

But I hadn't, because I had been a coward then. Now, not so much. But that didn't stop me from remembering how Simon had tried to paint a grotesque picture of Phillip, the kind of story which would make me want to kill him.

So what Augustus had just told me—maybe it was true,

maybe it was bullshit, but in the end it didn't matter, because I wasn't going to kill the man.

I started for the store when Augustus spoke in my ear.

"Take the gun with you."

"I'm not going to kill him."

"You say that now, but maybe you'll change your mind in the next minute. Maybe you'll begin to feel some sympathy for the man who is drowning in debt. Maybe you'll realize that while you might be taking his life, you'll also be helping his wife. If you think about it, Ben, you'll be a hero."

I continued toward the store.

Augustus shouted, "Stop!"

Sucking air in between my teeth, I stopped.

A soft clearing of his throat to compose himself, and then Augustus said, "Take the fucking gun with you, Ben. Don't make me tell you again."

I did another quick scan of the parking lot—the two cars by the pumps when I first arrived were long gone, a new car was at pump 5 and its driver was busy looking at his cell phone as he pumped gas—and then I returned to the Dodge. Opened the door, ducked down inside, opened the glove box, and withdrew the pistol.

It was a Smith & Wesson .38 Special. It was fully loaded, five bullets in the cylinder. I'd already checked before I'd left the Paradise Motel to see whether they were loaded with real ammunition or blanks.

Each cylinder contained a live round.

I backed out of the Dodge, stuffing the pistol in the waistband of my jeans and trying my best to hide it with my T-shirt, though I knew the weapon made a very noticeable bulge.

But that was okay, as I was going to be in and out of the store in less than ten seconds.

The electronic sensor above the door dinged twice when I entered again. Frank was still behind the counter, looking bored, or maybe he was just miserable with his life and this job and everything else in the world that had beat him down.

I went straight for the candy aisle. Grabbed one of the Snickers out of its cardboard tray. Held it up as I turned and started back toward the door.

"Sorry, Frank, but I'm stealing this."

I didn't look at him when I said it, still ashamed by the action but at least wanting to be up front with my intention. I kept my focus on the door, on the Dodge parked outside by the gas pumps, and I had taken only four steps when a commanding voice that didn't belong to Frank spoke loudly.

"Hey, buddy, stop right there!"

NINE

I paused for a beat, still staring out through the glass door at the Dodge. Then my gaze shifted to the pickup truck parked right in front of the gas station. Its driver was the one who had just spoken.

I started walking again, only seven more feet away from the door, and the pickup truck driver spoke again, more bite in his tone.

"I am a police officer, and I am ordering you to stop!"

I stopped, the Snickers still held up at my side, and shifted slightly to glance back over my shoulder.

The man looked to be in his early forties, clean-cut and lean. He wore khakis and a black polo shirt and on his belt he had his badge clipped to the left side, his service pistol holstered on the right. He held two diet sodas with one hand, and his other hand rested on the butt of his pistol.

I said, "Is this one of yours?"

The man frowned at me, clearly thrown off by the question.

"What did you say?"

In my ear, Augustus said, "I'm afraid not."

I glanced at Frank, who was watching me intently, and then I glanced back at the cop.

"I'm going to leave now."

The cop's eyes hardened. He probably wasn't used to having someone so blatantly disregard a command. Then his eyes shifted to the back of my waistband, and I thought, Oh shit.

The cop spoke again, his voice now even more on edge.

"Are you currently in possession of a firearm?"

I shifted again, so that my back was to the entrance. I still had the Snickers held up at my side.

"You have no idea what you're doing."

This apparently didn't sit well with the cop. Maybe he thought it was a threat. Suddenly his hand was no longer resting on the butt of his pistol; in the space of a second he'd unsnapped the holster and drew the pistol, metal whispering against leather, and aimed the gun at me.

"Put your hands on your head."

I glanced again at Frank, who looked frozen in place. It made me think about Simon and how he'd called me a man of wax, how he'd said everybody was a man or woman of wax in some way, just watching the world go by and not doing anything to change it.

The cop crouched slightly, to drop the two diet sodas to the floor. They were plastic bottles and not apt to break, but he still wanted to be cautious, and this, I realized, might be a good thing. A cautious police officer was much better than a reckless one.

Then again, Deputy Ray Porter had been cautious, too, and it hadn't mattered for him in the end. Like this cop, he'd been in the wrong place at the wrong time. Only Porter had been with his son who watched his father get shot to death by one of Augustus' men.

Having dropped the two diet sodas, the man now stood tall again, holding the pistol in an expert two-hand grip.

"I said put your hands on your head."

Augustus said, "You need to find a way out of this, Ben. We're not bailing you out of jail like last time."

I scanned the interior of the gas station—the racks of snacks, the cold cases of drinks, Frank still frozen behind the counter—but couldn't spot any easy outs. At least not one that didn't result in someone getting hurt. It was one thing to hurt or kill one of Augustus' people, but I didn't want any innocent civilians becoming collateral damage if I could help it.

I asked the cop, "What about the candy bar?"

His eyes didn't leave my face as he answered.

"Drop it."

I waited another beat, running through all the different scenarios, the potential avenues I could take where this man and Frank stayed alive, and then I decided to do what the man said.

I dropped the Snickers—and immediately drew back my foot and kicked the candy bar at the cop's face.

My aim was better than I'd hoped for. The Snickers hit the cop in the forehead, and he flinched, closing his eyes and taking a step back, and that was when I broke for the door, crashing through it as I yanked the .38 from the back of my waistband.

I hurried past the pickup truck, shooting once at the rear tire, and then I sprinted toward the pumps. The driver who'd been looking at his cell phone while he pumped gas hit the ground. He cowered as I approached, his hands on his head, his cell phone cracked on the pavement beside him.

I wanted to tell him not to worry, that I wasn't going to hurt him, but right as I reached the Dodge, the rear window shattered as a single gunshot split the air.

I tore open the door and dove in behind the wheel, staying low as I started up the engine and punched the gas.

The cop fired again, and part of the driver's side mirror

disintegrated, and I jerked the wheel as another car was pulling into the gas station and swerved up over the grass and nearly clipped a telephone pole as I fishtailed out onto the highway.

I took a moment to glance back and saw the cop standing by his pickup truck. He was tracking me with his gun, still holding the weapon in that two-handed grip, but the roadway was busy with traffic, and like I'd hoped, the man was cautious and didn't want to risk innocent lives, especially for a situation he didn't quite understand.

"Not bad," Augustus said calmly in my ear, and I was half-surprised that the earpiece hadn't fallen out in the melee. "I'm impressed, Ben, but unfortunately we weren't able to jam the cell signals at the gas station in time."

Both of my hands were on the wheel now, the revolver having been tossed on the passenger seat, and I was accelerating down the highway, going from fifty to fifty-five to sixty, my eyes darting from the road in front of me to the rearview mirror.

"What are you talking about?"

"It appears your friend Frank managed to call 911 before we could redirect the call. He reported what happened. As we speak, three units are headed in your direction. In fact, one is going to meet up with you in about ten seconds."

TEN

It was seven seconds later that I spotted the approaching police car—this one was an SUV, its roof lights blazing just as the lights in the grill strobed—and it was coming on fast in the opposite lane, probably doing close to sixty just like me, and two seconds later we'd passed each other in a blink but I managed to see the driver whip his head in my direction, and I glanced at the rear mirror in time to watch the driver slam on the brakes and maneuver a wide U-turn.

This wasn't a major highway, only one of those minor ones that was a single lane going each way, and I had to swerve around the slow-moving traffic in front of me, though there were instances—such as when a tractor-trailer was heading in the opposite direction—that I had no choice but to wait a few seconds for it to pass or try to overtake the vehicle in front of me on the right.

The SUV was gaining ground, as were the two units behind it. I was headed back in the direction of the 101, which meant traffic was soon going to become more congested.

"Augustus, you there?"

"I'm here, Ben."

"Any advice?"

"Yes. Don't get caught."

I nearly bit my tongue as I swerved around another car—but a pickup was turning onto the highway out of a strip mall at the same time headed in the opposite direction and I needed to swerve around the truck to the left, the Dodge's tires tearing up gravel, and then the hood clipped a sign and I squeezed the wheel tighter as I jerked it back and steered onto the macadam again.

In my ear, Augustus said, "They're getting closer, Ben."

"No shit."

"At this moment the only three units you need to deal with are those trailing you. They've radioed for additional units and so far we've managed to intercept those but that won't last forever. Word is already starting to spread across social media. A man who had been gassing his car when you came out is already posting live video on Facebook. We're working to delete that very soon, but as you can see, word is getting out, and if you care anything for your wife and daughter, you need to overcome this."

I glanced at the rearview mirror, saw the SUV even closer now, and started to pass another car but had to swerve back as yet another tractor-trailer blew past.

"I'm trying!"

"I know, Ben. I know you're trying. And I appreciate that. Which is why we're going to give you an out. Do you see the giant sign coming up on your left?"

BLACK VALLEY CASINO, the sign read.

"What about it?"

"That's your escape. Park at the door and go inside and head straight for the craps tables."

Another tractor-trailer was heading my way. I could wait for it to pass and then drift into the opposite lane and take the entrance into the casino, but instead I swerved into the oncoming lane and punched the gas to pass the car in front of me—the needle going from seventy to seventy-five to eighty—and heard the tractor-trailer blaring its horn as I jerked the wheel again and narrowly made it back into my own lane, and then at once I steered back into the other lane and tore into the casino parking lot.

My move had confused the SUV's driver, which hadn't been able to make the turn in time, but both of the police cruisers managed to follow me. By that point I had made it to the entrance and slammed on the brakes, and the Dodge skidded forward a few feet before coming to a rest.

Already a valet was approaching, shaking his head with disgust as I climbed out of the car.

"Hey, what do you think you're doing?"

I ignored him as I hurried past him up the steps to the glass entrance doors.

The valet shouted after me, panicked, "Hey, buddy, what the fuck?"

I realized then he'd spotted the gun in my hand. Plus he no doubt saw the two police cruisers speeding toward the entrance —their approaching sirens muffled the Muzak cascading from the outside speakers—and he was putting two and two together.

I hurried inside, once again tucking the .38 into the waist-band of my jeans. Like the gas station, the A/C was on high and the place was frigid, cooling the sweat on my brow. Maybe two dozen people were in the lobby, some checking in for a room, others coming and going from the casino which was off toward the right.

I never made it to the craps tables. The moment I stepped into the casino—all those bright lights and noises buffeting me like a heavy rain—I spotted two security guards coming my way. Both were heavyset and wore dark suits and had earpieces.

Augustus said, "I see them. Now do yourself a favor, Ben:

stand close to the wall right there beside you, and make your-self flat."

I did as he said, pressing myself against the wall while a slot machine dinged manically beside me.

Augustus' voice ticked down a notch.

"Get ready. It'll be any second now."

I could hear the police officers streaming into the lobby. It sounded like at least three of them. The security guards, which had spotted me and were headed in my direction, paused momentarily to swing their attention toward the cops.

That was when the lights went out.

For an instant, there was complete silence—every single slot machine had gone mute—and then somebody cried out "What the hell?" A few nervous chuckles as people waited for the power to come back on, but after a few more seconds the lights remained out, and as there were no windows it was pitch-black.

Augustus whispered, "Why aren't you moving?"

"Where should I go?"

"Back out into the lobby. But don't head toward the entrance doors you came in. I'll direct you to a side exit."

"What about the emergency power?"

"We've delayed the emergency power indefinitely. Now hurry."

I'd only gone five steps when I walked into a small moun-tain. Only the small mountain was one of the heavyset security guards, and the guard murmured an apology before he somehow sensed it was me. I heard him shift toward me suddenly but I ducked low as I felt his hand sweep over my head. I stomped down on what I thought was his foot and pushed into him, but it felt like pushing into a redwood tree and there wasn't much give and I realized that the guard could grab me in the next second and hold me there until the lights came back on and the police managed to find their way to us, so I did the only thing left to do.

I grabbed the .38 from my waistband, raised it high in the air, pointed at the ceiling, and fired two rounds.

Complete chaos.

Before, everyone had been nervously quiet and staying in one spot—a few lighting the area with their cell phones—but now half of them started shouting and screaming as they rushed for the nearest exit.

Suddenly hands gripped me from behind, held me in a giant bear hug, and I realized it was the other guard. He'd grabbed me with my hand still up in the air, and I considered letting loose another round or two but instead leaned back into him, bringing up my feet and kicking out at the other guard in front of me, thrusting both feet hard, using that momentum to drive the guard holding me to stumble back into the stampede.

The guard lost his balance and in doing so lost his grip, and I managed to wiggle out of his bear hug and hurried forward with the people pushing and jostling into the lobby.

The glass entrance doors and windows were tinted, meaning that there was light but it was still darker than outside. I spotted the three police officers—two of them were trying to push through the crowd into the casino while another was trying to create a modicum of order—and I broke in the other direction, away from those entrance doors and the Dodge parked right outside.

Augustus said, "Take the next hallway and keep going until I tell you to stop."

Ten seconds later, staying close to the wall and pushing past a few people, I came to a door and that was when Augustus told me to stop and to go through it. I pushed through the door but it led me into a stairwell that was pitch-black and I paused, unsure what he wanted me to do next.

"Head downstairs," he said.

I headed down the stairs. I could hear people a few flights up as they navigated their way to the ground floor. So far none were headed up the stairs from the bottom floor.

"We're going to need to turn the power back on very soon, Ben. It's the only way this will work. The door you'll be coming to is locked and can only be opened with an employee passkey."

"I don't have a passkey."

"Of course you don't. That's why we've already overridden their security system."

I made it to the door ten seconds later, told Augustus I was there, and at once the lights came back on, the quiet hum of the power circulating throughout the massive building.

Just as Augustus said, the door here needed a passkey. The overlarge lock by the doorknob currently had a red light blinking on it. Then, all of a sudden, it went green.

I pulled open the door and stepped through and found myself in a parking garage.

Augustus said, "This is where the valeted cars are parked. Head out one row and then turn right."

I did as he said and soon came to a row of carefully parked cars. Most of them were luxury cars—Mercedes and Maseratis and Jaguars and one Aston Martin—while a few were sports cars.

"Do you see the black Tesla off to the left?"

It was a sleek Model S. I started toward it but slowed as an important fact hit me.

"I don't have a key."

"You don't need one. We've already bypassed the system. It's fully charged and will get you to your next destination."

Dubious, I tried the door, thinking it would be locked, but it opened just fine. I slipped into the driver's seat, and at once the computer screen in the center dash lit up.

Without another moment's hesitation, I put the Tesla in

gear and pressed down on the accelerator pedal. The car glided forward like I was riding on air. I steered through the parking garage until I reached the ramp—which was blocked off by a metal gate.

Right on cue, the gate began to lift up into the ceiling, and I sped up the ramp and back into sunlight.

I drove down the side of the casino, past the mass of people waiting outside. A few other police cruisers had joined the fray but those officers were busy trying to create order and find the driver of the abandoned Dodge, not the man currently driving away in a Tesla.

"Where am I headed?"

"Get back on the 101 and head south. You've had a crazy morning, Ben. I'd say your evening will be even crazier."

ELEVEN

The Kid leaned back in his chair, and let out a breath.

"Jesus Christ, that was fucking intense."

Carver said nothing. The only image right now on the computer screen was from Ben's point of view as he drove south down the 101. After all, things weren't supposed to progress this way. There weren't cameras installed in the Tesla for the viewers to switch over to if they so pleased.

The Kid glanced back at Graham and Bae and Chin, who were still sitting in their seats, and then frowned at Carver.

"What is it?"

"Something doesn't feel right."

"Dude, this whole fucking thing doesn't feel right. It never has."

Carver looked feeble in his wheelchair, not the man the Kid had once known. His body had been broken, and so had his spirit.

"Kid, how many games would you say you've watched?"

Carver asked this as he kept staring at the monitor, his eyes narrowed, like he was trying to spot a hidden puzzle piece.

"I have no idea. Way too many, that's for sure."

"And in all those games, has Simon ever helped any of those players to the extent that we just witnessed?"

"Never. But what's your point? This isn't a regular game."

"I know. Still, something about this doesn't feel right. This feels like more than just a game."

The Kid stared at Carver, who was still watching the screen. He'd been watching it this entire time, not once shifting his gaze away. The Kid knew what Carver meant, but he wasn't quite sure where he was going with it. *Of course* this was more than just a game. Caesar and his people wouldn't be going to all this trouble for the hell of it.

"I told you, Carver, there's no way they're going to find us. I've got this system hooked up to over twenty different proxies all over the world. Besides, imagine how many of those fuckers are left in the Inner Circle. You gotta figure almost all of them are watching this. There's no way they can track us."

Carver nodded slowly, still staring at the computer screen, and then he blinked, looked around the basement as if seeing it for the first time.

"How's it coming with the laptops?"

Good question. The Kid popped up from his chair and squeezed between Carver and his wheelchair to the table where he had two of his computers right now trying to access the laptops. One of them they'd already accessed, but all the info on it was about the past games and the layout of the Fillmore. Still, the Kid had copied all of the info onto his computer to do another scan in case anything was hidden.

"The one laptop was easy, but these other two"—he typed madly at the keyboard, his eyes scanning the code scattered across the screen—"it'll take a while. But I'm gonna crack it. I can promise you that."

He drifted back over to the main table, grabbed the large plastic bowl that only had a few loose kernels inside.

"Think it's time for some more popcorn. You guys want some popcorn?"

For months the Kid had been going without, but these past several days had been extremely stressful, and he'd been stress eating like the overweight kid he used to be. Movie theater butter popcorn and Red Bull had become his diet.

Carver glanced at the microwave in the corner.

"I still don't get why you just don't use that to make your popcorn."

"I told you," the Kid said. "That microwave is strictly for tea. I can't use it for popcorn too. Didn't you ever hear about how you should never cross the streams?"

Nobody chuckled, or even cracked a smile. Apparently none of them were *Ghostbusters* fans.

Bae tapped his cane on the floor absently as he frowned.

"How long have they been in the air?"

He meant Ronny and Drew and Mason. And his daughter, of course.

The Kid glanced at his watch.

"Not even an hour at this point."

"When do they land?"

"I told you, the flight shouldn't be more than three hours."

"And they're flying to Reno."

The Kid felt his shoulders start to dip.

"Yeah, that's right."

"But Ben appears to be driving south."

That he was. Which certainly complicated matters. The problem was, while Fred was the pilot they always used, he worked for a private airline company. He flew their planes. Which meant that they couldn't just fly anywhere on a whim, especially once the jet was in the air. The Kid ordered the flight, and because he couldn't just tell them he wanted to fly west and would make up his mind halfway through the flight, there needed to be a predetermined destination. Which had been

Reno, as two years ago that was where Ben had ended up his first day in the game.

"Everything so far had me thinking they were going to do everything the same. Fact is, I'm pretty sure the plan was for Ben to end up in Reno, or at least head out in that direction. But you saw what just happened. Can't explain it, but that's okay, because once they land, Ronny will call me and I'll tell him what's up. I'll direct them from here. I doubt Ben will get that far. They'll manage to catch up with him in no time."

And then what would happen? Nothing, at least not right away. They had to figure Ben had escorts. They'd be on the lookout for Ben's team. Only this wasn't a normal game, so there was no reason to try to snatch the player out of the game. Still, Ben needed to have backup in case something happened. And based on what they'd just witnessed, it was clear something would happen.

"I'll be right back." The Kid started for the stairs, the plastic bowl at his side, but then paused. "Carver, when was the last time you used the bathroom?"

Carver didn't answer, still staring at the computer screen.

"Carver."

"I heard the question, Kid. I chose not to answer it."

The Kid glanced at Graham, who gave him a helpless shrug. The Kid set the bowl aside, nodded at Chin to help him.

Carver waited until they were only feet away before he slammed his fist down on the arm of the wheelchair.

"I do *not* need help."

The Kid stood silent, staring at him for a beat, and then sighed.

"Is that right? Because I'm pretty sure you aren't wearing diapers. And I'm pretty sure there aren't any toilets down here. And I'm pretty sure you haven't used the bathroom in at least twelve hours. You want me to bring you a cup to piss in?"

Now Carver flicked his gaze away from the computer screen again, only this time to glare back at the Kid.

"Fuck you."

"Yeah, and fuck you if you piss on my carpet. This is some vintage 1970s shit. It belongs in a museum."

"I don't need to use the bathroom."

"Carver, no offense, but you're a guest in my house. And as my guest, I'm ordering you to use the fucking bathroom."

Except it wasn't going to be easy. That's why he needed Chin's help. Before, Mason and Drew had helped carry Carver down the steps, with Ronny bringing down the wheelchair. Now, once Carver finally agreed, the Kid and Chin had to help him up the stairs, one slow step after another. It took almost five minutes, and then Chin had to hurry back down the steps to retrieve the wheelchair. Another couple of minutes later, Carver was in the guest bathroom, which was basically a closet with a toilet and sink and a Febreze air freshener plugged into the wall.

Before closing the door, the Kid said, "And just to be clear, I ain't wiping your ass."

The Kid turned to smile at Chin, but Chin had already headed back down to the basement. Where the Kid had left the popcorn bowl behind.

He started to head back down that way but instead drifted into the living room. His mom was in her usual chair, staring out the window. Carmen sat in the chair beside her, reading a book.

The Kid wanted to head back down to the basement, or wait for Carver, or make some popcorn, or do *something* other than see his mother this way. But this was how she was. How she'd been for a long time. And she would continue being this way until the day finally came when she took her last breath.

The Kid whispered to Carmen across the room.

"How's she doing?"

Carmen marked her place in the book with a coupon and set the book aside as she stood from the chair and crossed the room.

"She's having another one of her bad days."

"Shit."

"I don't think it helps that all this … activity is going on."

Carmen didn't exactly know what it was the Kid did other than that it dealt with computers. All she knew for sure was that she was hired to take care of his mother, and that she was paid on time, and so she didn't poke her nose in places it shouldn't be.

Still, the Kid knew the past couple of days had bothered her. All these different people suddenly here, some of them injured, not to mention the backyard … well, as far as the Kid knew, Carmen didn't know about the two bodies they'd buried in the backyard, but that didn't mean she didn't suspect something. She certainly wasn't stupid.

"Thank you for all your help, Carmen. I know everything going on … it doesn't make much sense, but trust me when I say I have everything under control."

It worried him that Carmen said his mother was having another one of her bad days. That often carried over into the night. More than once he'd needed to wake his mother from a nightmare, and it had always broken his heart when she freaked out because she didn't recognize him. She'd thought he was a burglar, who had broken into the house to steal and possibly do something terrible to her. He was tempted to ask Carmen to stay the night, but he knew Carmen had her own mother to look after, plus her schoolwork as she was doing night classes for her nursing degree.

The Kid said he would check in with Carmen before she left for the day and then drifted back into the kitchen. He'd opened one of the packets of Orville Redenbacher and popped it in the microwave and had just hit the popcorn button when he heard knocking on the bathroom door.

He headed down the hallway and stood outside the closed door.

"Carver?"

At first he thought he heard Carver crying behind the door, but then after another moment he realized it was laughter. What sounded like hysterical laughter.

"Kid, I need you to do me a favor."

"What's that?"

More hysterical laughter.

"I need you to wipe my ass."

TWELVE

It was close to five o'clock in the afternoon when I reached San Francisco. I followed the 101 over the Golden Gate Bridge—the Pacific vast and endless on my right, Alcatraz lonely off to my left—and then I followed the signs to downtown.

Augustus hadn't spoken for much of the past six or so hours, and it was only in the past ten minutes that he'd let me know where I was headed. Now that I'd gotten off the bridge, he continued to speak, his voice low and soft, telling me where to turn, what signs to look for.

He couldn't just tell me what my final destination was, let me input the address into the Tesla's GPS—or have one of his people remotely add my destination—because he wanted to keep it a secret, both for me and for those watching. As Simon once told me, it was all about the anticipation, the build-up, the thing that made people want to sit on the edge of their seats.

Plus, Augustus and his people wanted to give my people as little heads-up as possible, because surely they knew that a team was headed to my location right now. It might be another five hours, another ten hours, but they would already be in the air, mostly likely in one of the private jets the Kid managed to secure for us over the years. If that was the case, they would get here sooner than later, but right now there was nothing for them to do.

As I glided through the city streets, I said, "Are you ready to tell me yet?"

There was a slight pause on Augustus' end.

"Tell you what?"

"About the Pax Romana. I mean, you've been working on this for decades. You must have some grand master plan in place. It's not like telling me is going to change any of that, right?"

Another slight pause, and then a soft chuckle.

"Nice try, Ben. Oh, and make a right up at the next light."

I flicked on the turn signal as I slowed for the intersection.

"Then how about your real name? You know mine, so it's only fair I know yours."

Another beat of silence.

I said, "Your name isn't really Augustus Caesar, is it? Because I've met you, and you most definitely don't look like an Augustus."

A tired sigh, like he was getting irritated. Which was good. That was part of my plan. Somewhat. I wanted to keep him on his toes, but I also didn't want to do anything that would cause undue pain to Jen and Casey. Even though I had hope I would see them again, I still acknowledged the simple fact I may never see them again, that I could potentially die in the next hour or two. But unless I tried, I would never know.

Finally Augustus spoke.

"Are you trying to annoy me on purpose?"

"I'm just trying to have a conversation. Trying to learn what the big fuss is about. I always like hearing success stories.

So tell me: how'd you end up at the head of this vast evil empire? Like, did you answer an ad in the classifieds?"

Silence.

"You have a wife? Girlfriend? Husband? Boyfriend? *Any* friends?"

More silence.

I bit my lip, debating whether or not to keep pushing. Because there could be fatal consequences to my pushing. But the truth was I didn't know how much longer I would have access to the man. I didn't know if the Kid was having any luck on his end with the laptops. For all we knew, the laptops contained no important information, nothing that could help us try to understand what was going to happen next, so trying to push Augustus Caesar's buttons was all I had at the moment.

"What were you like as a boy?"

Another couple of seconds passed in silence, and then Augustus couldn't help himself.

"What was that?"

"I'm just trying to get a sense of your childhood. Did you have a loving family? Maybe your dad was abusive. Or maybe it was your mom. Or maybe you didn't have any parents. You led me to believe you're siblings with Congresswoman Houser, but from what we could tell based on our limited research, she doesn't have any siblings."

Silence for several seconds, and then another soft chuckle.

"I'm a bastard, Ben. Is that what you want to hear? My old man had an affair, got somebody knocked up, and when the time came to claim me as his own, he publicly wanted nothing to do with me because he was already married and had a child. After all, he was a U.S. senator. Back then, that kind of stuff was frowned upon."

"So it is daddy issues."

The chuckle this time was a full-hearted laugh.

"You aren't listening, Ben. I said he *publicly* wanted nothing to do with me. But he did provide support, both financial and emotional. He couldn't meet with me much, but when he did, I could tell he was proud of me. Don't tell my sister, but I think he had always been disappointed he only had a girl. He'd always wanted a boy, and now he had one, but a boy that needed to stay private. So he spoiled me."

I started humming Harry Chapin's "Cat's in the Cradle" but only got a few bars before Augustus fell silent.

"Sorry about that," I said. "The song was stuck in my head for some reason."

The smile had disappeared from Augustus' voice.

"At the next light, make a left."

As I made the turn, I said, "So then what was your childhood like? Were you bullied? Were *you* the bully?"

Silence, so I decided to try a different tack.

"It's got to be tough for somebody like you. What with having all that power, wondering if people under you really respect you or if they just fear you. Then again, for some it doesn't matter whether or not they're liked. They *like* being assholes. Is that how it is for you? Did you have to be an asshole to get where you are now?"

Augustus ignored me, as I expected he would.

"In the next one hundred feet make a left."

He had directed me to a charging station. There were six bays where cars could park and charge while their drivers presumably walked the city streets or got some coffee in one of the shops nearby. Three of them were currently occupied by other Teslas.

"The battery is going to need to be fully charged to get you to your next destination. We have a room waiting for you at the Ritz-Carlton, but it's not like you could drop this car off with a valet, what with you not having a key."

"Smart thinking."

Augustus ignored me again.

"In three minutes a Town Car will pull up along the sidewalk. Get in the back. Don't bother talking to the driver, as he won't say anything to you. You'll be driven to the hotel. You'll check in with the name on the ID that will be on the backseat. Are you following me so far, Ben?"

I backed the Tesla into one of the open bays, shut off the car.

"Yeah, I'm following you."

"Good. You now have two minutes."

I stepped out of the car and looked at the charging station. I'd never driven a Tesla before—had never driven any electric car before—but I wasn't an idiot. Well, most of the time. I did what I needed to do to get the car charging and then made it back to the street right as a black Town Car pulled up at the curb.

I climbed into the back, and at once the Town Car was moving. I glanced at the driver but his focus was on the city street; he didn't even bother glancing at me in the rearview mirror. I noted the leather wallet on the seat beside me. I opened it and looked at the ID inside.

It was my driver's license photo—at least the one from over two years ago, back when I lived in Lanton with my wife and daughter—but the name wasn't mine.

"Romeo Chase."

I whispered the name, and realized that my jaw had started to clench.

Two years ago, I'd ended up in Reno with that name. I'd met a beautiful young woman who went by the name Juliet. A beautiful woman that Simon had forced me to sleep with. A beautiful woman who I learned the next day had been murdered.

"I'm not killing anybody."

I spoke softly, almost a whisper, and if the driver thought I was speaking to him, he didn't show it, keeping his focus on the street.

In my ear, Augustus chuckled.

"We'll see."

THIRTEEN

The Town Car dropped me off at the corner, and I walked straight to the main entrance of the Ritz-Carlton, ignoring the sleek and impressive façade of the building and one of the valets who said hello to me as I walked past.

My sneakers squeaked on the marble floor, making me feel quite self-conscious, and I noticed one of the bellboys glancing my way. Was he trying to hide a smirk?

The desk clerk was a young woman in her thirties, dark hair and light dark skin. She didn't seem to care that my sneakers were squeaking on the marble floor or that I was dressed like I was ready to do some lawn work. With a smile, she welcomed me to the Ritz-Carlton and asked how she could help me today.

I told her I was checking in and handed her the ID that had my picture but not my name.

She glanced at the ID, and her expression changed all at once, the smile going tight, her eyes widening slightly. Then she kicked things up a bit, becoming much more chipper.

"Welcome, Mr. Chase. We've been expecting you. Your

luggage arrived earlier this morning. It's already in your room as instructed."

My room, I was told, was the Ritz-Carlton Suite, and again, thank you very much for being our guest today, is there anything that we can help you with?

"I'm fine right now, thank you."

The clerk waved over one of the bellboys, and it was the one who had smirked at my squeaking sneakers. He hurried over, lips a tight line as he tried not to smile, and then his expression changed just as quickly when he learned in which room I was staying.

Suddenly he was all business, his shoulders pushed back, and motioned to the elevators.

"Right this way, sir."

Five minutes later I was in the room, though to call it a room wasn't fair to rooms. It really was a suite—it not only had a master bedroom but a dining room and living room and a fully stocked pantry with a large refrigerator.

The bellboy gave me the quick tour, noting that my luggage was already in the bedroom, and then I found myself standing at the window in the living room and staring out at the view.

"That's Coit Tower," the bellboy said. "And if you look over there, you can see Alcatraz."

He was trying to be professional, friendly, maybe trying to make up for smirking at me in the lobby, and I didn't hold any hard feelings. Which was why I gave him one of the fifty-dollar bills and sent him on his way.

"That was very kind of you," Augustus said once I was alone.

I headed into the bedroom. I grabbed the black plastic-shell suitcase and set it on the bed and opened it. Inside were boxer shorts, undershirts, socks, an electric razor, and deodorant.

"Have to admit I expected more."

Augustus said, "The rest is hanging in the closet."

A garment bag hung in the closet. I zipped it open and found a gray herringbone suit jacket and slacks.

I checked the tag inside.

"Giorgio Armani. How much did this set you back?"

"As you probably can guess, the suit is your exact size. As are the shoes. You'll look quite spiffy, Ben, believe me."

"Where am I going?"

"Don't you worry about it. Right now you have some time to kill. A couple of hours, actually. Take a nap if you'd like. You've had a long day. Or take a shower and watch some TV, if you'd like to do that instead. Anything you want to watch, it's on us. Even porn. Tell me, Ben, when was the last time you watched porn?"

I didn't answer.

"At the very least, who would you say is your favorite porn star?"

Again I didn't answer.

Augustus issued a disappointed sigh.

"Okay, Ben. Do what you want to do. We'll let you know when it's time to get ready."

There wasn't any sound of Augustus' disconnecting, but I felt it, just like two years ago when Simon would hang up on me.

I took the earpiece out, turned it off, and set it on the bedside table. And then I pulled the phone from my pocket, held it in my hand, just stared at it. Not sure I wanted to use another one of my turns with the Peekaboo app. There was no telling how long this game would last. I'd already used up one of my turns, so I only had two left.

Still …

Taking a breath, I opened the phone and tapped the app. Immediately I started the countdown in my head.

Ten.

Again the single room. White walls, linoleum floor. Two beds in frame.

Nine.

Casey was on the same bed as before, her back against the wall. She didn't look as upset as before, like she'd been crying.

Eight.

Jen sat on the other bed, facing Casey, so her back was to the camera. Jen looked to be saying something to our daughter, but her voice was low, barely audible.

Seven.

"Jen, Casey, it's me."

Six.

Both of them reacted simultaneously, jerking at the sound of my voice. I hoped it was more out of surprise than fear.

Five.

Jen immediately twisted on the bed, stared up at the camera in the corner of the ceiling.

"Ben?"

Four.

"I'm coming for you. Okay? I love you both so much."

Three.

Jen jumped up from the bed, started to move toward the camera, and for the first time my eyes focused on her left hand and her missing ring finger.

Two.

"Ben, where are you? We—"

The screen went black. Just like that. The fastest ten seconds of my life.

I didn't realize I was crying until a tear slipped off my cheek and landed on the dark cell phone screen.

I was glad I'd taken out the earpiece, because I was sure Augustus would have spoken up just then, maybe with another chuckle in his voice, and I maybe would have said or done something that would have cost Jen to lose another finger.

Like before, the urge to tap the Peekaboo app hit me again, but I knew that I couldn't waste the final chance quite yet. Maybe I shouldn't have even used my second time, but I couldn't help it. Seeing my wife and daughter, even for a few seconds, had given me a second wind. Had given me a burst of fortitude.

Whatever Augustus had planned—not just with this game, but whatever he and the Inner Circle had cooked up to take over the world—I wasn't going to let it happen.

I was going to stop them, no matter what it took.

FOURTEEN

The ringing of a phone woke me.

Like déjà vu, I opened my eyes to an unfamiliar room, but I wasn't in Room 6 of the Paradise Motel. No, I was still in the Ritz-Carlton Suite, in the bedroom, stretched out on top of the expensive comforter. I was still in my clothes, still in my sneakers.

I leaned up and reached over and picked up the phone. I knew who was on the other end before I answered.

Augustus said, "Have a nice nap?"

I'd fallen asleep with the glasses on my face. I hadn't wanted to sleep at all, but I'd lain down on the bed for just a few minutes and then the next thing I knew the phone was ringing.

"What time is it?"

"Time for you to clean yourself up. Shave and take a shower. Put on the suit and the shoes. Your guest will arrive within the hour."

"What guest?"

"It's a surprise, Ben. One that I think you'll enjoy very much."

"Is this person coming to the room?"

"No. You'll meet your guest down in the Lounge. Consider it neutral territory. Then, if you hit it off ..."

I adjusted the glasses, stood up from the bed. Thought about the herringbone suit hanging in the closet, the leather shoes. How those items alone probably cost more than a month's mortgage payment.

"Who am I meeting?"

"You'll see. Now hurry up, Ben. You now have fifty-five minutes. Oh, and do remember to put back in the earpiece when you're ready to leave."

Without a word, I set the phone in its cradle and then started for the bathroom.

It was almost ten o'clock when I stepped into the Lounge.

The place was fairly busy. Almost all of the chairs and tables were occupied, as were the chairs at the bar.

Part of me felt like I would be overdressed, but there were several men wearing business causal dress clothes.

Augustus said, "Do you see her?"

I scanned the room.

"Do I see who?"

But as soon as I'd asked the question, I knew the answer. I even sucked air in between my teeth. It was an involuntary response, and I very much hoped Augustus hadn't heard. But he had, because he chuckled again.

"Oh yes, you see her. Back during your first game, Simon had asked you who your favorite porn star was. You'd never answered him. It's been a couple of years, and you inferred you never watch porn anymore, but you no doubt recognize her, don't you?"

She sat by a table near the window. Her blonde hair was pulled back in a tight ponytail.

"Remember," Augustus said, "we knew everything there was to know about you. We still have records of your Internet browsing history from all those years ago. You often deleted the history, but not before we had saved what we needed. There were certain porn stars you watched more than others. There was one in particular you seemed to return to again and again."

Even from across the room, I could see she was wearing a black dress with a straight neckline and spaghetti straps. One thin leg was crossed over another, exposing her black ankle strap heel.

"Tell me, Ben"—and here Augustus' voice seemed to tick down an octave—"how often did you imagine yourself fucking her? You can be honest with me."

She already had a drink, what looked like a Cosmopolitan. She reached for it with her right hand—her fingernails perfectly manicured—while she absently looked at her cell phone. Took a sip of the drink, set the glass back on the table.

Augustus said, "Ben, it's rude to stare."

I blinked, looked away. Took a step to the side as I scanned the room once again.

She had caught the eye of several other men, it was clear. Men who obviously knew her work. Furtive glances were thrown her way. One man had just surreptitiously taken a picture of her with his cell phone, was probably now texting the photo to all his buddies.

I glanced around the room once again, made sure nobody was watching, and then whispered just loud enough for Augustus to hear me.

"Why is she here?"

"To meet you, Ben. Why else?"

I swallowed. Wasn't sure what to say. I remembered being in that dive bar back in Reno, meeting the gorgeous woman who called herself Juliet and what I'd been forced to do to her in bed. I'd been mostly drunk, but I still remembered some of it, and I was still ashamed.

And then, of course, the next day I learned she'd been murdered.

"Why are you still standing there, Ben? Go over and introduce yourself. Buy her a drink. See what happens. She came all this way to meet you."

I opened my mouth but shut it. Wasn't sure what to say. I scanned the room again, noticed that a few people had glanced my way. Nothing alarming in their glances, just simply noticing somebody acting as a wallflower and maybe seeing if I was somebody they knew.

Any second, I knew, *she* would probably notice me too. What would happen if our eyes met? Would I feel compelled to cross the room, take the empty seat across from her? Shake her hand, or would she expect a hug?

I asked the question again, a little louder this time.

"Why is she here?"

"Again, she's here to meet you. She was told that you were her biggest fan. And she … well, she sometimes goes out of her way to meet her biggest fans. Especially after she's made several unwise investments over the years. The adult entertainment business can be tricky and doesn't always pay well. Everybody has a price. But don't worry about any of that, Ben. Just have fun."

I opened my mouth again but didn't speak. I moved from my spot against the wall, but it was only a few feet.

In my ear, Augustus chuckled again.

"Do not fiddle while Rome burns. Have you ever heard that expression? Back in 64 A.D., a great fire ravaged Rome for almost a week. Destroyed nearly seventy-five percent of the city. They said the emperor at the time, Nero, fiddled while Rome burned. It's not true, of course—the fiddle didn't even exist during Nero's time—and besides, Nero was reportedly not even in Rome when the fire started. He returned immediately and began trying to save the city, but the people didn't quite trust him. Some even believed he was responsible for setting the fire, what with the fact that he ended up using the land cleared by the fire to build his Golden Palace. He wasn't what people would call a good man—he was sadistic and cruel, had even had his mother and wife murdered—and maybe because of that he is falsely known as a weak and ineffectual leader."

Still scanning the room, I wet my lips.

"Is there a point to this?"

"Not really. I've just always found Nero's story interesting. Plus, I've always found it to be a warning of sorts about the kind of leader I need to be."

"And what kind of leader is that?"

"A smart leader. A fair leader. An effective leader."

"I'm not going to sleep with her."

"You don't have to, Ben. Of course, if you wanted to, you certainly could, but you don't have to. I'll be honest—we weren't quite sure just how long it would take before things fell into place. It's not like we had much time to get everything situated. But the next part of the game is already set. If you want to leave, feel free to leave. The Tesla is parked outside around the block. It's fully charged and it will get you to your next destination. Of course ..."

He let it hang there, forcing me to fill the silence.

"Of course what?"

"Of course, you don't have to go quite yet. You can buy her a drink. Tell her which movies of hers you like the best. Make her smile. Maybe even make her laugh. Won't that feel good, Ben?"

I was already turning away, heading back to the elevators.

In my ear, Augustus sighed.

"Very well, Ben. Stand up the young lady. Make her feel bad about herself if that's what you want to do."

I hit the button for the lobby, stepped back to wait for the doors to open.

"Where am I going next?"

The smile was once more in Augustus' voice when he answered.

"To see an old friend."

FIFTEEN

The Kid yawned, rubbed his eyes. He grabbed the closest can of Red Bull on the table—there were at least a half dozen—but it was practically empty, only a few drops left. Still he downed what he could, though the drink was warm.

On the computer screen, the image was still from Ben's point of view. Ben had been on the road now for just over an hour and a half. He'd headed east and then started to veer south, and he had just driven past Modesto.

It was almost 11:30 p.m. PST where Ben was, which meant it was 2:30 a.m. EST here. Three hours ago Graham and Chin had left to go back to their respective motels. Bae had been encouraged to go as well, but Bae had refused. God, the old Korean was almost as stubborn as Carver.

So at two thirty in the morning, it was just the Kid and Carver and Bae down in the basement. Carmen had left hours ago, once she helped the Kid's mother to bed, and the Kid had a baby monitor set up on her bedside table which would alert him if she called out for help. There was no telling how long this game would last, and the Kid had been up for almost twenty hours as it was. He needed sleep, but he didn't quite trust Carver or Bae to stay awake until morning. Somebody needed to monitor the game, because several hours ago Ronny and Drew and Mason and Ho Sook had landed in Reno, and after they'd split up and secured vehicles, they'd headed toward Ben. But Reno was over a four-hour drive from San Francisco, and they were an hour away when Ben had left the Ritz-Carlton, and so now they had redirected to head in Ben's direction.

Only there was no telling where Ben was headed. The Kid had to stay vigilant for all the highway signs, and then he would call Ronny with an update, and Ronny would then call Drew.

The Kid glanced back at Carver and Bae. Both appeared asleep. Bae's head was bowed, and it sounded like he was snoring. Carver's head wasn't bowed, but his eyes were closed. Both of them didn't look comfortable, and he thought about telling them to at least go upstairs and sleep on the couch or use his bed, but then he remembered just what a pain in the ass it had been to get Carver up the steps the first time around, and that had been with Chin's help, and the Kid didn't think Bae would be much help what with his cane and the fact he was even older than Carver.

"I know what you're thinking."

Carver's sudden, low voice in the silence nearly made the Kid jump.

"What am I thinking?"

Carver opened his eyes, stared straight back at the Kid.

"That I should get some sleep."

"We all should get some sleep."

"It'd feel wrong for me to leave at this point. Ben needs me."

The Kid wasn't quite sure that was accurate. Right now what happened to Ben in no way would be effected if Carver was in the basement or not. Still, he didn't feel like arguing. Mostly because he was too tired to argue.

"Any luck with the laptops?" Carver asked.

The Kid started to shake his head, knowing the answer, but climbed out of his chair anyway because he needed to stretch his legs. He went over to the laptops and checked his computer that was still trying to break the encryption on both of them.

"So far no luck."

"Okay."

The Kid heard the disappointment in Carver's voice, and turned away from the laptops.

"Carver, you know there's no guarantee anything important will be on any of these."

"I know."

"Like the first laptop, these two might be duds."

"I know."

"I'm not sure what—"

"I *know*, Kid. Trust me, I know. But at this point ... we don't have much else to work with, do we?"

No, they didn't, and it was depressing. After everything that they'd done so far, after all they'd lost, they had come no closer to figuring out what the fuck was going on. If the Kid wasn't so tired, maybe he'd be pissed, but as it was, he had to rub his eyes again as he stumbled back to his chair.

"By the way, Kid."

He glanced over at Carver who had suddenly gone quiet, like he wasn't sure what else to say.

"By the way, what?"

Carver took a breath, tried to smile but couldn't.

"Thank you."

"For what?"

"For everything. From day one. I was the one who initially arrested you."

"To be fair, that wasn't your fault. It was my stupid fault for getting caught in the first place."

"And even after all that, you still helped me. And not just me, but everybody else. Ben and Ronny and Drew and ..."

His voice faded as his eyes closed, and for an instant the Kid thought Carver was going to fall asleep. But then Carver's eyes opened, and he forced a smile.

"Without your help, we all would have been stuck in our games. We all ... would be dead."

The Kid was quiet for a beat, not sure what to say. While Carver may never have actually said the words before, not like this, the Kid had always sensed the gratitude. Even with Ben when the two of them would snipe back and forth at each other.

He thought about what he'd told Ben, nearly a week ago. How he'd told Ben the one thing he'd never told anyone else, and how he'd wanted to tell Ben because he wasn't sure they would all live through that night and he didn't want to die without telling anybody.

Ben had said Carver would accept him as he was, and he knew that was true, and he wanted to tell Carver but didn't think this was the right time or place. When all this was over, definitely, but not now.

"I appreciate it, Carver, but it's not me. It's you. Why do you think the team went to such lengths to rescue you from the Coliseum? You're the one who saved everybody. I'm just your sidekick. I'm like Gilligan, only much better looking."

SIXTEEN

In the middle of the night, there wasn't much traffic on the highway. A few cars, a few tractor-trailers, and that was it.

I kept the Tesla at just five over the limit, not wanting to attract the eye of any cop. By now the car would have been reported stolen by its owner, though there was a good chance that Augustus' people had made it so that report disappeared. At least until Augustus got bored and decided to mix things up. That could happen at any minute.

"Augustus, are you there?"

Silence. At least for about thirty seconds. Then his voice came through the earpiece, soft and direct as always.

"Yes, Ben?"

"Have you decided to tell me yet?"

"About what?"

"The Pax Romana. Your real name. Anything you want to talk about, really."

Another beat of silence.

"My real name is Andrew Kaufman. I faked my death in 1984 and have been working behind the scenes to change the world ever since."

"Interesting. I'm surprised you didn't go with Tony Clifton."

"Ah, are you a fan?"

"Not really. But I did like the Jim Carrey movie."

"I never saw it, to be honest. I don't watch most movies nowadays. Whatever magic Hollywood used to possess, they lost it long ago."

"So is that what all this is about, a bunch of old rich assholes yearning for the good ol' days?"

"I would say the Inner Circle is quite diverse, at least in terms of age. We may have some elderly members, but we also have members as young as twenty-two."

"How does one so young become a member of the Inner Circle?"

"Nepotism, of course. In the twenty-two-year-old's case, his father is a member. Or was a member. He died at the Coliseum last week."

"Aw, what a shame."

Another beat of silence, and for a moment I worried I'd overstepped things.

"Look, if you don't want to tell me your name, that's fine. I mean, it's not quite fair as you know my name, but whatever. At the very least, how does somebody like you—a bastard, no less—become the one and only Augustus Caesar?"

More silence, and I thought maybe I'd pissed him off good this time, that right this moment he was having men march toward wherever they kept my wife to tear off another body part.

But then he spoke, his voice still soft and direct.

"How does anybody become anything, Ben? How does somebody become a school teacher? How does somebody become a CEO? How does somebody become the president of the United States? They work at it. They *want* it. And eventually, if they're lucky—some more so than others—they get it."

"Wow, that's motivating. Do you have a DVD set you're hocking on the side to make a few extra bucks?"

"I have to say, Ben, I've enjoyed this more than I expected. Very rarely do I get to interact with somebody on your … level."

"Gee, thanks."

"However, I believe our time together is soon going to come to an end."

This made me sit up straighter in my seat, my hands tightening around the steering wheel. I glanced at the rearview mirror, saw a few cars behind me on the highway but nothing that raised a red flag, at least nothing yet. Then I remembered that the Kid and the others couldn't hear Augustus, so I made sure to repeat what he'd just said.

"What do you mean, you believe our time together is soon going to come to an end?"

"Well, no games last forever. There's always a starting point, and there's always an ending point. You're ending point is coming very soon."

I wasn't sure what to think about that. Obviously what he said was true—every game did come to an end—but I hadn't been expecting it to come this quickly. My eyes drifted to the time on the computer screen in the dash, and I saw it was 2:00 a.m. Not even twenty-four hours since I'd woken up in Room 6 of the Paradise Motel.

"You said before I was going to see an old friend. Who is it?"

A soft chuckle on his end, though there was something bitter in it, something dark.

"You'll see, Ben. You'll see. Now, take the next exit, and once you reach the stop sign, turn left. You're almost there."

I followed the directions off the highway, listening to Augustus' voice in my ear, making sure to always tilt my face toward the road signs so the Kid knew exactly where I was headed.

Except, suddenly, I worried maybe the Kid hadn't managed to find this game after all. I'd just taken for granted that he was the Kid, so he knew what he was doing, he was the best, and he could make it work. But maybe all this time he'd been poring over different websites or whatever it was he did to find the games, and so far none of the team knew where I was. Ronny and Drew or whoever wasn't right now headed in my direction. I was completely alone, headed toward the end of the game, and there was no way to know if any of my friends knew it.

The area was rural, fields dotted by houses and trees and the occasional business. I passed through a small town, which was all dark except for one ARCO gas station, and despite the bright lights even that looked empty.

Augustus had gone silent, just telling me to keep driving straight on this road, and so far five miles had passed and I worried maybe a signal had gone out, or the battery in the earpiece had died, or *something* had happened. Maybe this was just it—maybe the end of the game was to keep driving east until I eventually hit the Atlantic, and then what?

"Mr. Kaufman?"

Several beats of silence before his voice spoke in my ear.

"Yes, Ben?"

"I just wanted to make sure you're still there."

"Oh, I'm still here, Ben. I'm still here. In fact, your turn is coming up very soon."

The sky was clear, and the moon was mostly full, shining brightly on the sleepy landscape around me. It almost looked eerie at this time of night with no other cars on the road, as if I was the last person alive.

After another two miles—passing more fields, more houses and buildings dotting those fields—Augustus spoke again.

"Turn left at the next mailbox."

My foot immediately lifted off the accelerator. I leaned forward in my seat, craning to see the approaching mailbox. I hoped there would be a number on it for the Kid to make out, assuming he had managed to find this game after all.

When I spotted the mailbox—a simple black metal mailbox, nothing special about it—the anticipation I'd felt was immediately dashed.

The number on the mailbox was 738. The name under the number was LOCKHART.

I searched my brain, skimming through all the names in my memory rolodex for somebody with that last name, but nothing came up.

To see an old friend, Augustus had said, but who the hell was that?

The driveway wasn't paved. The Tesla slowly crawled over the stone gravel past some trees up a long drive.

A split-level house had been built into the side of a small hill. The Tesla's headlights lit up the side of the house and illuminated the blue siding and white trim. The bushes around the house looked like they hadn't been tended to in over a year. All the lights were off inside, so the house was dark.

A red Toyota Camry, an older model, was parked in front of the house. California tags. One of those Coexist bumper stickers.

I parked behind the car and turned off the lights. Just sat there in the sudden silence, staring up at the dark house, not sure what to do next.

That was when the porch lights came on. When the front door opened and a figure stepped into view behind the screen door.

Augustus said, "Don't be a rude guest, Ben. Go say hello. But first, take out the earpiece. Our time together has come to an end."

A chill raced through me. This was too soon. Way too soon. Whoever was in that house, either I would kill them or they would kill me. That was the only way I saw this ending.

I took out the earpiece, held it for a beat, then tossed it on the passenger seat. I unclipped my seat belt, reached for the door, but then remembered something.

Sliding the cell phone from my pocket, I held it tightly in my hand, took a deep breath, and then woke it from sleep and tapped the Peekaboo app.

Again, on the screen, the small room with the two beds. Jen was lying on the one bed, Casey on the other. They were both asleep.

I opened my mouth, wanted to say something, anything, but part of me didn't want to wake them. I didn't know why, but I imagined they didn't get many restful nights of sleep. I didn't want to disturb them if I could help it.

But then I couldn't help myself.

"Jen, can you hear me?"

She didn't move. Just lay there on her side, her back to the camera in the corner of the ceiling.

"Jen!"

My voice trembled on the single word. It sounded anxious. Desperate. I was afraid she wouldn't hear me, because I was afraid this would be the last time we'd ever interact. Whatever happened inside that house, there was a chance I might never come out.

My wife started to stir on the bed. Her eyes opened, and she looked up at the camera.

"Hello?"

Her voice was soft, dampened by sleep, and I found myself shouting at the phone.

"Jen, it's me! I love you so much! I love you and Casey! I—"

The screen went dark. Then the phone, a second later, shut itself off.

I held the dead phone for several more seconds, squeezing it even tighter, and then I tossed it on the passenger seat and opened the door. Stepped out slowly, scanning the area for … well, I didn't know what. All I saw besides the dark field were trees. Practically a forest. This house was a good half mile away from its closest neighbor.

I shut the door and started around the Tesla toward the walkway. Staring up at the figure standing behind the screen door as I took one slow step after another. Not sure what was going to happen next but already not liking it at all.

"Hello?"

The person behind the screen door didn't answer. I took a couple more steps, and at once I realized it was a woman watching me. A couple more steps, and her features behind the screen door started to take shape. I couldn't see her well, but I saw enough that it stopped me at once.

My sudden inhalation was barely audible.

Michelle Delaney unlatched the lock and then opened the screen door.

"Well, don't just stand there," she said. "Come on in before the bugs do."

SEVENTEEN

The Kid grabbed the disposable, dialed Ronny's number, and placed the phone to his ear. As soon as Ronny answered, the Kid blurted out the address, but in his excitement Ronny didn't hear him and told him to repeat it. The Kid did, and then asked where they were. Ronny asked Mason, who was riding shotgun, and once Mason noted the town they'd just passed by on the highway, the Kid looked up their location on the computer.

"You're about forty minutes away, a half hour if you drive fast enough."

"Kid, slow down a minute. What's wrong?"

"Ben said something that spooked me. He repeated a line that Simon or Caesar or whoever the fuck he's been talking to said."

"Which was?"

"That their time together was soon going to come to an end."

Ronny was silent for a moment, and then he cursed. Not a *bad* curse—not the kind that would have gotten the Kid's mouth washed out with soap when he was little—but still for Ronny, who almost never swore, it seemed like a big deal.

The Kid said, "I know. That's why you need to get to his location ASAP. It's a house in the middle of nowhere. A woman answered the door, but we don't know who she is yet. She just invited Ben inside."

On the computer screen, they watched from Ben's point of view as he stepped into a living room. The living room didn't look clean, but it didn't look dirty, either. It just looked *lived in*, if that made sense, like the woman picked things up every once in a while but never went out of her way to tidy up.

The woman motioned for Ben to sit on the couch. The couch was positioned near the middle of the living room; the TV sitting on a stand in front of it, a hallway and closet behind.

Ben appeared hesitant, looking around the living room slowly —no doubt to give the Kid and the rest of the team time to take it all in—and then he moved over to the couch to sit down.

Ronny said, "We'll call Drew now. He and Ho Sook are about two miles behind us. We'll get there ASAP."

The Kid clicked off and glanced back at the two men. Carver appeared much more awake now, leaning forward in the wheelchair. Bae had woken up too, his shoulders slouched forward as he leaned on the cane.

On the table where the laptops were set up, his computer chimed.

Carver jumped slightly. It was the second time the computer had made that sound with him here. The Kid wanted to chalk it up to exhaustion and nerves, but he knew what had happened to Carver had scarred him in so many different ways. The Kid had never suffered from PTSD himself, but he'd read up about it, and he knew that was what Carver was dealing with now. The way most people dealt with PTSD was to get therapy, address the issue, but he knew that wasn't an option for Carver. Carver might eventually talk to somebody about it —Ben, maybe, or even Graham—but in their line of work, going to a therapeutic professional just wasn't an option.

The Kid rose from his chair, hurried over to the laptops.

"We got into one of them."

He bent over the computer, typed at the keyboard, and then felt his shoulders sagging.

"Shit."

Carver asked, "What's wrong?"

"The system was only able to break into part of the laptop. Honestly, there's not much here."

"What is it?"

The Kid scanned the screen.

"I'm not sure. Looks to be some random locations around the country."

"Locations of what?"

"I don't *know*, Carver. Jesus Christ."

At once the Kid took a breath, looked away. He was coming up on twenty-four hours of no sleep, and it was definitely starting to show. Back when he was younger—God, he was only twenty-six and already thinking of himself as an old man—he'd once gone two days without any sleep, and he had been alert that whole time, chugging away at can after can of Red Bull, but now things were different. They were all stressed, and it didn't help that they were still mourning the loss of several of their friends.

The Kid opened his mouth, meant to apologize, but that was when the baby monitor on the main table made a noise.

A soft, sudden cry for help.

His mother.

The Kid sprinted for the stairs.

EIGHTEEN

"They told me you were there that night. That you were leaving some party and you heard us fighting and you hurried over to see what was wrong, but that you just stood there and watched Mike … you watched what he did to me."

Michelle Delaney's voice faltered, and she swallowed hard, looked away from me. Tears had already begun to well in her eyes. She wiped at them, shaking her head.

"Christ, I haven't thought about that night in years. I managed to put it behind me. It took a lot of therapy, a lot of work on my part, but I managed to just not think about it anymore. Until earlier tonight when they called and told me you would be coming here. They said that you were there that night. They said that … the whole thing has always haunted you."

She sat across from me in one of the easy chairs, leaning forward with her elbows on her knees. She was about my age, mid-thirties, but her face was drawn, making her look more like she was in her forties. Her dark hair was pulled back in a tight ponytail. She wore sweatpants and a T-shirt, what was probably sleep attire, though judging by her eyes she hadn't slept a wink all night.

Michelle snorted a soft laugh, shook her head again.

"I was in a coma, you know. Mike beat me so badly, I was in a coma for five days. After that, I still couldn't leave the hospital. He'd broken my jaw. He'd broken a couple of my ribs. It took a long time for me to heal. Even now, my jaw doesn't work right. I have trouble chewing. But I've learned to live with it. How else was I supposed to move on?"

The question was clearly rhetorical, so I didn't bother answering. I sat on the couch, watching her. The TV was across from me, but it was turned off. The house was silent except for the fridge in the kitchen kicking on.

"Who contacted you?"

"I don't know who they were. They didn't give me their names. But they did deposit money into my checking account. Two hundred fifty thousand dollars. When they told me that, I thought they were lying. I thought it was a stupid prank. But they told me to check my account online, so I did, because, well, I had that hope, you know? Like maybe I had finally won the lottery. Bobby plays those scratch-offs every once in a while, and sometimes he wins twenty bucks, but nothing too crazy."

"Who's Bobby?"

She blinked, lost in her story, and then she shrugged.

"Bobby's my husband. Been married now five years. He's a good man. Travels a lot for work. That's why he's not here right now. I'd considered calling him, telling him about the money, but …"

She drifted off and let the thought hang long enough that I felt the need to fill the silence.

"But?"

Michelle blinked again, made a face.

"He would've talked me out of it."

"Talked you out of what?"

"What they want me to do. What they want me to let *you* do to me."

Another chill raced through my body. Ever since I'd woken up this morning, I knew I was headed toward someplace dark, and right now I realized I had entered a very dark place.

"What do they want me to do to you?"

This clearly surprised her. Her green eyes squinted as she frowned, and then she shook her head again.

"Wait a minute. Are you sure this isn't a joke? Please tell me it's a joke. Like"—she looked around the room suddenly—"are there cameras hidden somewhere filming all of this?"

I didn't know if any cameras were hidden in the house, but there was certainly a camera in my glasses, though I wasn't going to tell her that. It would take too long to explain. Plus, I had more pressing matters to worry about.

"Michelle"—hearing myself say her name was staggering —"what do they want me to do to you?"

Her knee started bouncing, her entire body one anxious coil. Suddenly she popped up from the chair and started pacing back and forth in front of the TV. Despite the house being silent, despite her claim that her husband was away for work, I eyed the blank TV to see if there was any movement down the hallway.

"They arrested him, you know? Mike. But his parents, they had a lot of money, and they hired these fancy lawyers who managed it so Mike hardly spent any time in jail. Hell, I spent more time in the hospital than he did in jail. Can you believe that? And he wanted to see me while I was there! That was the craziest part. Despite what happened, despite what he did to me, Mike honestly believed that we were still together. It was my dad who told Mike I wanted nothing more to do with him, and one of the hospital security guards had to be there because they worried my dad was going to punch him in his face."

She paused a beat, shot me a devious grin.

"I wish he had, too. I wish my dad would've beaten Mike the way he beat me. But my dad … he was never a violent man. Neither of my parents were."

Michelle found her way back to the easy chair, setting herself down on it but still leaning forward, her knee still bouncing.

"Can we just get this over with? I just want to get this over with. They said I'd get another two hundred fifty thousand dollars once it was done. And since they've already paid the first half, I feel confident that they'll pay the rest. Do you think they'll pay the rest? Are they paying *you* anything?"

"Michelle"—I said her name slowly this time, trying to get her to focus—"I still don't know what it is they want me to do."

She gave me a new look, this one a mixture of surprise and confusion, and then she just came out and said it, her voice soft and tremulous.

"They want you to beat me like Mike did that night. They want … they want you to put me in a coma."

I opened my mouth to say something—to tell her there was absolutely no way I was going to do anything of the sort—but that was when the phone rang.

Its sudden trill in the silence was enough to make Michelle jump. She glanced down at the cordless phone on the coffee table, then glanced back up at me.

I said, "Maybe it's your husband."

She stared at the phone, shaking her head.

"No, it can't be him. He'd still be asleep, and I … I never told him about any of this."

She kept staring down at the phone, and then on its fifth ring she leaned forward and picked it up.

"Hello?"

Michelle held the phone to her ear for a moment, listening, and then her eyes shifted to meet mine and she extended the cordless to me.

"It's for you."

NINETEEN

The Kid practically kicked open the bedroom door and then he was beside his mother's bed, in an instant, clicking on the bedside lamp and leaning down over her as she writhed on the bed in what was obviously a nightmare.

"No, no, please, stop," she kept murmuring, and the Kid wasn't sure what to do at first, feeling helpless, feeling lost, wishing that he'd asked Carmen to stay the night because he had no idea how to deal with everything that was going on, and then he gently grabbed both her shoulders to try to hold her in place, which somehow made things even worse, because immediately she opened her eyes and saw him towering over her and that was when she started to scream.

"Mom, it's me," the Kid said. "Mom! Mom, stop!"

He finally let go of her shoulders, took a step back to give her space, and like that, she began to settle. Based on her expression, she was still terrified, thinking that he was that dreaded intruder, and he crouched next to the bed, hesitantly held out his hand.

"Mom, it's me. Everything's okay. You were having a nightmare."

She stared at him, her wrinkled face clouded with suspicion, and it broke his heart because he didn't know what to say to make her recognize him.

"Where am I?"

"You're home, Mom. This is your bedroom. This is your bed. I'm ... your son."

He had to swallow after he said this last part, afraid he might break down in tears. This wasn't the first time he'd had this sort of conversation with his mother, but it was the first time after he'd gone twenty-four hours with no sleep and nothing but Red Bull and artificially buttered popcorn in his system.

The confusion slowly faded from her face. She looked around the room once more, as if confirming to herself that it was indeed her own, and then she asked the question that nearly broke him.

"Has your brother come home yet?"

It was part of the Alzheimer's, his mother constantly waiting for his brother to come home. Only his brother had died over twenty years ago, back when they were both kids. He'd fallen out of a tree, having attempted to retrieve the boomerang their father had brought them from his trip to Australia. The drop was maybe ten, twelve feet, but his brother had tried grabbing for a branch as he fell, which threw off his center of gravity, and the next thing the Kid had known his brother had fallen straight down on his head.

The Kid remembered it vividly because it sometimes haunted his own dreams.

"No, Mom. He hasn't come home yet."

She stared at him, her expression not quite clear. Did she believe him? Did she think he was lying to her for some reason?

Yawning, she leaned back down on the bed, placed her head on her pillow.

"Do you think your brother will be home soon?"

The Kid gently took his mother's hand in his own, gave it a slight squeeze.

"Yeah, Mom. I bet he'll be home real soon."

It was a lie, but what else were you supposed to tell a woman who probably wouldn't even remember this conversation in the morning? He just needed her to fall back asleep. He needed her to have a restful night, and then Carmen could continue to watch her once she arrived in the morning.

Stepping out into the hallway two minutes later, after making sure his mother had fallen asleep again, he quietly closed the door and headed back toward the basement. Ben had just entered that house, and the Kid needed to know what was happening.

He eyed the red box of Orville Redenbacher on the kitchen counter. It was a six-pack, and there was only one packet of popcorn left. His anxiety had gone into overdrive, and the only remedy was to eat, and so he tore open the cellophane packet and threw it in the microwave and then headed down the basement steps.

"Did I miss anything?"

Both Carver and Bae had moved closer to the computer monitor. Based on what was currently on the screen, Ben looked to be on the couch in the living room, listening to the woman talk.

"The woman?" Carver said. "It's Michelle Delaney."

The Kid picked up the empty popcorn bowl, watching the monitor.

"You're fucking kidding me."

"No, it's definitely her."

"Why did they send Ben there?"

"Not sure yet. She just started talking. Is everything okay with your mom?"

"She's fine. Just had a nightmare. I'll be right back."

The Kid hurried up the steps with the popcorn bowl. In

the kitchen, he set the bowl on the counter, turned to the sink to wash his hands. He glanced out the window over the sink, out at the dark front lawn, and then he dried his hands on a towel and opened the microwave door right as it started beeping.

The Kid took the hot bag out, pinching it at one end so not to burn his fingers, and as he closed the door he immediately paused. Stood still for several seconds, not breathing. Then he moved over to the light switch on the wall, and flipped the kitchen lights off.

Still with the bag pinched between his two fingers, the Kid crossed over to the sink, slowly now, trying not to make any noise.

When he'd glanced out the window, he hadn't really been focused on the lawn, was just glancing outside as his mind ran through everything that had just happened. Breaking into the one laptop, finding a bunch of random addresses, then his mother crying out, dealing with her, and now learning that Caesar and his people had directed Ben to Michelle Delaney's house. None of it made sense, at least not to his tired mind, so he hadn't been thinking much at all when he glanced out the window. It was only a few seconds later, once his mind caught up with his eyes, that he realized he'd spotted movement out in the dark.

Moving closer to the window, the Kid once more glanced out at the front lawn. The sky was mostly clear, and the moon was bright, so it wasn't entirely pitch-black out there.

Which meant the Kid easily spotted the two men as they moved up the driveway. They both wore black, both carried assault rifles, and one of them started toward the front door as the other veered off toward the side of the house.

The Kid spun away from the window. His first impulse was to race back downstairs but he paused for a beat, thinking of his mother. He wanted to see her one last time, wanted to kiss her forehead. Christ, why didn't he kiss her before he'd left her? What kind of fucking son was he?

But no—there was no telling how much time they had left. So the Kid continued forward, tearing down the basement steps, realizing once he hit the landing that he still had the bag of popcorn pinched between his two fingers and tossing the bag aside.

Carver, his focus on the computer monitor, spoke without looking up at the Kid.

"So now we know why they sent Ben to the house. They want him to beat Michelle Delaney like her boyfriend had beat her back in college. Apparently they've already paid her a quarter million dollars. She lets Ben beat her, she gets another quarter million. I can't believe they—"

Carver paused then, realizing the Kid was barely paying any attention.

The Kid, who had hurried over to the table in the corner, was busily typing away on one of the laptops. He grabbed a flash drive off another table, inserted it into the laptop, and turned back to Carver and Bae, his body shaking and his face ashen.

Carver said, "What's wrong?"

"They're here."

"Who?"

On the computer monitor, a phone started ringing.

Just as upstairs, the front and back doors were simultaneously kicked open.

TWENTY

I stared at Michelle Delaney, not ready to take the phone but knowing I had no choice. I placed the phone to my ear, but all I heard was silence.

"Yes?"

Augustus Caesar said, "Are you enjoying your visit?"

"Aren't you watching?"

"I'm in the middle of something right now, so I'm afraid not."

"I'm not going to beat her."

As I said the words, I noticed a flash of disappointment cross Michelle's face.

"That's up to you, Ben. That's the beauty of these games. From the very beginning, we wanted to make sure the players all had free will. Granted, there are times where it seems as if they're forced into one situation or another, but when you dig right down into it, each player always has the opportunity to say no."

I was silent, not sure where he was going with this. Michelle still stood in front of me, her back to the TV. I kept glancing at the reflection of the room behind me, at the dark hallway.

"Why did you call?"

"Because I decided I wanted to tell you a story. An origin story, to be exact. That's what you kept asking about, isn't it?"

I didn't answer. Still staring up at Michelle. Still not sure what the fuck was going on but not liking it one bit.

"So, Ben, this story is about a boy. A bastard, if you will. A bastard who saw his father every once in a while, but who mostly was raised by his mother. But his mother wasn't around much, what with her job, so he read a lot, and he watched TV, and he would cross the field to the high school to watch the older kids interact. The boy always watched from a distance, worried that the older kids would beat him up if they thought he was some kind of weirdo. In fact, there were times when he even had to run away because the older kids chased after him, but that only intrigued the boy even more."

Michelle, looking uncomfortable, took a step back and lowered herself down on the chair.

"The boy was fascinated by these older kids. How they interacted with the older girls. How they interacted with each other. How they interacted with adults. Keep in mind, the boy was just a boy, only ten years old, and these kids were at least sixteen, some of them seventeen. Kids the boy's age often notice older kids, but hardly any of them actually *study* those who are older. The boy quickly understood what motivated the older kids. How they craved power within their circle of friends. How they especially craved sex. Again, the boy was fascinated by all of it, but he wasn't sure what to do with that knowledge. Then the years passed, and he realized just how predictable the kids his age now were. There were no surprises for the boy. The boy had already figured out human nature, so to speak."

On the easy chair, Michelle watched me, her knee bouncing again.

"The boy was smart, and he attended a good college—the same college his sister attended, in fact—and he decided to join a fraternity, the same fraternity his father had been a member of. The boy was allowed to try out during rush week, but it turned out the fraternity never had any intention of letting him join. You understand, there was no way they could have known who the boy's father truly was. That was a closely held secret. To the fraternity, the boy was just some random kid. He came from a poor family, was smart so he got scholarships, but that didn't matter to the fraternity. What they respected was the same thing that those older kids the boy had used to spy on respected: power and sex."

Michelle's knee kept bouncing, up and down like a piston.

"The fraternity decided to have some fun with the boy. They pushed things farther than they typically did. In fact, things got so out of hand the boy nearly died. I won't go into the details, but the boy was in the hospital for two weeks. During that time, the boy heard from his father. It was one of those rare occasions when his father actually came to see him. His father did not show the boy compassion. Instead, his father told him he was an embarrassment. The father said that he was glad the boy didn't have his last name. The father said if the boy were him, he'd kill himself. I'll tell you, Ben, it wasn't your usual pep talk, but it was in fact a pep talk. That's just how the old man was. He left the room and didn't even say goodbye."

Her knee still bouncing, Michelle ran her hand through her hair, looking everywhere but at me.

"Once the boy healed enough to be discharged from the hospital, he returned to school. The boy didn't have any friends. The only person he saw every once in a while outside of class was his sister. The boy told his sister about their father's visit. She knew how their father could be. She said she was sorry for what their father had said to him, but the boy told her their father was right. And then he told his sister he had a plan."

Michelle rose from the chair and started pacing in front of me, her thumb to her mouth now, biting at the nail.

"Stories are powerful things, Ben. Stories can make and break empires. The boy knew this, and he decided to use it to his advantage. He started some stories—some rumors, if you will—and they quickly circled around campus. About an exclusive club. Something even more sacred than the fraternities. The boy made sure those in charge of the fraternity—only three young men, those who were responsible for what had happened to the boy—heard the stories. Word reached them fast. Now, this was before the Internet, so messages had to be sent through the campus mail. The boy manipulated things so that his identity was kept secret. But the boy teased those in charge of the fraternity for weeks, giving them bits and pieces that made them become obsessed with the idea of joining this exclusive club. What's more, the boy managed to make sure those in charge of the fraternity kept word of the club to themselves, and never even hinted about it to their closest friends."

Michelle kept pacing, kept biting at her nail. I glanced again at the blank TV screen, at the dark hallway behind me.

On the phone, Augustus Caesar let out a heavy sigh.

"I don't want to draw this out much longer, Ben. Let's just say things fell into place for the boy. He managed to get those in charge of the fraternity on the hook. He convinced them to come to an exclusive party hosted in an abandoned warehouse. He convinced them to wear masks to hide their identity. He convinced them that they were going to ... well, remember when I told you the boy understood just how much the older kids respected power and sex? The boy convinced them that they were going to have the best sex of their life."

Augustus paused suddenly, and then made a noise as he remembered something.

"I forgot to tell you the best part. The boy convinced those in charge of the fraternity that they needed to pay to get into the exclusive club. They had come to believe the club was so exclusive that they were willing to pay whatever it took. The boy managed to bring in a hefty amount of money. He used some of it to get things prepared in the warehouse for the party. It was three o'clock in the morning when those in charge of the fraternity arrived. They wore masks, so none of them knew who each other were. They climbed to the second floor of the warehouse, where hundreds of candles had been lit. And in the middle of the room was a young girl, lying on a table, her legs and arms bound. She was naked, of course, but her mouth was taped shut and a blindfold was over her eyes. In the middle of the night, in the dark room with the candles, the girl looked to be maybe eighteen, nineteen years old. But she was really four-teen. The boy had abducted her earlier that day, having watched her for the past month. And now that those three young man in charge of the fraternity—those who had orches-trated the beating that the boy took—had finally arrived to this exclusive club, had gone up the stairs to find this naked child … that was when the police arrived."

Augustus paused again, and I knew he was smiling.

"Oh, Ben, I can't tell you just how much trouble those young men got into. Of course, they tried to explain about how they'd been contacted about the exclusive club, but there was no evidence. The letters that were sent to them had to be sent back. Photocopiers were available at the time, but the letters were sent on dark paper, which meant there was no way for the young men to make copies. The young men's parents were quite rich, and they hired expensive lawyers, but it was impossible for them to get out of trouble. After all, the girl who was abducted? Her father was a judge."

Augustus chuckled, soft and low, and when he spoke next his voice had become thoughtful.

"It was after that the boy realized just how easy it was to manipulate others. He'd learned the trick to gaining power was to tell people what they want to hear, and that, when you're really skilled, it's making people believe what you tell them is what they've believed all along. It came natural to the boy. And moving forward, he understood the importance of those two basic tenets: power and sex. That's what drives every man and woman, deep down inside. It's that dark nature I believe Simon once told you about. Everybody has it. Some manage to keep it hidden all their lives. Others ... well, sometimes that dark nature comes out. Everybody just needs an excuse to let it out. And everybody—and I mean *everybody*—can be manipulated. The more you do it, the easier it becomes, until ... well, until you've created your very own empire."

Augustus fell silent, and as I watched Michelle continue to pace back and forth in front of the TV, I asked him the only question that made sense right then.

"Why are you telling me this?"

"It's simple, Ben. I've never told anybody that story before. Only my sister knows it, and that's because she was involved in what happened. All these years, all these decades, I've kept it a secret and, well, I don't know why, but I just wanted to tell you. After all, it's not like you're going to be able to tell anybody my story. And even if you did, what would it matter? Nobody knows who I am. That's the genius of it. The more invisible you can make yourself, the more power you can have. It's just that ... Okay, Ben, here's a secret. Are you ready for the secret?"

I was silent for a beat, watching Michelle, my entire body on edge.

"What secret?"

"This game? Nobody in the Inner Circle has been watching. There's only a handful of people who know about it—us and … well, you and your team. I'll tell you, there was never any guarantee that this was going to work. We knew that hacker friend of yours is smart and that he keeps himself well hidden. But you have to understand just how wide our reach is. We have people everywhere. Tracing your friend's location, no matter how many proxies and VPNs he uses … well, we figured it would take days, but it barely even took twenty-four hours."

I stood up from the couch suddenly, and Michelle immediately froze, her eyes wide.

"If you hadn't stolen those laptops, Ben, maybe we wouldn't have bothered to do any of this. Yes, that's right, we saw you take those laptops. We had cameras all over the Fillmore that were still recording before the place blew up. I'll be honest, we aren't quite sure what information may have been on those laptops, since the rest were destroyed in the explosion, but we couldn't take any chances. Plus … I thought it would be fun to throw you back into the game one last time. I would have preferred Carver, to be honest, but in his current state there wasn't much he could do. Plus, he had no motivation to come back into the game. Both his wife and son are long dead. Your wife and daughter, however, are still very much alive. We always thought we might need them in the future, once we realized just how much of a problem you had become, and so we've kept them alive ever since."

Augustus paused to let out a soft sigh of relief.

"Now, Ben, it's time for you and me to part ways. The truth is, my men have been securing the hacker's house for the past ten minutes. There was some gunfire earlier, I believe. I assume Carver and whoever else is inside tried to defend themselves but without any luck, as I'm getting the signal that everything is clear so I can make my entrance. Is there anything you want me to tell Carver and your hacker friend?"

Standing there, the phone to my ear, I shouted, "Carver, Kid, they know where you are!"

Augustus Caesar chuckled again in my ear.

"Nice try, Ben. But like I told you, my men have already secured the house. There's nothing you can do to save your friends. And by the way, what Michelle told you about beating her for the second half of the money? That's what we told her to tell you. We knew it would rattle you, the idea of doing that to the poor girl whom you didn't help so many years ago. The truth is, Michelle and her husband get the second half of the money as soon as they kill you. Nice knowing you, Ben."

Something must have changed in my face, because a realization flickered through Michelle's widening eyes, and she shouted, "Bobby, now!"

And in the reflection of the TV, the closet door swung open and a large man with a beard stepped out, a shotgun in his hands.

I spun at once, raising the phone over my head as Bobby raised the shotgun. I threw the phone right at Bobby's face. Like the cop back at the gas station, it clipped him on the forehead, only the phone was heavier than a candy bar, plus the distance between us was much shorter. It was enough to cause some damage, and Bobby stumbled back just as I vaulted over the couch and slammed him into the wall. The shotgun went off, into the ceiling, and I was so close that it nearly ruptured my eardrum. I grabbed the barrel of the shotgun and shoved it back into Bobby's face, shoved it hard, and at once blood squirted from his nose. Through the ringing in my ears I heard Michelle cry out and the next thing I knew she was hanging on my back, trying to pull me off her husband. I wrestled the shotgun from Bobby's grasp as Michelle scratched at my face and tried to dig her teeth into my ear, and I pivoted to the side, slamming her into the wall with enough force that she lost her grip. Bobby charged at me, pushing me back deeper into the house. I stumbled over Michelle's foot and fell back, nearly losing the shotgun in the process. The back of my head knocked against the floor, enough for me to momentarily see stars, and Bobby stepped close to kick me in the stomach. I had just enough time to pump the shotgun and squeeze the trigger. I jerked the shotgun at the last second, so it wasn't aimed at his face. After the massive blast, he cried out in pain and fell back against the wall. Michelle shouted out his name and immediately rushed to his side. Much of his left shoulder had been torn apart.

Crouched beside him, Michelle quickly inspected the wound before she directed her glare in my direction.

"You bastard! You almost killed him!"

I pumped the shotgun again, held it steady on her as I managed to climb to my feet.

"You crazy bitch, you two were going to kill me."

"Fuck you! We need that money!"

I stepped past them into the living room, Bobby on the floor groaning in pain.

"Yeah, well, you might want to call an ambulance before your husband bleeds out."

The cordless phone was near my foot, and I kicked it over in her direction.

Tears in her eyes, Michelle picked up the phone and threw it back at me.

"Fuck you! Why'd you have to hurt him? Why you'd have to go and shoot him like that?"

These people were fucking nuts. I kicked the phone back in her direction, and it skidded to only a few inches away from her.

"If you don't want him to die, call an ambulance right now."

Michelle was in tears now, completely hysterical, and Bobby's face had become pale. If I were a better man, I would have called the ambulance for them, but I have a rule about not calling 911 to help people who just tried to kill me.

I backed to the front door, keeping the shotgun aimed at them, and then stepped outside and hurried down the walkway.

I had just reached the Tesla when headlights appeared at the bottom of the driveway. First one car, then a second.

Escorts, I thought and aimed the shotgun at the approaching vehicles.

I had no idea how many shells were left in the shotgun, but I was going to use all of them. It probably wouldn't be enough, but at least I'd take out a couple of Augustus' men.

God, at least let me take out a couple of his men.

The first car came to a sudden halt, and a voice shouted from the driver's-side window.

"Ben, it's me!"

I stood there for a moment, breathing heavily, and then I lowered the shotgun.

"Ronny?"

He stepped out of the car. As did Mason.

The second car stopped behind the first car, and Drew and Ho Sook climbed out.

Ronny regarded the shotgun in my hands, then glanced up at the house.

"What happened? The Kid sent out an SOS because you were in trouble."

I shook my head, tears stinging my eyes, and headed for the car.

"Not me. It's them. The Kid and Carver and whoever's at the house. We need to head back there right now."

Ronny stepped in front of me, placed both of his hands on my shoulders to hold me steady.

"Slow down, Ben. What do you mean?"

I nearly hit him with the shotgun, so much rage was coursing through me, but I dropped it to the ground and wiped at my eyes.

"Caesar and his men, Ronny. They found the Kid's place. At this point ... they're probably already dead."

TWENTY-ONE

The man who called himself Augustus Caesar stepped out of the SUV and handed the cell phone to one of the men standing nearby. They were parked in the driveway, and he looked down at the closest house maybe one hundred yards away. Far enough that if the neighbors were looking outside— or had heard the faint gunfire, which was doubtful, as it wasn't even six o'clock in the morning yet—they might see the two SUVs but couldn't tell what else was going on.

He appraised the ranch house before him, its brick siding and weathered roof, and he found himself shaking his head that this was the base of operations for the people who had caused him such aggravation these past five years.

He stood there, waiting, until Zach appeared through the front door and headed down the walkway.

"We're all clear, sir."

"How many?"

"Four. Carver Ellison and the hacker are downstairs in the basement, along with an old Korean man. An old woman is in one of the two bedrooms upstairs. We believe it's the hacker's mother."

Zach spoke quickly and confidently, having accepted the new role as Augustus' first in command. Augustus knew Zach had been part of the Legion program, that from the day Zach was born he'd been tasked with taking up the cause. Zach had been put in charge of eliminating a problem several years ago that dealt with a pair of old employees; in the process many people had died, including Oswald Matheson, who Augustus had known from the very start. Oswald had been a good, intelligent man, but stubborn, which was probably the cause of his eventual demise. From there Zach had worked on the game side of things and eventually faded into the background, until last weekend when he was stationed at the Fillmore. As soon as the lights went out, Zach was the first one to reach Augustus and pull him off stage, rush him out of the building to safety.

Considering the attack that occurred soon after, Augustus may very well have been killed if Zach hadn't acted so quickly. Augustus owed his life to the man, and so he decided to put him in charge, at least for the time being. Zach's first task was tracking down those damned laptops that Ben Anderson had stolen. Augustus had been assured there was no way to break into those laptops, but the Council didn't want to take any chances.

"The laptops?"

For the first time Zach looked hesitant. He glanced at the other men standing nearby before clearing his throat.

"They've been destroyed."

"Excuse me?"

"Destroyed, sir. All the laptops have been smashed with a hammer. So has all the hacker's equipment. Apparently as soon as they heard us breach the house, they went about destroying everything."

This revelation made Augustus grit his teeth. He didn't like it. Not one bit. Now there was no way to determine whether or not any information had been found on the laptops. At least, he didn't think so. That would need to be determined from their own techs. He supposed there was a way to salvage the parts.

He nodded at Zach and started up the walkway toward the house. As he reached the door, he paused.

"I had heard gunfire. Was anybody injured?"

"No, sir. Carver had a Glock on him, and fired when our men went down the stairs. But he soon exhausted his magazine, and we've secured everybody down in the basement. Except the old woman, of course."

Augustus noticed one of the men standing off to the side, holding a digital camera aimed at them.

"What is he doing?"

"The Council, sir. They requested video documentation. We're to upload it to them once we depart."

"I didn't approve that."

Zach once again looked hesitant. He took two steps to the side, blocking Augustus from the camera's view, and then lowered his voice.

"We received notice from the Council ten minutes ago. You were on the phone. I apologize—I assumed you were speaking with them."

Augustus motioned for Zach to stay put and stepped up onto the porch, in full view of the camera. He didn't like the idea of the Council micromanaging him, and he especially didn't want to appear weak, so he paused a beat and then turned back around.

"The hacker's mother—is she awake?"

"She is, yes."

"Wait five minutes, and then bring her down into the basement."

"Yes, sir."

Augustus continued into the house, marveling at just how *ordinary* everything looked. The furniture, the décor, the carpet—it was all rather bland, like it had no personality whatsoever.

The fading odor of popcorn caught his notice, and he saw the box of Orville Redenbacher on the kitchen counter. He remembered reading in Ben Anderson's story that the hacker—who they called the Kid—liked eating popcorn. Apparently the hacker had kept up the habit.

He went down the carpeted steps, taking his time, savoring the moment. Carver Ellison had been a pain in his ass from the very beginning. Last week he'd thought it would all be over—Carver would be dead, his part in this saga completed—but then the attacked happened, and many of those in the Inner Circle perished, and that just wasn't acceptable.

When he reached the bottom of the stairs—the cameraman two steps behind him—Augustus surveyed the tiny basement area, the tables and the destroyed computers on top, as well as the hacker and the old Korean man, before his gaze settled on Carver sitting in a wheelchair.

"Hello, Carver. It feels like we just saw each other yesterday."

Carver said nothing. Neither did the hacker or the Korean man. Probably because his own men were standing behind them, aiming pistols at their heads.

Augustus scanned the basement once more, making a face as he shook his head.

"This base of operation you have here is rather … pedestrian."

The hacker said, "Fuck you, you old piece of shit."

The man standing behind him knocked the hacker in the back of the head with his pistol. A quick, blunt jab, nothing more.

Augustus focused his attention on the Korean man.

"And who is this?"

Glaring back at him, the man wet his lips.

"My name is Bae. I woke up in one of your games."

"Is that right? Must have been one of our international games. I'll be honest, I never paid close attention to those. Coming up with a plan to save the world takes up a lot of your time."

Carver's expression didn't surprise him. It was indifferent, like back at the Coliseum. Then, Carver knew he was probably going to die and had accepted it. Here, he most likely knew that he was going to die and had accepted it again. Only this time, it was a certainty.

"Cat got your tongue, Carver?"

When Carver answered, his voice was low and flat.

"Just get it over with."

"Oh, we will. Typically, I wouldn't even make an appearance at something like this. But I felt the need to be here this time, if not for any other reason except for all the people who died."

The hacker said, "Boo-fucking-hoo to those assholes."

Which prompted another jab against the back of his head with the pistol.

Carver said, "You can kill us, but there are others. People will always keep rising up against you."

"Maybe," Augustus said. "But without someone like your hacker friend in their corner, there isn't much they can do."

Carver grinned, and shook his head.

"You have no idea what my team can do."

"Oh, I think I have an idea. Many of them are dead already. Ben is probably dead by now too. Whoever you sent after him might not suffer the same consequence, but that's okay. They'll certainly get the message once they return here."

Footsteps at the top of the stairs, and a tired, weak voice asking what was happening.

The hacker attempted to jump up from his chair but was

held down in place, the barrel of the pistol digging into the back of his head.

Zach and another one of his men brought the old lady down to the bottom of the stairs. She was wearing wrinkled pajamas. Her gray hair was a mess. Her wide eyes took in everybody down here, including the guns, and then her gaze shifted up to meet his.

"Do you know when my son will be home?"

Augustus was very aware of the cameraman standing in the corner. Filming every single moment for the Council to review and dissect. Especially his sister, who he knew would search for any signs of weakness.

So he decided the old woman would be the first.

He gave a slight nod to Zach, and Zach raised his pistol to the back of the old woman's head.

The woman looked around the basement, completely oblivious, until suddenly recognition filled her face seeing the hacker in the chair.

"Avery? Who are these men? What is happening? Have you seen—"

Gunfire filled the basement like a savage symphony.

PART II

PAX ROMANA

TWENTY-TWO

I had the passenger-side door open and was jumping out before the car had even come to a complete stop.

Graham stood on the porch, leaning on his cane, looking more beaten down than I'd ever seen him—even after Augustus' men had burned down the farmhouse and killed all his bees just over a week ago.

The midday sun was bright, forcing him to squint as he watched me charging forward. When he realized I didn't intend to slow down, he raised a quaking hand.

"Ben, just wait a—"

I stepped past him, went straight for the front door. But Chin waited just behind the screen, shaking his head slightly.

I took a breath, feeling my fingernails digging into my palms, wanting to scream out my frustrations. We'd been on the road for the past two days, only stopping for gas. We no longer had the luxury of the Kid hiring Fred to fly us wherever we pleased.

Because the Kid was dead.

And so was Carver.

And so was Bae.

And so was—good God—the Kid's mother.

In my mad dash to be the first one inside, I hadn't properly noticed Chin behind the screen door. He wore a surgical mask over his nose and mouth, and blue nitrile gloves on his hands. And in his hands were two boxes: one with more masks, the other with more gloves.

Chin opened the door, and held out the boxes.

Impatient, I put on the gloves and a mask and then glanced back at Ronny and the others as they hurried up the walkway. Even Mason was back there, and I was sure he wanted to return to the motel, see his wife, but he felt the need to be here, too, though I honestly wasn't sure what his being here would accomplish.

I wasn't sure what any of us being here would accomplish.

Graham cleared his throat, and spoke quietly.

"We haven't touched the bodies. We've done our best to keep the house closed up, because we didn't want flies getting everywhere, but because of that"—he made a face—"down there is a godawful stink. That's why when we knew you'd be here soon, we opened the windows to try to air the place out. But it didn't help much. My God, I worked as a police detective and saw my fair share of dead bodies, but nothing like—"

He cut himself off, shaking his head. I lightly touched his shoulder, though it was less out of comfort than just acknowledging that this entire situation was fucked up.

Once again I regarded everybody—Ronny and Drew and Mason and Ho Sook, all now wearing masks and gloves—and my eyes settled for a moment on Ho Sook. Her father was down in the basement. A father she may never had been very close to but her father nonetheless. She was trying her best to hide the pain but still her eyes were glassy in the early morning light.

Graham cleared his throat again.

"The woman who took care of the Kid's mother is getting

suspicious. We'd waited for her down at the end of the road. We told her that the Kid decided he didn't need her services for a couple of days but would pay her anyway. She probably tried calling the Kid, but of course he didn't answer. Eventually her suspicion will grow, and that's when she'll probably call the police. So before that happens, we have to work on a plan. We can't just burn this house down, but we can't quite leave it as it is either, can we?"

"We'll bury them."

My voice, deep and tremulous, sounded so different I didn't realize I'd spoken at first.

Graham tilted his head, studying my face.

"Is that what the backyard is now, a graveyard?"

"You have a better idea?"

He didn't. He made sure that everybody wore a mask and gloves and then he put them on himself and we entered the house.

Even with the mask, the smell was repugnant, and I hadn't gone any farther than the kitchen.

The front door had been kicked in, that much was evident, but the rest of the first floor didn't look any different than it had the day I'd left to drive straight to D.C.

In the kitchen, I noted that the Kid's popcorn bowl was on the counter. A clear plastic bowl marked by dried butter and grease and some kernels.

We'd debated whether or not all of us needed to go downstairs, and in the end it was decided that we did. Carver and the Kid were family to us. Bae we didn't know much at all, but he was most certainly family to Ho Sook. And the Kid's mother … Christ, even thinking about it made me want to punch a wall.

Chin went down first. I followed. Ronny followed me.

Then Drew. Then Ho Sook. Then Mason. Graham came last, taking his time as he slowly climbed down the steps, holding onto his cane with one hand and the banister with another.

We'd been told what to expect, but still the sight of the four dead bodies nearly knocked me off my feet.

Ho Sook pushed past us to hurry over to her father. Somehow he was still in the chair, slumped but still in a seated position.

He'd been shot in the back of the head.

They'd all been shot in the back of the head.

My eyes watered, both from the stench but also from the sight of the four dead bodies.

Carver in his wheelchair.

The Kid in his leather office chair.

The Kid's mother crumpled on the floor.

"As you can see," Graham said, standing back near the steps, "they took all the hard drives. It's unclear whether or not they destroyed the computers or if it was the Kid who did it."

I stared down at the bodies and the countless scattered pieces of glass and plastic littering the floor, and said, "It was the Kid."

"How can you be so sure?"

"Caesar's people wouldn't have destroyed the computers and then taken just the hard drives. The Kid must have gotten some kind of tip off that they were coming. He destroyed as much as he could as fast as he could."

A retching noise came from Mason's direction.

"I'm sorry," he said, backing away toward the stairs, "but I gotta get out of here."

He pushed past Graham and hurried up the steps and went straight for the bathroom. Even from down here we could hear him throwing up in the toilet.

Drew said, "I'm going to head up too."

I nodded at him and watched him climb the stairs. He

didn't move as quickly as Mason, but he was clearly in a hurry. I didn't blame him. I didn't want to be down here either. But I felt I had no choice.

Graham said, "Well, they didn't appear to take anything else. Chin and I searched the basement the best we could. We were worried that maybe Caesar's people would have left a bomb behind, or some cameras, but Chin scanned the entire house and didn't find anything."

Still staring down at the bodies, I shook my head.

"Blowing the house would cause too much attention. As for the cameras, I think Caesar and his people are done with us. They came for what they wanted. They could have killed us, but without Carver and the Kid, they know we're no longer a threat."

There was a beat of silence, and then Graham issued a heavy sigh.

"I almost stayed that night. I wanted to be here, but I was too tired. Part of me wonders if things would have been different had I stayed, but I know that's not true. I ... I would just be another body on the floor."

I kept staring at the bodies, in a trancelike state. For the past two days while we'd driven down one highway after another, I'd thought about what Graham had told us had happened. But I'd also thought about Jen and Casey. They were still alive, or at least they had been early Saturday morning. Now it was Monday, and there was no telling what had become of them.

Ronny asked, "You said you searched the basement and didn't find anything?"

Graham said, "That's right. There wasn't much down here to begin with now that all the computers are gone. You've got the microwave over in the corner, and there's still a bag of popcorn inside, but besides that, there's nothing else."

I kept staring down at the bodies, thinking about everybody we'd lost, including Maya who was buried in the backyard along with Mason's son, and then I found myself blinking as I turned back to Graham.

"What did you say is in the microwave?"

"A bag of popcorn. The Kid must have made it right before Caesar's people showed up."

I stared past the dead bodies at the microwave in the corner. Then I moved suddenly, stepping over the Kid's mother, edging past Carver and Bae, and as I reached the microwave I realized my hands were shaking.

Graham shuffled forward a couple of feet, his voice cautious.

"What is it?"

I opened the microwave door, considered the popped bag of Orville Redenbacher inside.

"The Kid never used this to make popcorn."

"Maybe he did that night."

"No. His bowl is upstairs on the counter. He must have been making it when they showed up and hurried down here and still had the bag."

"Okay," Graham said slowly. "But if that's the case, why did he put the bag in that microwave?"

I didn't answer. I had no idea. I didn't know much about anything anymore other than the fact that half our team was dead and my wife and daughter may very well be dead now too.

I pulled out the bag, held it in my hand for a beat. It was mostly sealed except for the slit near the top that was partly open to let out steam.

The bag didn't feel any different from any popcorn bag I'd ever held, though it had been a while since I'd made any popcorn in the microwave.

I opened the bag, my heart pounding, certain that there would be something inside.

But there wasn't. Just two-day old popcorn, crusted over with artificial butter.

I jerked the bag, shuffling the popcorn, but there didn't appear to be anything inside.

"Goddamn it."

I wanted to throw the bag across the room but knew that wouldn't remedy my frustration. Instead I took the bottom and tipped it over, let the popcorn cascade down to the carpet as I shook the bag angrily.

Only it wasn't just popcorn that fell out of the bag.

Something else fell out of it too.

Something that bounced on the carpet and then was covered in a pile of popcorn.

Tossing the bag aside, I crouched down and reached into the mess and then came back with what had been inside the bag.

The thing the Kid had specifically hidden there moments before he was murdered.

A flash drive.

TWENTY-THREE

I had just lit another cigarette when Mason stepped out of the motel room.

"Can I have one of those?"

I handed him the pack and lighter and watched him as he lit up and inhaled and blew a stream of smoke out into the parking lot. A soft breeze drifted through, and the smoke dissipated into the air.

By now it was late afternoon. The sun was steadily dipping toward the horizon, the sky awash in orange and purple, and the temperature was that nice sort of in-between where it wasn't too hot and it wasn't too cold.

"How's your wife?"

Mason let out another stream of smoke, tapped the end of his cigarette on the railing.

"Not so great."

"Maybe we should take her to the hospital."

"I'm not sure what more they can do. Beverly has done everything she can. She's made sure Gloria has gotten all the attention she needs. It's just ... sometimes a body becomes so broken it's impossible to fix it."

I imagined he was thinking of his son right then, broken and beaten to the point he was practically dead. I imagined he was thinking of his son because I was thinking of his son and how he hadn't been that way when he and his mother were introduced to the crowd in the Torture Room at the Coliseum —with me standing in the back of the room, a gun hidden underneath my cloak, powerless to save them.

"Mason—"

I couldn't seem to push out any more words, no matter how hard I tried. Mason read the expression on my face, and nodded solemnly.

"I know, Ben. Ronny told me. You did what you could, but the truth was there was nothing more you could have done."

I felt he was letting me off too easy. Telling me what I wanted to hear. But I knew that wasn't true. It just wasn't Mason's style. I didn't know the man well, but I at least knew that much.

"I'm sorry."

He nodded, took one final drag, and flicked the butt out into the parking lot.

"Me too. I've been through hell the past two weeks, but I can't imagine what you're going through. Losing Maya, and then learning your—"

But he cut himself off, shaking his head. Not wanting to voice what I'd been trying to grapple with the past couple of days. A betrayal of sorts.

For nearly two years I'd believed my wife and daughter were dead. It was a knowledge that allowed me to move on, though it had been difficult, nearly impossible. Maya had helped me get past it. She'd helped me see that I was able to love again. Because I had loved Maya. I had been *in* love with her, if I was being honest with myself. I was ready to share everything with her, but then the Coliseum happened, and she stepped in the way of a bullet meant for me.

Then, not too long later, when I believed I'd lost the only thing in the world I truly loved, I learned that my wife and daughter were in fact still alive.

It had been jarring, the kind of revelation that makes you lose your balance, the kind that threatens to rip apart your soul, and immediately there was the sense of betrayal, that while I'd moved on from loving my family—who had apparently been alive all this time—I had gone and fallen in love with someone else.

I had of course still loved my wife and daughter, but it was a passive love, the kind you give your departed loved ones. I still thought of them every day, but I thought of them as they had been and not as they were now because I'd been lied to, manipulated by Augustus Caesar and his minions for no other reason than to fuck with my head.

Mason spoke again, his low, deep voice pulling me from my thoughts.

"They're back."

I blinked and looked up to watch the car parking in one of the open spaces. Drew stepped out of the car along with Ho Sook and Chin. They'd gone to a Best Buy to purchase a computer.

I touched the outside of my jeans pocket; the bulge of the flash drive was still there. Then I turned and tapped lightly at Beverly's door, and Ronny spoke from inside.

"It's open."

I pushed the door open. Ronny was sitting on the bed beside Beverly. Graham sat across from them. What was left of the sunlight streamed into the room, stretching my shadow across the carpet.

Ronny asked, "Help you with something?"

"They're here."

That got them moving. They pushed off the beds where they'd been talking to make room for Drew and Ho Sook and Chin. I waited out on the walkway and touched Ho Sook's arm to stop her before she followed everybody else inside.

She paused, looking at me with her dark eyes. Silent.

I whispered, "I'm sorry."

She just stared at me. Her expression blank.

Though I was pretty sure beneath that blank expression was the bubbling lava of fury. She was tamping it down, letting it get hotter and hotter, so that eventually—when she was ready —she'd let the volcano of her fury explode.

"I am sorry as well," she whispered finally, and entered the motel room.

I didn't follow her in. I had them keep the door open so I could stand outside and smoke another cigarette. I noticed Ronny give me a look, and it reminded me of the look Maya had sometimes given me when she felt I'd had too much to smoke for the day.

The trio had purchased a Dell Inspiron laptop. Drew opened the box and got out the laptop and the cords and plugged it in, everybody standing around watching silently.

Mason said, "I still don't get why we couldn't just use one of the laptops we already have."

Drew opened the lid of the laptop, powered it on.

"Like Ho Sook said, it's better we use an air-gapped computer for this."

"Okay. But I still don't get what air-gapped means."

Ho Sook took over, kneeling beside the bed as the prompts came up to set up the laptop. She skipped several of the prompts until she arrived at the main screen.

"An air-gapped computer has never been connected to the Internet or any other network. I know a bit about computers, but not nearly as much as your friend."

She paused, and looked up at me.

"The flash drive?"

Keeping the cigarette between my lips, I slipped the drive from my pocket and tossed it on the bed beside the laptop.

Ho Sook took the drive, undid the cap, and inserted it into the computer. She stared at the screen, as did everybody else inside the room.

She'd had the right idea, Ho Sook. It was something I never would have thought of, and probably nobody else. She pointed out that computers that have already accessed the Internet might still have traces of the network on the Internet, or something along those lines. The main concern was that depending on what was on the flash drive, it might send out a signal to Augustus' people depending on what was on it. That was why we'd waited nearly two hours to get the new laptop.

I stayed out on the walkway, still smoking. I watched the rest of them inside as they crowded around Ho Sook. They were quiet, which probably meant nothing had come on screen yet.

The reason I was still standing out here—the reason I hadn't joined the others—was because I feared nothing would come on the screen. That all of this had been a waste of time. That the Kid hadn't managed to get anything useful off the laptops, and that this was just some sick joke by one of Augustus' men or even Augustus himself. Maybe they'd left the flash drive behind just to fuck with us. And that when we did access it, all we would see was the murder of our friends and family.

There was a long beat of silence, and then Mason grunted.

"What the fuck is that supposed to mean?"

I flicked my cigarette over the railing and entered the room. Moved close enough to see the screen.

It was an image of a giant demon or some kind of creature that looked like a demon. It had giant horns and was engulfed in flames and looked to be holding a sword.

The words BOW DOWN BEFORE SARGERAS appeared above the demon's head.

I shook my head, and returned to the walkway. Pulled out another cigarette but didn't light it.

Drew mumbled, "This is bullshit."

Ronny said, "Ho Sook, do you have any ideas?"

She used the trackpad to try to find something on the image to click on but then shook her head.

"I do not know. It appears to be a game, or ... some kind of encryption I have never seen. Again, I know computers well, but I am not nearly as knowledgeable as your friend."

Ronny tilted his head down, touched his fingers to the bridge of his nose to stifle a headache.

"Now what the heck do we do?"

"Nothing," Drew said. "It's over. There's nothing we can do. We don't know anybody who can break this encryption."

There was a silence—a thick, heavy silence full of frustration and anger—and then I stepped back into the room, stuffing the unlit cigarette back into the pack.

"I think I might know someone who can."

TWENTY-FOUR

As he did during many of his frequent grocery store treks, Titus carried a plastic shopping basket down the dairy aisle.

It was early morning, not even an hour after the store had opened, so many of the employees were still stocking the shelves. One of the employees had a U-boat out stacked with egg cartons and was busy rotating the cellophane containers. The employee noticed Titus out of the corner of his eye, but the employee didn't smile at him like he typically would do to other customers.

Titus wasn't surprised. He'd lived most of his life like somebody's shadow: people knew he was there, but they often ignored him.

He came to the cheese section and set the plastic basket on the freshly waxed linoleum floor and started grabbing packages of Kraft American cheese and loading them into the basket. He typically grabbed six at a time—what usually got him through a week—but he saw that they were currently on sale, 2 for $5, so he grabbed ten packages in all and then hefted the basket and started down the aisle again.

An old woman was headed his way, who looked to be about

sixty or seventy with a bob of curly white hair. She stared at
him, like she had never seen a little person before, especially
one with thick glasses and a hearing aid, and that urge to snap
at her raced through him. Years ago he'd been more apt to do it
—to stop and say, Hey, lady, why don't you take a fucking
picture, it'll last longer—but in his old age (only twenty-eight,
but still) he had come to understand there were better ways of
living your life.

Only, as he neared the woman, walking almost lopsidedly
due to the weight of all the processed cheese, he realized the
woman hadn't been staring at him at all but checking out the
butters in the display case above him.

Titus snorted, wanted to laugh out loud.

His snort drew the old woman's attention, and she gave
him a curious frown. Like she hadn't even realized he existed
until that moment. Which felt even worse than being stared at,
to be honest.

Again, that urge to snap at her streaked through him, but
Titus forced a smile and gave a little wave and continued on
down the aisle.

He had a couple more stops to make before it was time to
leave. He needed to buy some canned soup, and some cereal,
and some snacks. It probably wouldn't all fit in the basket,
which meant he would have to go without, but he knew that
was probably for the best. He'd been meaning to cut back on
the junk food for a while now, but it was just so hard, especially
when the stores kept having sales on all that delicious, artificially flavored, often-high-in-fructose-corn-syrup junk food.

Buy one get one free chips! How could he possible say no
to *that*?

But again, there was only so much space in the basket. The
carts were obviously too tall for him to push on his own,
though he had done that once or twice, but he felt absolutely
ridiculous, like a child, and during those times when he'd

succumbed to the siren-sound of a squeaky-wheeled cart that allowed him to stock up on way too many snacks, people most certainly *had* been staring at him.

Titus had tried one of those kid carts, the kind that were tiny and had the plastic banner hanging off a pole proclaiming FUTURE SHOPPER IN TRAINING. The truth was, those carts were perfect for him, but then he had definitely felt like a child, and it didn't help that one time some teenagers had been in the store, probably skipping school—Titus purposely did his shopping in the mornings, when school was in session—and they had taken pictures of him, including a video, and it had taken Titus nearly a week to track down the video the kids had posted on social media and delete it.

So, yeah, he'd tried different carts before and found that the best course of action was with a plastic basket. Even if it meant he couldn't put too much in said basket.

Anyway, he knew that he could have the Publix or Winn-Dixie deliver groceries, but that would mean somebody coming to where he lived, and he didn't like that idea at all.

Which was why he used the smaller chain stores, the ones that were family-owned. This store in particular was one of his favorites. Some of the staff was nice of him, others were more indifferent, which, to be honest, was just as well.

Titus went down the canned aisle and grabbed several cans of tomato and chicken noodle soup. He hefted the basket again, chuckling to himself that this was when he got his true workout, and as he started back down the aisle he had that weird feeling you get when you're being watched

He paused, and glanced over his shoulder.

A man was standing down at the end of the aisle, a tall, dark-skinned man with a scarred face.

The man might have been scanning the shelves for some-thing on his shopping list, but Titus didn't think so, especially when the man seemed to realize he'd been spotted and quickly moved to the next aisle.

Okay, then. Time to leave.

Titus made his way to the front of the store and waited in line for his favorite cashier. He'd typically use the self-checkout, even when it was sometimes a pain in the ass due to his height, but the cashier here—Brenda, a bespectacled woman in her fifties who was the sweetest person in the world—was so kind that Titus didn't mind waiting in line until he was close enough to the conveyer belt to start unloading the items from his basket.

As he waited for the old man ahead of him to pay for his groceries—he was actually writing out a check!—Titus had that feeling again that he was being watched.

He scanned the front of the store.

There the man was again, down near the bakery. As soon as he noticed Titus looking his way, he turned toward the rack of fresh bread and slid a cell phone from his pocket, typed what appeared to be a text message.

Titus didn't like it, though he wasn't certain why. All he knew was that he'd gotten a bad feeling. He was used to people staring at him at times, but those were almost always ignorant assholes who didn't know any better. This ... this felt different.

"Good morning, Titus. How have you been?"

Brenda was beaming a smile down at him as she started scanning his items.

He glanced back toward the bakery once more, but the tall black man with the scarred face was gone.

"I'm doing okay, Brenda. How about yourself?"

She told him about her cats—she had three, two tabbies and a Balinese—and he smiled at her story regarding one of the cats, how it had been acting silly with an empty box just the other day, and for a moment the thought of the man in the bakery had left his mind and he remembered why he still ventured into town from time to time, for these rare moments when somebody spoke to him like he was just another person, a *normal* person, and not the little person he had been his entire life.

Then, just as quickly, that moment was over and Brenda had bagged his groceries and handed him his receipt and wished him a nice day and Titus was headed out into the parking lot.

His orange VW Beetle was parked in the third row. He made a beeline directly for it, suddenly worried that the man with the scars was going to come after him. He was carrying his items in the plastic bags, having left the basket behind, which meant he was using both hands, which meant he wouldn't be able to reach into his pocket for his keys if he were attacked.

Was it a silly thought? Maybe. So far in his twenty-eight years he'd never been attacked, especially in the parking lot of a grocery store during the week, but he'd become especially unnerved since the night he had driven all the way to Miami Beach to pick up Ben Anderson, who had literally been running for his life from Caesar's people.

Titus had always known those people were out there—at least he'd known for as long as he knew about the games—but until that moment it hadn't really registered. But when he heard that Carver had been shot and killed, and that dirty cops had been involved, it had suddenly made everything so much more real, and terrifying.

He loaded up the Beetle as quickly as he could, and he was about ready to climb up into the driver's seat when a shadow appeared on the car from somebody walking up behind him and a voice he faintly recognized spoke.

"Hey, there, Titus. Long time, no see."

TWENTY-FIVE

Titus didn't move for several seconds, standing beside the Beetle with the door open looking like he wanted to jump in. Then, slowly, he turned and looked up at me. Stared for a beat, and then frowned.

"Ben?"

I forced a smile. I could tell he was on edge and didn't want to spook him more than I already had.

"I need your help, Titus."

He quickly scanned the parking lot. I wasn't sure what he was looking for until his gaze settled on something behind me, and I turned to glance over my shoulder to see Drew stepping out of the grocery store.

Titus whispered, "Is he with you?"

"Yes. His name is Drew Price. He came down here with me to find you."

"Find me? Why? The Kid could have just—"

"The Kid is dead."

His eyes became large at this, and his face started to ashen. He adjusted his glasses and then squinted up at me.

"Were you involved in what happened up in New York City?"

"In a way, yes. But the blackout wasn't our doing. It was Caesar's."

His eyes widened again, and then he blinked.

"The Kid is really dead?"

"Yes."

He swallowed, looking away. He opened his mouth, tried to find words to express his sudden grief, and then just asked one question.

"How?"

"Caesar and his people. Look, a lot has happened in the past two weeks, more than I can get into right now. I really hate to have to bring this to you like this, but there's nobody else we can turn to."

"Bring ... what to me? How did you find me in the first place?"

"It wasn't easy. I remembered the Kid saying you weren't really from Immokalee, but we figured you were at least living around the area. And I remembered you like cheese—a lot of cheese. So we checked all the groceries in this town and the surrounding towns. Asked the people retrieving the shopping carts if they recognized an orange Beetle. Said we had scraped it with our car and wanted to find the owner to pay for the damage. Most people claimed not to have seen your car. A few others were a bit cagier. Anyway, it took three days—one full day driving all the way down here from Ohio, the other two driving around the area keeping an eye out—but now here we are."

I didn't feel like adding that while Drew and I had been trying to find Titus everybody back in Ohio had been working on securing and burying the bodies in the Kid's backyard. It wasn't a large backyard, but once they were done there would then be six bodies in it.

Titus was quiet, his bottom lip trembling. He shook his head again.

"The Kid … is really *dead?*"

"Again, Titus, I'm sorry to bring the news to you like this. But we're in a bind."

"You need my help."

Saying it more to himself than to me, as if trying to process the notion.

"Yes."

"Help … with what?"

I reached into my jeans pocket, pulled out the flash drive.

"Help opening this."

He stared at the flash drive, his brow slightly furrowed.

"What's on it?"

"No idea. But I believe the Kid left it behind for a reason. The problem is, there appears to be some kind of encryption that we can't break. I'm hoping you can."

"What kind of encryption?"

"The only thing that comes up on the screen is what looks like a large demon and the words 'Bow down before Sargeras.' Any idea what that might mean?"

For the first time a grin cracked Titus' ashen face.

"Of course," he said. "I'm the one who wrote the program."

We followed Titus out of town, down one highway and then another, cypress trees and sawgrass stretching out around us, and then, in the middle of nowhere, the Beetle made a sudden turn.

There was a drive here, unpaved, and if you were speeding down the highway at seventy miles per hour you would miss it.

A quarter mile back, set in the shade of trees, was a trailer home.

Titus parked in front of the trailer, and we parked

behind him.

The first thing Titus asked when we got out of the car was, "You guys wanna see Hercules?"

He led us around to the back of the trailer. He carried one of the plastic grocery bags, I carried the other. Insects buzzed in the trees all around us, making me wish I'd packed bug spray.

At the back of the trailer was a large fenced area made of chicken wire. In the corner was a small wooden structure, like a doghouse.

Titus set down the grocery bag, dug inside for one of the packages of cheese, extracted a slice, rolled it a bit, and pushed it through the chicken wire.

"Hercules, come get a snack!"

Nothing. No movement from inside the enclosed area.

"C'mom, Hercules! I've got cheese!"

Still nothing. At least for another thirty seconds. Then, through the opening in the wooden structure, a small raccoon appeared. It stayed low to the ground as it approached, eyeing the cheese, though when it realized Titus wasn't alone, it paused.

"It's all right, Hercules. They're friends."

The raccoon clearly wasn't convinced. He eyed the cheese again before eyeing us. Then, in a flash, the raccoon moved forward, plucking the cheese from the chicken wire and hurrying back toward his enclosure. He moved fast, but probably not as fast as a typical raccoon moved, what with the fact he was missing his right front leg.

Titus picked up the grocery bag, turned to the trailer—which I now saw had several satellite dishes positioned on the roof.

"I came across Hercules when he was just a baby. He'd gotten caught in a trap. That's how he lost his leg. I think his momma had abandoned him. He was all alone. I took him to the vet, and they said they could amputate his leg and that might save him, but it might be best just to put him down. I couldn't do it. I felt he needed a chance, and it's been four years now since I brought him home with me. I figured he probably wouldn't last by himself out in the wild, what with only having three legs, so I put together this area for him. There are days when I think maybe I should let him go, like that's what's best for him, but ... he does love cheese."

The temperature inside the trailer was comfortably cool. Titus went to the tidy kitchen area and started putting away the packages of cheese in the fridge.

There were two step stools in the kitchen, I noticed—one by the sink, the other by the stove.

I set the bag I was carrying on the small table near the sink, then glanced back at Drew.

"So, Titus—"

"How did they kill him?"

The question caught me off guard, the bluntness of it, and it took me a moment to steady my voice.

"They tracked him down."

"I find that hard to believe."

"It's the truth. These people ... they're extremely powerful."

"If they tracked down the Kid, that probably means they can track me down too."

"Yes."

"That means they could kill me just like they did to the Kid. They could kill Hercules."

I nodded, not sure what to say, because of course Titus was right. It wasn't fair bringing this to his doorstep. There was no reason he needed to get involved.

I opened my mouth, meaning to tell him this, that it was okay if he didn't want to help us, that we would figure something else out, when he took a heavy breath and held out his stubby hand.

"Well, let's see that flash drive."

TWENTY-SIX

The living area of the trailer had been set up for Titus' computers. Like the Kid, he had several—three desktops, two laptops —spread out on three tables.

The tables weren't regular height, which made sense. The same with the chair Titus climbed onto. It was lower to the ground than most office chairs, making it easy for Titus to push himself from one computer to the next.

Grateful Dead posters and other paraphernalia adorned the walls, and a record player sat off in the corner. Based on the empty sleeve, it appeared Titus had recently been listening to *Terrapin Station.*

A sunglasses case on one of the tables caught my eye, and I stepped over to it and opened the case. The same pair of glasses that Titus had shown me in his Beetle after he'd picked me up from Miami Beach were inside. I remembered Titus told me how the Kid had sent him the pair from my first game, the pair that the Kid had snapped in half once everything was done. Titus had seen how Simon and his team made those glasses, and he'd made his own, only this pair had very thin frames and the camera was so well hidden you couldn't even tell it was there.

"These are the ones you made for me," I said.

Titus paused, looking all at once uncomfortable.

"Yeah."

"And I didn't take them with me. Sorry about that. At the time, I was just—"

Titus cut me off.

"I know, Ben. And it's okay."

I closed the case and set it back on the table. Then, as Titus started to insert the flash drive into one of the computers, something occurred to me.

"Are any of your computers air-gapped?"

This made him pause, and grin back at me.

"Did the Kid teach you about that?"

"No. Somebody else mentioned it. That's how we accessed the flash drive, with a brand-new laptop."

Titus inserted the flash drive, moved the mouse to wake the screen.

"It's always best to be cautious, but my network is extremely secure. Besides, if this drive has the Sargeras encryption, that means the Kid copied whatever information he found onto it, which means we don't have to worry about triggering some kind of notice for anybody looking out for it."

On the screen, the same image appeared of the giant demon. The large horns, the fire, the sword.

Titus started typing at the keyboard, and as he did, he kept talking.

"You're probably wondering who Sargeras is, right? He's a dark god of chaotic magic, a demonic titan who created the Burning Legion. It's from *World of Warcraft*. Remember, I told you that's how I met the Kid? We'd play a lot online. When I hadn't heard from him in the past two weeks—when I didn't see him online—I started to worry. So I guess when I saw you in the parking lot, I just instinctively knew, you know?"

He turned in his chair to glance back at me, and something changed in his eyes.

"You already knew who Sargeras was, didn't you?"

"I may not be a hacker, but I know how to use Google. I figured either the Kid or you created the program, and if not either of you, I simply hoped you'd be able to crack it."

As if on cue, Titus' computer chimed.

He swiveled back around, moved and clicked the mouse a bit, then typed at the keyboard, and then lifted his hands at the computer screen.

"Ta-da!"

Drew and I stepped closer to the table. I wasn't sure what I'd been expecting, but the simple text on the screen—what appeared to be just a couple of addresses—deflated me.

"That's it?"

Titus clicked the mouse a couple more times, and nodded.

"Looks to be, yeah."

"There's no way anything else could be hidden somewhere on the drive?"

"I'm afraid not. Why, doesn't any of this look familiar to you?"

It didn't. There were six addresses on the screen. One was in Lawen, Oregon. Another in Silver City, Arizona. Another in McLaughlin, South Dakota. Another in Mt. Pleasant, Michigan. Another in Woodbury, Vermont. And then one in Addison, South Carolina.

I asked, "Can you do a Google search of those addresses?"

"Of course."

Titus highlighted the Lawen, Oregon, address and right-clicked the mouse to copy it. Then he minimized the program, brought up Google, pasted the address in the search bar, was about to hit ENTER but then paused.

"Where did these addresses come from?"

"What do you mean?"

"The Kid placed them on this drive for a reason. He encrypted the information for a reason. He didn't want it easily found. And if you have no idea what these addresses are, then where did they come from?"

I glanced at Drew. He glanced at me. We stared at each other for a beat, and then I sighed.

And told Titus everything. From the moment I left him at the Immokalee Airport two weeks ago when Maya and Fred picked me up in the jet to the moment we finally tracked down Titus in the grocery store's parking lot an hour ago. Surprisingly, it didn't take too long, not when I stuck to the basic facts, and then there was a heavy silence as Titus took time to process all of it.

Finally he said, "So Carver didn't die in that hotel in Miami Beach, after all."

"No. They kept him alive only to kill him later. But we managed to save him. Only … we just delayed the inevitable."

Titus' eyes had started to fill with tears. He wiped at some of them with the back of his hand as he turned away in his chair, ashamed for us to watch him cry.

"How many of you are left?"

That was a good question. I hadn't really taken the time to count how many of us were left. Mostly because I didn't want to face that reality.

"Not many."

"And the addresses on the flash drive, where do you think they came from?"

"My guess? The Kid managed to crack one of the laptops I stole from the Coliseum. Obviously he didn't get much off of it, but he did get those addresses."

"And you said the reason Caesar forced you back into

another game was to track down the Kid. Because of the laptops you stole."

I felt my own eyes threatening to tear up at this. In many ways, it was my fault that the Kid and Carver and Bae were dead. Christ, and the Kid's mother—that one was on me too. If I hadn't stolen those laptops, maybe Augustus never would have gone to such lengths. Which only reinforced the idea that those laptops contained vital information.

"That's right. So those addresses there—I imagine they're important to Caesar's cause. That's why I want you to find out what they are."

"But that's the problem, Ben. If those addresses are important to Caesar's cause, they'll probably be flagged. Which means if anybody searches for those addresses—or even addresses nearby—Caesar and his people will be alerted. You said they're crazy powerful, right? They can police the Internet like that. Like I said, my network is extremely secure, so I'm not worried about them tracking me, but if those addresses are flagged and we were to search them—"

I finished the thought for Titus.

"That would tip off Caesar and his people to the fact that we now know the locations."

"Exactly. Right now, if you were to go to one of these locations, at the very least you'd have the element of surprise."

Titus had pulled up the addresses again. My eyes focused on one in particular.

"Addison, South Carolina. That's the closest, so I guess that's where we'll head next."

Titus asked, "Just the two of you?"

"No, the rest of our team is up north. They can meet us there. It'll probably take a day or two for us to connect. With the Kid gone, we no longer have the luxury of flying around the country on private jets."

"Why not?"

The question made me pause.

"What do you mean, why not? The Kid had the money. He financed the flights."

"Okay," Titus said. "Well, if you need somebody to help pay for the flights to get you places quicker, I can help out with that."

I briefly remembered the Kid telling me that when money was tight he would hit up Titus, but I didn't want to go down that road.

"I appreciate it, Titus, but we can't take your money."

"Why not? I have way more than I need. Just because I live in this trailer out in the middle of nowhere doesn't mean I don't have a lot of money. I just like being out here in the middle of nowhere. What am I going to do with a mansion? It's not really my style."

I glanced again at Drew. He gave me a slight nod.

"Drew, you want to go outside and give Ronny a call and tell him what's going on?"

Drew nodded again. He knew I wanted to be alone with Titus. He headed for the kitchen, pulling his cell phone from his pocket, and stepped outside.

I turned back to Titus, who spoke before I could even open my mouth.

"You're trying to protect me. I get that, and I appreciate it, but I don't need protecting."

"These people, Titus … they're merciless. They won't think twice about killing you. They won't think twice about killing Hercules."

I felt bad bringing the raccoon into it, but I was hoping that would sway Titus into my line of thinking. But it was clear it only reinforced his resolve.

"Do you know why I named him Hercules? Because even though he's small, even though he was abandoned, even though all the odds were stacked against him, he managed to keep living. He's a tough little guy. So am I. I can handle this, trust me."

I glanced again at the screen. At the six addresses listed there.

"We don't even know what these places are. If you want to help us get there faster, that would be great, but until we have a better understanding of what's going on, I don't want to bring you in any more than you already are."

Titus stared back at me, chewing his lip. It was clear he was trying to make up his mind about something. After a moment, he seemed to make a decision.

"I think I might know somebody who can help you."

I started shaking my head, but Titus pushed on.

"It's somebody I came across on the Internet a couple of years back. I've had minimal communication with him, but I think it's just the person to help you. I even tried telling the Kid once, but the Kid wanted nothing to do with it. Like I think I told you before, the Kid was always worried about me. He made me swear not to dig into this stuff. But I couldn't just *not* dig into this stuff, you know?"

"I appreciate the thought, Titus, but the truth is I barely know you. The only reason we came down here is because, well, we were desperate. We already had somebody on our team betray us, so I'm having a lot of trust issues right now. I'm sure this person is great, and you trust them a lot, but that's not something I'm willing to bet my life and the life of my team on right now. Do you understand?"

Titus nodded. He didn't look disappointed so much as simply resigned.

Something occurred to me, and I grinned.

"Actually, while we're gone, there is something you could look into for me. Two things, in fact."

TWENTY-SEVEN

Addison, South Carolina, sits southeast of Spartanburg, close enough to Croft State Park that you can smell the pine trees when the breeze is strong enough. The town is small, only a couple thousand people, a handful of schools, and a variety of businesses.

At 2:47 a.m. that Saturday morning, a black Mercedes-Benz Sprinter cargo van coming down the highway slowed to make a turn.

A sign at the entrance announced HARRIS WORLD INDUSTRIES. The sign was large enough to be seen by passing pedestrians, but not large enough to attract too much attention.

The property sat near the edge of Addison, in that limbo space between towns that was mostly highway and hills and a plethora of trees.

The only thing locals knew of Harris World Industries was that it was a regional office for an international company and that they weren't currently hiring. In a town as small as Addison, that was all that really mattered.

Two men sat in the front of the cargo van. The driver's name was Brendan. The passenger's name was Stevens. They wore jeans and sweatshirts, baseball caps pulled low on their heads. Both men had worked together several times in the past, but they weren't friendly, which both had agreed was just fine by them.

So it was quiet up front in the van, no radio playing, no small talk, just the noise of the six-cylinder diesel engine and the highway humming underneath the tires, which meant that they could easily hear the woman in the back start to scream.

Of course, the woman was bound and gagged, and when she'd been loaded into the back of the van she was unconscious, knocked out by a heavy dose of whatever the hell it was she was given before Brendan and Stevens arrived for the pickup.

They typically didn't ask those kinds of questions. Their job was simply transporting the subjects. Had been for the past three years. It was easy work but tedious, and Brendan some-times wished he could just do the transports on his own. He would feel more comfortable that way, for sure. Plus, he could listen to an audiobook, or a podcast, or *something* other than the continuous drone of the van's heavy engine and Stevens's heavy breathing.

"Christ," Stevens murmured. "You think her gag came off?"

It didn't sound like it. What it sounded like was the woman was screaming as loud as she could with the gag still in her mouth. So it wasn't loud, but it definitely made a noise, enough so that they could hear it up front.

"Doesn't matter," Brendan said. "We're almost there."

The drive to the building was moderately maintained and was nearly a quarter mile long. Trees stood tall like sentries on both sides of the drive, momentarily blocking out the moon so that all that lit the aged pavement was the van's headlights.

Soon they crested the incline and the headlights swept across the building.

It was pretty large for a building that was basically just cover. Two stories tall, white brick, about one hundred yards long. The parking lot was mostly empty with four cars parked in the employee spaces, and the lamps posted around the area emitted a weak glow, enough so that swarms of bugs jittered in the light.

Brendan slowed as they approached the building. He steered the van toward the side, where there were two large garage doors. He aimed for the door on the left and halted the van right in front of it.

A camera was positioned near the corner of the roof, staring down at him.

Brendan gave a small wave at the camera, and a minute later the garage door started to lift up into the ceiling.

Once the door was fully open, Brendan coasted forward into the bright light.

Diaz and Cross were already waiting there. They wore khakis and polo shirts, stood tall and straight like they'd been taught growing up, though maybe *taught* wasn't the right word for it. *Drilled into their skulls* might be more apt; it was just part of the training, the day-in and day-out training all of them had gone through to learn how to become the perfect soldier.

Radios were holstered to their belts, but no pistols.

Brendan had always thought that strange. All of them were trained in firearms—had been trained from a very young age, to become accustomed to not just pistols and rifles but knives and explosives—but Diaz and Cross didn't seem to find it necessary to carry, at least when Brendan and Stevens did their drop-offs.

He guessed he knew the reason why. This site was so secure there was no worry about it ever being found. And if some hapless townsfolk came down the drive, or maybe one of the highway patrol officers, the last thing they needed to see was somebody wearing a gun on his belt. It would raise too many questions, and in their world questions of any kind were not acceptable.

Brendan shut off the van and opened his door as the two men approached.

Stevens, stepping out of the van on the other side, said, "We've got a loud one tonight."

Diaz and Cross paused to listen. Then Diaz glanced at his partner, turned away, and headed back toward the elevator.

Stevens asked, "Where's he going?"

Taking off his glasses and holding them up to the bright lights to check for smudges, Cross said, "To get Rachel."

They were going to have to knock out the woman again, Brendan knew. Which meant Rachel—who was basically a nurse—would appear with one of her syringes to make it happen. Usually the subjects Brendan and Stevens transported never woke up, but it did happen on occasion.

Brendan leaned back inside the van for his cigarettes. He grabbed the pack of Pall Malls and headed out through the open garage door to the parking lot.

Outside, he lit the cigarette and watched as Stevens opened the rear of the cargo van and Cross shined a flashlight inside to inspect the woman.

The woman was still bound to the gurney, but the sight of the two men outside was enough to cause her to start screaming even louder as she bucked and jostled on the gurney.

Brendan had no idea where they'd found her—he didn't know where they found most of the subjects—but she sure had grit. Which he guessed was one of the reasons she'd been picked to come to this location. Brendan didn't exactly know what they were working on down below the building, but he knew those who entered alive always came back out dead.

The elevator doors opened, and Diaz returned with Rachel. She was good looking for a middle-aged woman, dark skin and short dark hair and sharp cheekbones.

Brendan took one last drag of his cigarette before flicking it away to join them.

Once it was over—once Rachel had applied another shot of whatever it was that knocked the woman out, and once they extracted the woman from the back of the van and wheeled her to the elevator—Brendan and Stevens were told to wait.

A few minutes later two bodies came up on gurneys, just like the woman that went down below, only these were dead and wrapped in black body bags. Brendan and Stevens would transport them to another location, where they would be disposed of.

They loaded the dead bodies in the back and shut the door and climbed back into the van, and Brendan started the engine and backed the van out of the garage, watching as the door was already closing in front of them, and then they were headed back down the quarter-mile drive toward the highway, the only noise that of the diesel engine making its low growl, until Stevens suddenly leaned forward in his seat.

"What the fuck is this?"

A car was parked across the entranceway. It was a blue Toyota Prius, with its hood up. A young Asian-looking woman was bent over with a flashlight inspecting the engine. She wore tight pants that nicely showed off her ass.

Brendan knew Stevens was going to say something stupid right before he said it.

"Damn, would I love to hit that."

The woman heard them coming and stepped back as Brendan slowed the van. He didn't have much choice; her car was blocking them in.

He kept the headlights on but killed the engine, and both he and Stevens stepped out of the van. He had to admit, the woman was striking, squinting back at them in the harsh glow of the headlights, and he was worried that Stevens would say or do something stupid, something that would raise questions about who they were and who they worked for and what they were doing out at this time of night.

The woman let out a heavy sigh of relief.

"Oh my *God*, do you think you can help me? My car, it just crapped *out* on me. I tried calling for help but I'm not getting a *signal*. Do either of you have a cell phone that *works*? Or maybe you can figure out what's wrong with the *engine*?"

Her English was pretty good but it was tinged with the trace of an accent that Brendan couldn't quite place. He figured she was a local college student, visiting on a visa, though what she was doing out here after three o'clock in the morning was beyond him.

Before Brendan could answer, Stevens eagerly stepped forward, his voice full of bravado.

"Sure thing, miss. What's your name, by the way? I bet it's as pretty as your face."

Brendan wanted to groan, both inwardly and outwardly, but before he could even blink, the woman swung her flashlight at Stevens's face.

It was enough to stun him, to cause him to stumble back. A beat of uneasy silence, like they were all frozen in place, and then Stevens's training kicked in and he went right for her, reaching for her neck, but incredibly the woman was faster, dodging him and using the flashlight to smack at the top of his head. She kicked out the back of his knees, sending him to the ground, and then took his head and bounced it against the side of the car.

All of it happened in the space of three seconds, more than enough time for Brendan to react, but he was stunned that this woman was actually doing this, here on the side of the highway, and besides, he knew it didn't matter, because while Diaz and Cross didn't carry weapons, Brendan always did, and he reached now for the Sig he kept in the holster on his hip, and that was when he sensed movement behind him and felt the barrel of a gun press against the back of his head.

TWENTY-EIGHT

"The van's back."

Cross looked up from the newspaper spread out in front of him on the table. Diaz was sitting in front of the security monitors, leaning back in his chair, pointing at the monitor in the corner.

Just as he said, the cargo van was right now edging the parking lot.

Cross adjusted his glasses as he stood up from the chair and approached the security monitors.

"Did they forget something?"

Diaz thought about it for a beat, and then shook his head.

"Not that I can think of."

"We have their number?"

Diaz made a *phsss* sound as he shrugged.

"Probably, but I don't know where it is."

Cross watched as the cargo van eased to a stop in front of the left garage door.

In the driver's seat, Brendan waved like he did every time he came to drop off a new subject. Only he'd already dropped off a subject twenty minutes ago, and not once before had he ever circled back.

"Can we zoom in on his face?"

On the screen, it was impossible to get a good view of the driver's face, what with the baseball cap and the angle of the camera.

Diaz was already pushing back his chair and getting to his feet.

Cross said, "I think we should confirm it's him."

"Of course it's him. They were just here, for Christ's sake."

Diaz had just opened the security room door when Cross spoke.

"At least take one of the Glocks."

"Are you serious?"

Cross only pointed at the locker in the corner, and Diaz, knowing not to argue with Cross as Cross was technically in charge, did his best not to roll his eyes as he tracked over to the locker and inputted his code and grabbed a Glock 17.

"There," he said. "Happy?"

Cross didn't answer. He just tilted his chin toward the door and watched Diaz disappear through it. Then he drifted over to the security monitors and studied the screen that showed the cargo van.

Brendan—or somebody who looked like Brendan—just sat there staring at the closed garage door.

Cross leaned forward, clicked the mouse, and the angle changed to show the other side of the van.

Stevens sat right there in the passenger seat as always.

At least, Cross thought it was Stevens. Why wouldn't it be? Maybe Cross was being overly paranoid. But after what had happened at the Coliseum, why wouldn't he be paranoid?

He hadn't heard the whole story, but word had drifted down from those who had been there. How it had been attacked by those assholes Carver Ellison had pulled out of the games. Apparently their whole purpose was to save Ellison, and while the official word was that Ellison and his team had died in the explosion at the Fillmore, Cross had heard rumblings that Ellison and his people had managed to escape.

Cross shifted his gaze to another monitor that showed Diaz in the elevator. It had reached the garage and the doors opened and Diaz stepped out. He went over to the control panel on the wall and hit one of the buttons, and the garage door started to rise.

The cargo van drifted forward, its headlights bathing Diaz in bright light as he approached. Diaz kept the Glock at his side, but Cross could tell by his body language that he wasn't on full alert.

The driver's door opened and a man stepped out of the van, a man who clearly wasn't Brendan, and in the space of an instant the driver lifted a pistol and fired two shots into Diaz's chest, then one shot at his head.

Expertly. Like a goddamned pro.

Cross didn't see the rest. He leaned over and smacked the emergency button beside the keyboard, and then grabbed the radio from his belt.

"Code red! I repeat, code red!"

He knew Diaz's radio was transmitting the alert, but that was okay. The people who had just broken into the building—the people they'd *just fucking let in*—knew what the situation was. Besides, the alert was for Rachel, and for Fisher, though what good the tech would be in this situation Cross didn't know.

Next he sprinted over to the locker and extracted a Glock 17, just like the one Diaz didn't even get a chance to raise, as well as a Heckler & Koch HK416. He slung the assault rifle over his shoulder, grabbed another HK416, plus two magazines, and hurried to the door.

He only paused when he glanced back at the security

monitor and saw somebody stepping out of the passenger side of the cargo van. A big man, it looked like, much bigger than Stevens, though somehow he'd squeezed into Stevens's clothes.

The back of the van opened, and a man and a woman jumped out.

The woman and the driver headed toward the elevator, the driver leaning down to grab Diaz's badge as they stepped past him, while the big guy and the man from the back of the van both drew guns and headed outside.

Cross was tempted to see where the two men were headed, but he had more pressing matters at hand. Namely the fact the driver that wasn't Brendan and the girl had just gotten into the elevator.

The elevator couldn't reach the upper floors. The only numbers on the panel were for the garage and basement. Which meant they would be arriving any second.

There was a camera in the elevator. The girl noticed it at once, and fired one round into it.

Shit.

The door to the security office opened, and Cross nearly shot Rachel as she poked her head in.

"What the fuck's going on?" she said.

"Intrusion. Two are coming down the elevator as we speak."

He tossed her the HK416 and spare magazine—each weapon in the locker was already primed and loaded—and they hurried out into the corridor. The elevator was at the far end of the corridor. They stopped about thirty feet away, standing side by side, and aimed their rifles.

The moment the doors opened, Cross and Rachel would tear the intruders apart. After all, the HK416 fired at a rate of almost nine hundred rounds per minute at full-auto. The magazines held thirty rounds, which would be more than enough to take care of their problem.

Well, their problem down here. There was still the two men somewhere up top.

The light above the doors lit up, signaling that the elevator had arrived, and even before the doors opened, Cross and Rachel opened fire.

They moved forward as they did, the empty shells littering the floor at their feet, and they both dropped the empty magazines as the same time and slapped in new magazines and continued firing as they advanced, twenty feet away, ten feet.

Silence then, as they each exhausted their second magazine.

What was left of the elevator doors had finally opened the entire way to reveal—

Nothing. The elevator was empty.

Cross muttered, "What the fuck?"

That was when the girl appeared from the ceiling of the elevator. She didn't drop straight down, onto her feet, but instead her head and torso appeared as she leaned through the opening in the top of the elevator, a pistol in her hand.

Cross never had a chance to reach for the Glock secured in his waistband.

The girl fired twice, each bullet skillfully placed for a head-shot, and Cross and Rachel dropped dead without a sound.

TWENTY-NINE

In her previous life, Ho Sook must have been a fucking Olympic gymnast.

It was her idea for us to climb up into the ceiling, knowing that by then those in the basement probably knew we were here and would no doubt open fire the second the elevator doors opened. Then, once the salvo was over, she practically fell headfirst into the elevator but used her legs to stop herself and fired two shots and that was that.

Seconds later, she'd contorted her body to the point that she dropped gracefully into the elevator.

It took me a bit longer, afraid I was going to twist my ankle on impact, but then once I'd dropped down we both stepped into the corridor, our guns held at the ready.

A man and woman lay dead in the corridor ten feet away. Both had been firing HK416s before they were killed, and the assault rifles lay on the floor next to them in a scattering of spent shells.

It was funny, but the man I once was two years ago had never even fired a gun, let alone touched one, and now I could identify the make and model of practically any firearm on the market. I knew the caliber, how many rounds each magazine held, whether they were semi or full auto.

Simon had stolen my life, but Carver had turned me into a soldier.

Each of us—Ho Sook and I inside, Ronny and Drew and Mason and Chin outside—were equipped with earpiece comms.

I toggled my radio and said, "We made it to the basement. You guys having any luck up top?"

Mason answered.

"Doors were all locked so we broke a window. Chin and I are checking the first floor now, but most of the place is empty. It's a total cover."

We'd figured as much but it was good to get confirmation.

"Good. How about you, Drew?"

Drew was currently positioned with his sniper rifle somewhere in the trees on the hill overlooking the building.

"So far all's quiet."

That was even better, though we all knew the quiet wasn't going to last. It was a safe bet a distress signal had been sent the moment we killed the guy upstairs. How long it would take before a strike team arrived was impossible to say, but they would be coming fast, and they would be heavily armed.

I toggled my radio again.

"Ronny, how are things on your end?"

"Kind of boring, to be honest."

"Let's hope it stays that way."

Ho Sook crouched down and took the badge from the woman. Now we both had a badge which would open doors for us, and maybe even let us access computers.

I nodded at her, and we started down the corridor, leaving the two dead bodies behind us.

The first room we checked appeared to be the security

room. It was empty, and I started to back out but the open locker of weapons caught my eye.

In the rack were two more HK416s. I took one, slung it over my shoulder, and handed the other to Ho Sook. I gave her two magazines and kept one magazine for myself, and then I nodded again at her and we started back down the corridor.

The next room we checked appeared to be an office with two desks and several different computers and a half-dozen filing cabinets.

Ho Sook went to one of the computers, but it was soon clear that the badge wasn't going to help us. Once she moved the mouse, it asked for a username and password, and so far the only people who might have helped us out with that were now dead.

Still, if we had time, we would take the computers. We would take as much as we could to help explain what the fuck this place was and why Augustus and his people wanted to keep it so secretive and secure.

The next room was empty, though it smelled of bleach and looked as sterile as a hospital room.

The next room was pretty much the same, only this one had a woman lying on a gurney. I checked her pulse. She was alive, but unconscious.

So far the rooms we'd seen were pretty small. The next one was much larger. It looked like some type of laboratory.

It was bright and clean with computers everywhere, as well as stuff you typically see in labs—microscopes and test tube racks and beakers and Petri dishes—and the sight of all the equipment caused a stirring of dread in the pit of my stomach.

Whatever they did here, it certainly wasn't good.

On the other side of the lab was a long, tinted window.

Ho Sook and I approached the window, passing by all the lab equipment, and when we got close enough, we saw that somebody was on the other side.

A man who looked to be in his forties, dressed in sweat-pants and an undershirt. His undershirt was drenched in sweat. He was lying on the floor in a fetal position, moaning as he writhed in pain. It looked like he was suffering from a severe stomach cramp, but that didn't explain the tears of blood drip-ping from his eyes.

I stepped closer, spotted a door on the other side of the small room. Based on how the corridor had stretched out, it looked as if this room was accessed by a room just off the corridor.

I found myself speaking quietly, more to myself than to Ho Sook.

"We need to help him."

But before we could turn away from the window, a voice spoke behind us.

"I wouldn't do that. Not unless you want to die too."

We spun around, aiming our guns at what looked to be a skinny college kid with curly brown hair and glasses. He wore khakis and a polo shirt, just like the two men we'd killed, though he didn't look like security.

His hands shot up at once.

"Don't shoot me!"

Keeping my gun aimed at him, I tilted my head back at the window behind me.

"What's wrong with him?"

The college kid offered up an incredulous expression, like he couldn't believe we were so dense.

"That guy? He's infected."

"With what?"

The kid only stared, bemused, like he couldn't believe we hadn't figured it out yet.

I took a step forward, aimed at the spot between the kid's eyes.

"If you don't want to end up like your friends, tell us what the fuck is going on here. What's he infected with?"

The kid shook his head, as if at a loss for words, and then answered simply.

"The Pax Romana."

THIRTY

Ben's voice came through their earpieces.

"Are you guys done sweeping the first and second floors?"

They were standing out in the parking lot now, under one of the lamps and the army of bugs swarming around it. They both carried FN 15 SRP Tactical rifles with FNX-45 pistols holstered to their belts, looking like proper militiamen.

Though, if Mason was being honest, the incongruity of the two of them as militiamen—Mason standing nearly six-five, weighing close to 350 pounds, his lazy face and bald head and tattoos of swastikas and racial slurs all over his body while Chin stood several inches shorter, a lean face and build, his English not the best—was downright hilarious.

Except Mason knew what was happening now was no laughing matter.

"Yeah," he said into his mic. "Both floors clear."

"Okay. In that case, I need Chin to return to the garage. Ho Sook will meet him in the elevator. They'll finish sweeping the basement. Mason, I need you to get the car. There are computers down here that we need to load up."

They had come in two vehicles (or three, if you counted Ronny's). The one car was parked about a mile away, hidden behind a billboard; the other was parked near the end of the quarter-mile drive, just far enough from the highway that anybody passing by couldn't see it.

Mason said, "Will do."

He nodded at Chin. Chin nodded back. They broke apart, Chin heading around to the side of the building, Mason heading back toward the drive leading to the highway.

Mason had gone only a couple paces before he paused and glanced up into the trees on the hill.

"How are things looking, Drew?"

Drew's whispered response came back a moment later.

"Nice and quiet."

Mason started moving again. He was forty years old and should have been in better shape than he was. He hadn't been on this team long—and to even think of it as a team was weird, as he barely knew these people—but he saw how dedicated they were to their mission. Ben and Drew usually exercised every day, from what he could tell, though of course the past couple of weeks had disrupted that.

He thought about Gloria, back at the motel being looked after by Beverly, and how those bastards had cut out his wife's tongue. He remembered the nights he and Gloria would go out drinking, and how Gloria was always keen to sign up for karaoke. She didn't really have a great singing voice—always seemed to be off-key, no matter the song—but her energy was so kinetic it got the rest of the bar going, and pretty much every time she finished her last note the whole place would erupt with applause.

The night was still and quiet, the sky clear and the stars bright.

As Mason jogged up the drive—a steady jog as he could

already start to feel a pain in his side—he thought about Anthony and how those bastards had killed him.

Mason still couldn't believe that his son was gone. It wasn't one of those things you worried about when you became a father. Sure, you wanted to keep your kid safe, and you knew that there were certain dark realities that he might face—a school shooting, for instance, because this was America and school shootings were as plentiful as the stars and stripes on the flag—but you did your best to try to make sure he was as safe as could be.

And then one day you wake up completely naked in a bathtub in Alma, Georgia, a state you'd never even visited before, and soon you're told that if you don't play some twisted game your wife and son will die.

Despite the cool temperature, sweat beaded his brow. He wiped at it with the back of his arm as he pushed on.

Mason found himself thinking about his brother-in-law, Adam. Mason had gone to jail to protect the man. It was dumb —Mason had simply been transporting meth with Adam, trying to be part of the biker gang because he was tired of just being a mechanic—and not a day went by that he wished he'd stayed home that night.

He had begun to believe that had he stayed home and not agreed to help Adam which then landed his ass in prison, then maybe he and Gloria and Anthony would have moved away from Bakersfield much sooner than they had. Had that happened, Mason was convinced he wouldn't have one day woken up naked in that bathtub, but maybe he was kidding himself.

Maybe, no matter what he did or how good he tried to live his life, Mason had always been destined to end up in Simon's game—just as Anthony had always been destined to lose his life, and Gloria to lose her tongue.

Soon he reached the car parked along the side of the drive.

It took him a few minutes to catch his breath, leaning down with his hands on his knees, and then he opened the door and slid in behind the wheel.

He nudged open the sun visor, just a bit, and the key dropped down into his hand.

Mason headed back down the drive, and despite knowing that the building had been secured, he only drove with the running lights on.

He parked by the open garage door and climbed back out of the car.

Chin was already waiting with four hard drives stacked up on top of each other. He was holding them like a towering pile of books.

Mason popped the trunk and helped Chin load the hard drives, making as much space as they could because Chin said there were a couple more hard drives to bring up.

"What's Ben doing?"

Chin slowly answered in his broken English, taking his time to find the right words.

"One man still left alive. Ben asking him questions now."

This surprised Mason. The initial plan was to infiltrate the building, learn as much as they could, and then hightail it out of there. Spend not one second longer than was needed.

Assuming this place was so important, and assuming they were successful with their attack—and so far it appeared that way—then a strike team would be headed to their location. The longer they waited, the more likely they would get caught.

Chin's face had tightened, and despite the color of his skin, he looked pale.

Mason said, "What's wrong?"

Chin looked back toward the elevator, then shook his head.

"I did not hear much ... but I heard enough. I asked Ho Sook, and she told me. It is ... scary."

"How so?"

"The Pax ... Romana."

"Well, what is it?"

Chin looked away again. Swallowed. Said one word that instantly caused Mason's blood to go cold.

"Plague."

THIRTY-ONE

Once Ho Sook had gone up in the elevator and retrieved Chin and they returned to the basement to continue sweeping the rooms, I motioned at the kid with my gun to sit on one of the stools.

He just stood there, trembling like a child afraid he was about to be whupped with a belt.

"Come on, man, don't kill me. I'm just a tech, okay? It's not like I created this stuff!"

I motioned again at the stool.

"Take a seat."

He swallowed, looking around the room like there might be some escape, but the only exit was the door on the other side of the room and he knew he would never reach it alive, so he finally relented and climbed up onto the stool.

"Good," I said. "You do as you're told and you'll stay alive. Now, what's your name?"

"My name?"

He looked at me again, his face pale, like telling me his name would rob him of his soul.

"Don't make me repeat the question."

"My name is Eric. Eric Fisher. People just call me Fisher."

"Okay, Eric. So what's that man dying from?"

"I told you. The Pax Romana."

"And what is the Pax Romana?"

He stared at me, like he wasn't sure how to answer the question.

"Again, Eric, don't make me repeat myself."

"It's the end game! You know, the thing they've been working towards for decades. Caesar and all the rest of them."

"What rest of them?"

"You know, the Inner Circle. At least, those who are still alive. I know who you are, you know. I heard you got killed at the Coliseum—you and the others—but I guess that was just some bullshit they told us to try to keep us calm. How'd you find this place, anyway?"

"The Pax Romana, Eric. What is the plan for it? What is the end game?"

"Fuck, man, I don't know. I don't even know if it is the end game. That shit is above my pay grade. But we've all been speculating about it for a while. Like, what do you *think* they plan to do with it? Especially with Caesar always talking about changing the world and shit. My guess? They're going to let it loose."

"When?"

"Shit, man. Again, I'm just a tech. They don't tell me shit. But this stuff, it's been perfected for a while now. But from what I hear, Caesar isn't ready to pull the trigger. So we keep running these tests because I guess why the hell not."

I glanced back at the window. I couldn't see the man in the room, but I pictured him still writhing on the floor, blood dripping from his eyes. If I couldn't save him, at the very least I needed to put him out of his misery.

"The man in there, the one who's dying … is there a way I can expedite the process?"

"You mean like killing him? Like he's a horse who broke his fucking leg and you want to put a bullet in his head? No, that really isn't an option. Besides, he's coming up on almost forty-eight hours. Pretty soon it's going to be over for him."

"Who is he, anyway?"

"Hell if I know. They just bring us the subjects. We inject them with the Pax Romana and wait for it to do its magic."

The way he said this was so flippant, so casual, that I wanted to slap him across the face with my gun. Maybe use the handle to smack the back of his skull a couple of times. But he was talking, which was good, and he seemed to be giving me answers, which was even better.

"What is the Pax Romana, exactly?"

"It's basically a virus. What kind, I don't know; they had started working on it way before I came along."

"And you said it's been perfected for a while now."

"Yeah, from what I can tell. At least a year."

"But they keep running tests."

"That's right. I guess with something this massive, Caesar wants it to be more than perfect, if that's even possible."

"How many people has it killed so far?"

"Shit, man, I don't know. Hundreds. Thousands. Who knows? Like I told you, I'm just a tech. All this is way above my pay grade. I didn't come up with it!"

"Who did?"

"I don't know. Caesar, I guess. Or maybe somebody in the Inner Circle. Like I said, it's all above my pay grade!"

"Eric."

"Yeah?"

"Say pay grade one more time, and I'm going to beat you to death with the butt of my gun."

He swallowed and didn't say anything else, looking around the room again like he was searching for an escape hatch.

I was faintly aware of Ho Sook and Chin out in the corridor. They'd done the sweep of the basement and were now taking what they could from the different rooms. I'd noticed Chin pausing briefly outside the door to hear what the tech had to say before moving on with several hard drives in his arms.

"How does it work?"

The question seemed to surprise him, causing Eric to jump, and his wide eyes swung back to me.

"Huh?"

"The Pax Romana. Keep up, Eric. You're testing my patience."

"How does the Pax Romana work?"

"Yes."

He paused a beat to take a breath, and then pushed on.

"Okay, look. You remember the Ebola scare a couple years back? They practically quarantined people coming in from outside the country. I mean, if you're going to try to spread a virus, that's how you'd do it, right? You'd release it to somebody on a plane, or a cruise ship, or even somebody in a football stadium. The Pax Romana? It's highly contagious. Just like the flu. And like the flu, it doesn't hit you right away. There's at least a twelve-hour incubation period where it just spreads into your system. After that period, you become contagious, and you spread it to your family, to your friends, to your coworkers, to the people at the grocery store. It's, like, designed to spread really fast."

I swallowed, not sure what to say at first. My legs were feeling weak and I wanted to sit down, try to steady myself, but then I remembered we were working on borrowed time and needed to get as many answers from this kid as possible.

"What happens after the initial twelve hours?"

Eric's eyes shifted toward the window, and he shrugged.

"Basically that."

"What does *that* mean, exactly?"

"The body starts to shut down. All the major organs. Your body keeps trying to fight the virus, but it's way too weak for that, and eventually you just … die. From what I heard, they initially tried to figure out something that would be painless, like dying in your sleep, but there was just no way that was going to work. The way I've heard it described, it feels like your insides are eating the rest of your body apart. The pain is excruciating. I mean, they had the best chemical engineers working on this. They tried a lot of different things, but in the end, they realized they just needed it to be simple and to the point."

"And what point is that?"

"To kill people. A lot of people. I mean, isn't that obvious by now?"

It was, and it staggered me. I'd spent the last week or so racking my brain trying to think what the Pax Romana might be. Augustus had asked me what was the greatest thing the Roman Empire gave the world, and I had guessed roads, and he had just smiled, and so for some reason I thought I'd been on to something, but clearly he had just been amused by my guess.

The answer, it turned out, was in its name.

Pax Romana.

Roman Peace.

That was the greatest thing the Roman Empire had given the world, Augustus believed. Peace. And this was his way of accomplishing that now. Killing off a countless number of people.

Except—

"Wait a minute. Back up. If this thing spreads, what's to keep Caesar and the Inner Circle and whoever else they want alive?"

Eric gave me that look again, the one that said I was an idiot asking stupid questions, and my grip tightened on the pistol.

"I mean, isn't that part obvious? They also developed a vaccine. When the time comes, Caesar and the Inner Circle and the Legion and the rest of us will take it, so that we'll be fine."

"What's the Legion?"

Eric gestured at the corridor.

"You killed two of them already. You know, Cross and Diaz. They were part of the Legion program."

"I'm not following."

"Shit, man, I don't know how to explain it. One of the scientists years ago, his name was Matheson, he came up with this way to make these … like, super humans. People who weren't afraid of anything. Anyway, they were raised from babies to be soldiers in all of this."

I had no idea what he was talking about, but it didn't matter. This entire time I'd been wanting to figure out what the Pax Romana was, and now I had my answer. And it was terrifying.

"What about the woman?"

"What woman?"

"The one that came in the cargo van tonight."

"Oh, her. She's just another subject. We've been testing subjects for years. Honestly, at this point I don't know why they keep bringing in more. We know what the Pax Romana does. We know how it works. Like I told you, it's been perfected for a long time now. But still, they bring us subjects, we infect them, they die, and then we ship them out and new ones come in. To be honest, it's gotten kinda boring."

My pistol was an FNX-45. It was stainless steel and weighed about six pounds. The barrel was four and a half inches long. The front sight on the barrel stuck up just a bit that when I backhanded Eric with the gun, it tore open his cheek.

He cried out, falling off the stool which tipped over, and shouted up at me.

"What the fuck, man? *What the fuck*?"

I stepped close to him, aimed the pistol at his face.

"If you're so fucking bored, I'll go ahead and put you out of your misery."

He raised his right hand while with his left hand he pressed at the wound on his cheek. It was already bleeding heavily. He would need stitches if he made it through until morning.

Eric said, "Christ, man, what the fuck do you want from me? I answered every question you asked!"

I was barely aware that both Ho Sook and Chin were standing in the doorway, watching. Neither seemed concerned that the tech was lying on the floor holding his bleeding cheek.

That was when I noticed the stainless-steel door in the corner. It looked to be the entrance to a walk-in refrigerator. I'd seen it when I first entered the room but didn't think much of it at the time.

I gestured with the pistol toward the door.

"Is it in there?"

"Is *what* in there?"

"You know what."

Something changed in his eyes. Something that confirmed the virus was indeed in the fridge, but something that also questioned whether or not I planned to inject him with it.

The idea hadn't crossed my mind, but now it was starting to feel like a good idea.

I nodded at Ho Sook, and she hurried over to the door. But when she got close, she saw that you couldn't just open it. It was locked, and her stolen badge wasn't going to do the trick.

She said, "It needs a code."

I crouched down beside Eric, tapped him on the forehead with the gun.

"What's the code?"

He glared back at me. Whatever had been keeping him talking was now gone. He was pissed, that much was clear, but he also knew I would keep hurting him if he didn't give me what I wanted, so he finally relented.

Eric rattled off six numbers, gritting his teeth as he did, and Ho Sook inputted those numbers, but the door still wouldn't open.

I kept the pistol aimed at the tech's face.

"What's the deal, Eric?"

He grimaced, said, "It requires a fingerprint scan too."

I stepped back, motioned with the pistol for him to get up, and soon he was on his feet and trudging over to the stainless-steel door. Without being told, he inputted his code and then pressed his thumb against the scanner, and a green light on the keypad lit up.

Ho Sook opened the door and stepped into the walk-in fridge. It wasn't very large. There were several racks, but only a few looked to be occupied.

Keeping my pistol trained on Eric, I called into the fridge, "Anything?"

Ho Sook answered.

"Yes. Five vials."

I said to Eric, "Where's the vaccine?"

He glared back at me, defiant, and nearly spat the answer.

"Not here. It's in Rome."

This threw me for a second.

"You mean Italy?"

He made a face which clearly pulled at the cut on his cheek because he clenched his teeth against the pain.

"No, not fucking Italy. Rome is what Caesar calls head-quarters or the base or whatever. They keep the vaccine there. It's where everything is. The server farm too. It's where—"

In my ear, Drew's whispered voice came through, quick and urgent.

"Strike team's here. I didn't even see them. They've got Mason and—"

A new voice came over the line, one that didn't belong to anyone on our team.

"That's right. We have your friend Mason. And we've accessed the security feed, so we can see there are three of you downstairs right now, as well as one of ours. Now, Man of Wax, if you want Mason to stay alive, you and your friends dispose of your guns and come up to the garage with your hands up. Bring along our guy too. You have one minute, and then we will shoot your friend in the head."

THIRTY-TWO

When the elevator doors opened, I expected the strike team to be waiting for us in the garage.

They weren't.

But I saw two men standing outside the open garage door. They were wearing black tactical gear. One of them carried what looked to be an M4, aimed at us. The other held a pistol at the back of Mason's head.

Mason was on his knees in front of the two men. His hands were behind his back, presumably zip-tied.

I nudged Eric out of the elevator. I held him close, my left hand squeezing his shoulder, my right hand holding the loaded syringe and the needle right against his neck.

Ho Sook and Chin followed us out of the elevator.

We'd disposed of our guns, as requested. If they could access the security feed, it meant there was no use trying to hide them anyway. But as soon as the new voice had come over the radio, Ho Sook had moved quickly, grabbing all of the vials, as well as a syringe, and in the elevator she'd distributed them around, tasking with me the syringe.

Now I led Eric out past the cargo van to the parking lot.

The kid was trembling, knowing exactly what would happen if I injected him with the virus.

The man with the pistol to Mason's head spoke in a deep, angry voice.

"I said no weapons."

"No, you said no guns."

Eric Fisher suddenly shouted, his voice shaking.

"They have the Pax Romana! Do whatever they say! Let that guy go! Jesus Christ!"

The kid was panicked, and I was sure he would try to bolt at any second. Only if he did that, I might inadvertently inject him with just a bit of the virus, and I was sure he didn't want to chance it.

When we were about ten feet away from the two men, I squeezed Eric's shoulder tighter to make him stop.

Ho Sook and Chin stopped behind me. They'd had their hands up this entire time, though their hands had been clenched in fists. Now they opened their fists to reveal the small vials in each hand.

I eyed the two men, keeping the needle snug against Eric's neck.

"If it's your job to protect this building, then you know exactly what's inside it, which means you know exactly what's in these vials. You want to kill us, fine, but we're going to make damned certain one way or another you become infected. Just think of those little vials as grenades."

Eric Fisher was practically close to tears.

"Do what they say! Jesus Christ, you know what this shit does! Just let them go!"

On his knees, Mason stared up at me.

"Ben, if I don't make it out of here, tell my wife—"

"Stop it, Mason. You're going to make it out of here. All of us are. Isn't that right, fellas?"

Both men were silent. Their gazes were heavy, calculating.

The man with the M4 kept it trained on us, while the other man kept his pistol trained on the back of Mason's head.

Something suddenly occurred to me, something that caused a sour taste in the back of my throat.

"Where are the others?"

The hard stare of the man holding his pistol on Mason momentarily lifted, and he grinned.

"Oh, they're almost here. And yes, we know what that shit is. We know what it does. And we're not fucking afraid of it."

Okay, fuck this.

I shouted, "Drew, light 'em up!"

The man with the pistol would be the first fatality, I was sure. Drew had been watching us this entire time from the trees, crouched low with a Barrett M95 sniper rifle aimed at the two men, and the moment he squeezed the trigger, the man's head would explode.

Then, two seconds later, his partner's head would explode.

Except ... nothing happened. The area was still and silent, just the sound of the insects in the trees and the bugs swarming the parking lot lamps.

The man grinned again.

"Oh, me and my buddy aren't the only ones here. Another one is up in the trees with your friend. Shit, your friend is probably dead by now. Hate to say it, Man of Wax, but you're no longer a prized commodity. None of your team is. Which means our orders aren't to capture you, but to make sure you're all fucking dead."

THIRTY-THREE

Drew was entirely still. He didn't even breathe. It had been maybe five seconds now since he felt the barrel of a gun poke him in the back of the head, and he hadn't taken a breath since.

A voice whispered, "Take your fucking finger off the trigger."

Drew had found solid cover behind a fallen tree. It wasn't a large tree, but it wasn't a small tree either. There was just enough room for him to lie flat with the Barrett aimed down toward the parking lot. Which meant he was in no position to try to wrangle himself out of this sudden mess.

Ben and the others had just exited the garage. They had somebody else with them, somebody that Ben was holding close to him with what looked to be a syringe against his neck.

It had been surprising to see only two men down there. They had come out of nowhere, grabbing Mason before Drew could take them out, and once they had Mason, Drew quickly scanned the parking lot, searching for others. And by then the men had called for Ben and Ho Sook and Chin to come up, and so Drew had planned to wait to take out the two men.

Only he hadn't. Because it had been suspicious. They'd

expected the strike team to consist of more men, assuming they were still here when the strike team arrived. So only two men didn't make sense.

Now Drew knew why.

Because at least one was behind him, holding a pistol to his head.

The man whispered, "Don't make me tell you again."

Drew removed his finger from trigger.

"Now move away from the rifle and stand up."

Drew closed his eyes. He knew that this was it—that he was going to die tonight. He'd never been a good man. He'd been unfaithful to his wife, which was why when he woke up in Simon's game he learned that not only had his wife been taken but his girlfriend as well. Both were now dead, long gone, and soon Drew would be too.

The man whispered again, a bite in his tone.

"Fucking do it now."

Drew slowly leaned away from the rifle. He'd been lying on the ground so long one leg had fallen asleep, which made standing painful.

"Hands out at your sides."

Drew did as he was told. Slowly he lifted his hands out to his sides while he stared down through the trees at everybody in the parking lot. Ben had been talking to the two men, and one of the men had been saying something back, and then suddenly Ben's voice echoed in the night as he shouted.

"Drew, light 'em up!"

But Drew couldn't light 'em up. Not like this, seconds away from being killed himself. He would never light up anybody ever again.

The man whispered, "Turn around slowly."

Drew did. His eyes had adjusted to the dark enough so that he could make out the man and his partner with no trouble.

The man wore dark tactical gear, a black baseball cap, and held the pistol right at Drew's face.

His partner stood right behind him, a knife in his hand.

Drew said, "If you're going to kill me, then one of you just fucking get it over with."

This clearly threw the man with the pistol. Even in the dark Drew saw the confusion flash across his face.

The man turned his head, suddenly realizing that somebody was standing behind him, and that was when the second man—not the partner, Drew realized—stepped forward and drew the knife across the man's throat.

The first man jerked standing in place, started to fall down, and the second man stepped forward and grabbed the gun from him and tossed it to Drew.

Drew stood stunned, the pistol that he was so certain was going to kill him now in his hands.

The new man stood back up and stepped past Drew to peer down into the parking lot. Then he turned back to Drew and spoke quietly.

"Okay, look, we don't have much time. You don't know me, I don't know you, but I'm here to help you and your friends. This team has been here for almost ten minutes already. You see up there in the sky? That's the drone that they've been flying. My guess is it senses heat signatures. That's how they knew where to find you. Soon they're going to realize there's one more person than they anticipated, but I don't think that matters anyway, as the rest of the strike team will be here any second. Still, do me a favor and shoot that fucking thing out of the air. Then open up on the rest of them when I give you the signal."

Drew just stared at the man in the dark, having no idea how to process what had just happened. He opened his mouth but couldn't speak. Swallowed and tried again.

But the man suddenly held a finger to his lips.

Drew heard it then too. The oncoming rumble of engines. It sounded like at least two vehicles, and they were coming fast.

"Shit," the man said, unslinging the rifle strapped to his shoulder. "Start firing, now. Oh, and do me one favor."

The man was already moving away from him, silently headed down the hill.

Drew whispered after him, "What favor?"

The man paused to glance back.

"Whatever you do, don't shoot me."

THIRTY-FOUR

I pressed the tip of the needle into Eric's neck, enough so that the kid started crying.

"Holy shit! Holy shit! Just let them go, okay? I don't want to die!"

The man with the pistol glared back at him, disgusted.

"Shut your fucking trap, you whiny piece of shit."

"Fuck you! You're going to die too! All of us are going to die!"

The man with the M4 said, "I'm tempted to take him out first just to shut him the fuck up."

Eric didn't take too kindly to this idea. He started trembling even more as he sniffed back tears.

"Fuck you! Fuck you both! If you want to die, then be my fucking guest. You don't know what's going to happen next, do you?"

"I do," I said. "These two assholes are going to let us go. Our friend up in the trees too. We leave alive, you leave alive, everybody is happy and lives to fight another day. What do you say, fellas? Don't be fucking stupid."

That was when I heard the low rumbling of engines coming

up the drive. The man with the pistol heard it too, and again his face split into a grin.

"Like I said, our orders aren't to capture you."

Two black SUVs came speeding down the drive. They looped around the front of the parking lot and came to a stop. Doors opened, and more men in tactical gear climbed out.

Keeping Eric right where he was in front of me, the needle in his neck, I spoke to the men standing by the SUVs.

"We have the Pax Romana. We're ready to infect all you assholes if you don't let us go. You really willing to take that chance?"

None of them answered. They didn't need to answer. Of course they were willing to take that chance. Especially if it was true there was a vaccine for this shit.

"Oh well. I guess that means we'll have to go with Plan B."

Everybody's focus was on me—especially the men from the SUVs—that nobody noticed the Kenworth T680 semi-truck that was creeping down the drive.

The SUVs still had their engines running, so maybe that was why nobody noticed. Plus the semi's lights were off. But now that it was coming down the incline, the headlights bloomed brightly and the engine roared as it started to pick up speed.

Ronny had been stationed across the highway, maybe three hundred yards south, this entire time, just waiting in case the strike team arrived while we were still here. Once they did, he was going to follow them up the drive with the lights off until he reached the parking lot, and then he was going to do the only thing he could do since we couldn't get our hands on an actual tank.

He was going to ram them.

Which he did, hunched behind the steering wheel, his boot pressing the pedal to the floor, going what looked to be twenty miles per hour, then thirty miles per hour, then forty miles per hour, while the men by the SUVs pivoted away from us to open fire on the truck. But we had anticipated this part, and that was why Ronny was wrapped with Kevlar, enough to keep him as safe as possible as he veered closer and closer to the strike team.

In the same moment, the two men we'd been dealing with were momentarily distracted, their attention on the oncoming semi, that Ho Sook saw an opening. She launched herself at the man with the M4, doing a roundhouse kick at his face just as he turned back to her.

The man stepped back, went to aim at Ho Sook, and that was when Mason issued an animalistic cry as he shot up from where he'd been kneeling, forcing his body straight into the man with the pistol and driving him back to the ground.

A second later, something fell from the sky, a large, black quadcopter drone. It landed only a couple yards away from us.

Then I spotted somebody running out of the trees, somebody that wasn't Drew, and this man fired at the strike team as he sprinted forward, then tossed what I realized was a grenade at the closest SUV.

This was confirmed two seconds later when part of the SUV exploded, tipping it onto its side and taking a few of the men with it.

Meanwhile, the semi smashed right into the second SUV. The impact nearly flipped the SUV over, instantly killing several of the men who had taken cover behind it.

Chin, I realized, had launched himself forward much like Ho Sook, only he was headed into the fray. Slipping the vials into his pockets, he swept up one of the discarded M4 rifles and immediately opened fire.

Ho Sook had knocked the M4 out of the man's hand. He was trying to get up and she knocked him back down. He tried once more, and she kicked at his head but he caught her foot and threw her aside. She bounced back up a second later and launched herself at him again.

Mason was dealing with the man with the pistol. The man had regained his footing and still had the gun. He aimed it at Mason, and Mason charged at him, his hands still bound behind his back, issuing another animalistic cry, and used his shoulder to knock the weapon just as the man fired.

I pushed Eric away and hurried over to Mason and the man with the pistol. I tossed the syringe into the bushes and tackled the man right as he tried to fire again at Mason. We hit the ground, and I elbowed the man in the face, then pressed down on his neck, hard enough to crush his windpipe. He tried to aim his gun at me, and I knocked it from his hand, then elbowed him in the face once more before leaning over and grabbing the gun and leaning back and shooting him in the head.

Up in the trees, Drew was taking out as many people as he could. The sound of the Barrett was a bit different from the chaotic melody of the M4s. Besides, there weren't many left of the strike team. Either they'd been crushed from the semi or injured from the grenade, or had just been shot by Chin and the new guy.

Ronny was out of the semi now, had stripped himself of the Kevlar padding, and returned fire at the few remaining strike team members.

I helped Mason to his feet. His face was strained, entirely flushed, and the cords in his neck popped out, and the next thing I knew he'd snapped the zip-ties apart. They'd bit deeply into his skin, enough so that he was bleeding, but he didn't seem to care.

"My brother-in-law sometimes called me the Hulk. He said you didn't want to know me when I got fucking angry."

"Are you fucking angry now?"

Mason only grunted. He saw Ho Sook still dealing with the

other man, and took the pistol from my hand and charged over and shot the man in the face. Then he picked up the discarded M4, handed it to Ho Sook, and they headed past me toward the others.

I surveyed the parking lot. Not many of Augustus' people were left alive, and it looked like those who still were wouldn't be alive much longer.

I started to hurry forward when I was tackled from behind. I hit the pavement, hard, and managed to look back at who'd hit me.

It was Eric Fisher, pressing his entire weight onto my chest. He was small, but there was a madness in his eyes that momentarily made him unstoppable. He had the syringe in his hand, the one I'd tossed in the bushes, and brought the needle down quickly toward my neck.

I managed to grab his wrist at the last moment, the needle only an inch or so from my throat.

He growled, "Fucking tried to infect me, motherfucker? Then I'm gonna fucking infect you!"

The madness was driving him, making him stronger than normal, and that combined with the adrenaline flooding his system made it difficult for me to push him off. I was only able to keep the needle at bay, but it was still only an inch or so from my neck, and any false move would cause him to stab me, and once he did, it was game over.

Then, suddenly, half of his face disappeared.

I heard the echo from the Barrett a second later, along with the sporadic gunfire behind me and the blood pounding in my ears.

In my ear, Drew asked, "You okay, Ben?"

I only nodded, and pushed Eric Fisher's dead body off of me, carefully taking the syringe from his hand.

That was when I heard footsteps close by, and a figure stood over me, momentarily blocking out the light from one of the lamps.

It was the new guy.

He leaned down, and held out his hand to help me up.

"Nice to finally meet you, Ben. I'm John Smith."

THIRTY-FIVE

At just after one o'clock in the afternoon, the helicopter touched down in the parking lot on the west side of the Addison, South Carolina, regional office location of Harris World Industries.

Already several SUVs dotted the parking lot, including several cargo vans. What could be salvaged went in the cargo vans. What couldn't be salvaged would burn with the building once it exploded.

Gas leak would be the official word once everything was said and done. Just one of those freak things. Nobody could have predicted it. Thank God nobody was inside at the time.

Etcetera, etcetera.

Tarps had been set up, too, not quite tents but they played the same role. The last thing they wanted was somebody flying over to spot the destruction. Or a satellite that they didn't control snapping and uploading a picture to some database. The chances were minimal, but they couldn't risk it.

Zach climbed out of the chopper and scanned the area for Davis. Several people watched the chopper, but none headed his way. They knew he was a proxy for Caesar, and after a fuck-up like this, they wanted to avoid him at all costs.

A tall man with glasses and neatly combed hair rounded the corner of the building and then started to jog toward him. He carried a tablet at his side, and met Zach halfway and extended his hand.

"Davis, sir. Apologies for not meeting you promptly."

Zach ignored the man's extended hand and kept walking straight for the building.

"Show me."

Davis nodded and led Zach around to the side where there were two garage doors.

Now that he'd neared the extended tarps, Zach had a better view of the wreckage of the two SUVs and the semi and all the dead bodies.

Around the corner, by the garage doors, were more dead bodies. Two big men, who were part of the strike team, and a skinny man wearing khakis and a polo shirt, who was one of the techs stationed at the site.

"We found another body up in the trees," Davis said. "Apparently he'd gone up there to take out their sniper. The drone caught two heat signatures—our man and the sniper—before suddenly there was another heat signature. Our best guess is the other person was cloaked in a thermal blanket until he showed himself."

Zach said nothing. Thermal blankets weren't anything new, and they were easily accessible, though their own people had advanced the technology a bit. Zach couldn't help but wonder if the person had in fact used a blanket, and if so, if it was one of theirs. Because if that were the case, then that meant the person who'd used it was a traitor or, somehow worse, it had been stolen.

"Speaking of which"—Davis gestured toward the wreckage—"you can see what's left of the drone over there.

From what we can tell, the sniper shot it out of the sky before…"

The man fell silent, not wanting to voice the simple fact that their own people had been slaughtered.

They entered the garage. Another cargo van was parked here, its back doors open. Two dead bodies were inside. It looked as if they'd been stripped of their work clothes.

Two more dead bodies, wrapped in body bags, were in the back as well.

Davis said, "These two were transport. They dropped off a live subject and picked up two dead subjects. From what we've ascertained from the security footage, the van left and then returned about twenty minutes later. We believe they were somehow stopped before they reached the highway. Then the people who killed them returned in the van."

Another man in khakis and a polo shirt lay dead on the floor several yards away. He'd been shot twice in the chest, once in the head.

Zach followed Davis to the elevator. When he'd first entered the garage and scanned the space, he thought the elevators doors were already open but now realized that much of the steel had been obliterated.

"What happened here?"

"Cross and Rachel—you'll see their bodies once we get downstairs—opened fire on the elevator once it became clear the intruders were headed down."

"So our people meant to ambush them."

"Yes, sir."

"How the fuck did the intruders survive an onslaught like that?"

As they rode down to the basement, Davis told Zach about how one of intruders had dropped down from the ceiling of the elevator and opened fire on Cross and Rachel once there was a pause in the gunfire.

Zach said, "He did this upside down?"

"Yes, sir, though it was a she. After the strike team was eliminated, the intruders shot out all the security cameras, but the footage was still saved in the cloud so we were able to review all of it. I'm surprised it wasn't sent to you."

It was but Zach didn't want to view what happened on a tablet. He wanted to see it for himself. Stand in the place where the attack had occurred and smell the rank odor of death and destruction that had been left behind by their enemy.

"It's still unclear to us how they managed to find this location," Davis said. "I was under the impression that this site was top secret. Have you heard anything on your end, sir?"

Zach didn't answer. He was thinking about being in the Kid's house only days ago. How the Kid had destroyed all his equipment, as well as the three laptops Ben Anderson had stolen from the Coliseum. Their own people had attempted to see if any of the hard drives had been accessed but so far they'd had no luck. Now Zach was starting to worry the Kid had been successful after all.

In the corridor just outside the elevator were the two bodies, Cross and Rachel. Each of them had been shot in the head.

"The woman who killed them shot them like this hanging upside down in the elevator?"

"That's right, sir. Again, I can show you the video if you'd like."

Part of Zach did want to see the video. Clearly Davis wasn't lying—the two dead bodies proved as much—but still it was hard to believe it was true.

Instead, he tilted his head down the corridor.

"Show me the rest."

Davis did. He took Zach through the security room and the other rooms, including the main lab.

"From what's logged in the system, the site only had a

supply of five vials of the Pax Romana. All of it was taken, as well as several hard drives. They also took the woman with them."

"Who?"

"The live subject the transport team brought in last night. The intruders dropped her off at a hospital two counties away. Local law enforcement has since gotten involved. We don't believe she can tell them much. As far as we can ascertain, she had no idea where she was taken, or by whom or for what purpose."

"After the strike team was eliminated, what else happened?"

"Another woman arrived."

This caused Zach to pause, and he turned away from taking in the lab to regard Davis.

"What woman?"

"It's probably better if you see for yourself. You only see her briefly, because, again, the intruders destroyed all the security cameras. At least, the ones down here. They didn't manage to destroy all the ones outside."

Davis tapped at the tablet several times and then tilted it so Zach could see the screen.

The camera angle showed a car coming down the drive and parking near the wreckage of the SUVs and semi. A woman in her early thirties stepped out, and was met by a man. They were far enough away that Zach couldn't make out their faces, but once they hurried into the garage to get onto the elevator —accompanied now by another man—Zach felt his entire body go tense.

On the tablet, Zach watched as the trio quickly moved through the underground, the woman taking pictures and video with her phone, but he didn't see much, because that was when the two men started firing rounds at each security camera.

Davis closed out the tablet, cleared his throat.

"As you can see, after that everything goes dark. We tried tracking where they may have gone afterward, but ... well, we lost their trail. Even after they dropped the woman off at the hospital. Tell me, sir, you recognize the woman who showed up at the end, don't you?"

Zach did. He recognized Ashley Walker because years ago he and Hogan had been tasked with tracking her down. But then things went sideways, no thanks to John Smith and Eli Craig.

Craig was dead—had died back in one of the black sites along with Dr. Matheson—but John Smith was most certainly alive. Over the years, he'd been as much a pain in their ass as Carver Ellison had been—Carver Ellison who had, at the Paradise Motel two years ago, shot Hogan in his face.

Only difference was John Smith had been part of the Legion program. Though he hadn't gone through the same training as every other man and woman in the program—the weapons training, the hand-to-hand combat training, all the different languages they'd been forced to learn—that didn't mean Smith wasn't as strong, fast, or fearless as the rest of them.

Which was a terrifying combination when you understood John Smith wasn't on your side.

And then, to top that all off, you had Ben Anderson along with them.

How the fuck Ben had met up with John Smith and Ashley Walker was something Zach didn't know, but what he did know was bad enough.

Without another word, Zach headed back to the elevator and returned to the surface.

When the pilot saw him coming, he started up the chopper. By then Zach already had his phone out and had dialed Caesar's number, and he shouted over the building roar of the rotors as he climbed into the helicopter.

"We have a major problem."

THIRTY-SIX

"I'm sorry, Ben. Really. I don't want you to think I betrayed your trust, though I guess that's what I did. But remember, I tried telling you about John and Ashley, and you said you didn't want to hear about them. And I just, well, I knew you needed help, and I knew that they could help you, and I just—"

"It's okay, Titus. I'm not mad."

"Really?"

I was mad, but I didn't want to get into it with Titus at the moment. There was a betrayal, though the fact was I barely knew Titus so it was silly of me to expect a certain level of loyalty. The same with John Smith and Ashley Walker, who seemed to have come out of nowhere, though on the drive so far—they drove with me and Ronny while Mason and Drew and Ho Sook and Chin traveled in a different vehicle, on a different highway headed north, in case we were being tracked —they'd told us the story about what happened to them years ago. Much of it sounded outlandish, but then again I had to remind myself of what all had happened to me in the past two years.

It was midafternoon, and it would be another five hours or so before we reached Ohio. We'd pulled off for gas and it was the first chance I got to get out to stretch my legs while Ronny gassed up the car. Then I'd grabbed the disposable cell phone and called Titus.

"How did you come across them, anyway?"

"It was a couple years ago. I'd been doing my own research into the games. John and Ashley had been searching the message boards, trying to find somebody who would know more about the organization or people who were fighting back against them. I honestly don't remember what I said—I think I mentioned reading your story after you'd posted it—and they had sent me a private message. Just testing the waters, I guess. They didn't give me much information, and I didn't give them much information, but as time went on they started filling in the pieces, like who they were and what they were doing. I confirmed it all, by the way, everything that they told me. How John's sister, an ADA in Manhattan, supposedly killed her family before jumping off her building. The courier company John worked for. His roommate getting killed. Even the fire at the bookstore where John worked, and the crash that happened at the coffee shop. They told you all of that, didn't they?"

"Yes. But still, they—"

"Could have created their story around those real-life events? The thought had crossed my mind. But everything else about their story checked out too. Like what happened to Ashley's parents' place on Martha's Vineyard. And then that black site in Maryland. The state trooper who Ashley killed? His death was in the papers, though of course they didn't say how he'd actually died. That was one of those deaths that didn't quite match up unless you remember that Caesar and the Inner Circle are really powerful. Then it makes a lot of sense how they were able to just cover up the death like it was natural causes."

Ronny had finished gassing up and moved the car beside the truck stop. John and Ashley had gone inside to get some food and now came out with plastic bags full of water and premade sandwiches.

John spotted me standing off near the bushes with the disposable to my ear. He didn't nod, didn't make any gesture. He just saw me, made sure I knew he saw me, and then continued on to the car with Ashley.

I decided to switch gears.

"Any luck on those two things I'd asked you to look into?"

Titus let out a soft sigh of relief. He knew I was still angry but I was moving on from it, at least for now.

"Yeah, the one thing was easy. The other wasn't."

"Which one wasn't easy?"

"Finding out more information about the fraternity. It helped that I could figure out which school, since Congresswoman Houser attended the same college, but records going back decades like that aren't readily available on the Internet. Besides, based on what you told me, I imagine the school would have tried their darnedest to hide what happened. If I had more time—or if I were able to go there in person, see the physical files—maybe I could figure it out. But as of right now, I can't tell you who Caesar really is."

"That's fine. I knew it was a long shot, anyway. What about the other thing?"

"Again, that was easy. After the Manhattan Blackout, Congress has been holding emergency hearings for the past week. Congresswoman Houser has been in D.C. all this time. She even did TV spots on all three cable networks yesterday. Jeez, Ben, you should have seen it. She looked so concerned, so angry about what had happened and all the people who were affected by the blackout. It's sick."

I watched the traffic on the highway surge past. I glanced

over and saw Ronny was in the car with John and Ashley. All of them watching me, waiting.

"Any chance you can find out where Congresswoman Houser stays when she's in D.C.?"

There was a beat of silence on Titus' end.

"I can. But … can I ask why?"

"Just wondering where she lays her head at night."

"You're thinking about going for her next, aren't you? It makes sense. She's Caesar's sister, after all."

"I'm thinking a lot of things right now, Titus. Just find me the address. And if you can, see if you can determine how she gets to the Capitol every day. But be careful, because like those locations on the flash drive, I imagine Caesar has alerts set up for when people search anything about his sister online."

I disconnected the call and returned to the car. Ronny was behind the wheel. John Smith was in the passenger seat, with Ashley sitting in the back behind Ronny. That was how we'd agreed to drive, since as we didn't know each other well it didn't seem safe to have one set sitting behind the other set.

When I slid into the backseat, John tilted his head to the side.

"How's Titus holding up?"

I said nothing. I just stared out my window as Ronny got us back on the highway.

Ashley pulled out one of the premade sandwiches.

"They didn't have much selection. Ham and cheese, and turkey and cheese. Since you're the last one in the car, all that's left is turkey and cheese."

I took the sandwich with a nod but said nothing. I was starving, but I was also trying to process everything that had happened in the past twenty-four hours.

After another couple of miles in silence, I spoke.

"Where have you been living?"

John Smith shifted in his seat to look back at me.

"What do you mean?"

"It's a simple question. Where have the two of you been living all this time?"

Ashley said, "We don't stay in one place very long."

John nodded, taking a bite of his ham and cheese sandwich.

"We're constantly moving around the country. Usually stay at motels, or we sleep in the car. We have storage units in several different states. Sometimes we stay there a week or two at a time if we can."

"What do you keep in the storage units?"

"Vehicles. Weapons. Money. Basically anything we can steal from Caesar and his people."

"How many of their locations have you tracked down?"

"A good bit. They keep them well-hidden. And well-guarded. So it takes a lot of time to find one, and then when you find one, it takes a while to surveil and find the best course of attack."

"So which places have you found?"

"Mostly places where they keep children or other people used in the games. That's where we found a lot of their tech. In fact, I managed to hide myself from that drone with the blanket I showed you. We managed to take a lot of other stuff, too. Some really high-tech stuff. I'm talking James Bond, *Mission: Impossible* level high-tech shit. But even after all the stuff we've seen and taken, this Pax Romana ... it scares the shit out of me."

"You have all this tech, and Ashley has been taking pictures and video of all these places, so why not finally take it to the press?"

"We've tried," Ashley said. "More than once. The same thing happened that happened when your friend Carver contacted people in the press. They died, which meant the story died. We considered leaking everything online, to

YouTube or even Facebook, try to make it go viral, but we know that as soon as it hits the Internet, Caesar and his people will scrub it entirely, make it like it never existed. Besides, nowadays, they can just point at it and say it's fake news. Nobody will believe it. And those who will believe it … it won't matter, because nobody is powerful enough to go up against them."

There was another lengthy silence, and then John Smith cleared his throat.

"That guy in the lab—Eric—he told you the base of operations is called Rome?"

"That's right."

"And he said the vaccine for the Pax Romana is there?"

"Yes."

"And the server farm?"

I nodded but said nothing else. I could tell the gears were turning in his head, just as they were turning in mine.

Ronny asked, "What's a server farm?"

Ashley said, "It's a collection of computer servers. It must be the central hub for everything the Inner Circle does. They may have people working at server farms all over the world, but they can't hide all that data in those places. So they keep it at their base."

"Rome," John said thoughtfully. "I can't believe they fucking call it Rome."

Another beat of silence, and then I released a breath.

"Do me a favor. Tell me what happened next."

John shifted in his seat to look back at me.

"Are you fucking kidding? We already spent the past couple hours telling you what happened."

I held his stare. He knew I was testing him and he didn't like it, but I didn't care. Not when the safety of my own people was on the line. Not when the safety of the entire world was on the line.

"You told me the first part of what happened, everything leading up to you saving those kids and taking them to the orphanage. But I want to hear what happened after that in more detail. How the two of you got to where you are right now."

THIRTY-SEVEN

Sister Sara had offered them a place to stay, at least for a couple of days, and while it had been tempting, John and Ashley decided they needed to get back on the road as soon as possible.

Staying stationary too long was a risk. It could be dangerous. Could cause them to become complacent. To let their guard down.

No, they needed to keep moving, needed to keep looking over their shoulders, and the longer that they stayed at St. Nicholas Home for Children, the more chance that the Legion and the Inner Circle and whatever else was out there would find them.

So after three games of checkers—Evelyn, who Eli Craig had hidden away at the orphanage, had kicked John's ass in each game—they said their goodbyes and loaded back into the minivans and drove away.

They headed north and abandoned the minivans in a mall parking lot. A used car dealership was down the highway, and after some spirited negotiating they purchased a ten-year-old Ford Escort for an even $1000.

They filled the gas tank, stopped for some greasy fast food, and then headed west.

Where were they going? Well, among the items in Eli's storage unit in New Jersey, John had found a journal with years of chicken-scratched notes. Over one hundred locations all over the country. Some of them had been crossed out, which John figured meant that Eli had determined there was nothing there, but still there were several other locations that hadn't been crossed out that they could try ... though the *what* and the *how* were still up in the air.

Eli had told John about other storage units he had scattered around the country. Like the storage unit in New Jersey—the one John and Ashley had gone to after the incident on Martha's Vineyard, when Eli had more or less offered himself up as prisoner to the people who were hunting them—these storage units contained vehicles and weapons and money. Eli had been planning to go to war for many years, so he had been carefully putting together a long game, setting up bank accounts that were linked to the storage units that would automatically deduct payments every month.

As long as the storage units were paid every month, nobody seemed to care, and every storage unit that they came across over the next year—seven of them in total—hadn't been vacated.

Their first week on the road, they stopped at motels and got two separate rooms, but soon they realized this sometimes raised eyebrows from the clerks. It made more sense to the motel employees that John and Ashley were a couple, and so to keep up appearances they would get a room with two twin beds. Besides, it was cheaper that way, and there was no telling just how much money Eli had squirreled away in his storage units.

They had to be smart, but they also had to be frugal with the cash.

One night after the first week, after they'd driven to California to check out the second storage unit, they had both been in the motel room and on their separate beds well past midnight. John hadn't been able to sleep, and neither had Ashley, and after a while—after the air conditioner kicked on for the umpteenth time and a distant car alarm eventually quieted—Ashley had whispered his name.

"John."

Staring up at the ceiling, at the mishmash of cracks in the paint, he whispered, "Yeah."

"Just what the hell are we doing?"

It was a good question. A very good question. They had each led two entirely different lives, and now those lives had been upended to the point where they could never return to them. They could try, sure, but already too many people had died in their wake, and if the people hunting them didn't kill them, then the authorities would most likely take them into custody.

When John didn't answer right away, Ashley said, "Are you still awake?"

"I am. And I don't know."

She was quiet for a beat, and then whispered, "I'm scared."

He wanted to tell her he was scared too, just to say something, to ease her worry, but the truth was he wasn't scared at all. He had never truly appreciated the fact that he had no fear. It wasn't until Eli explained to him about the Legion program that he understood why he was different. The truth was, he wanted to find the people hunting them. He wanted to take the fight to those who had killed his siblings. Only problem was, from what he could tell, the number of the Legion was vast, and there were only two of them, John and Ashley, and despite how she'd managed to protect herself against the state trooper who had attacked her, Ashley wasn't a killer.

To go up against these people—to survive—John Smith knew that you had to be a killer.

But … was he a killer? To stay alive this long he'd obviously been forced to kill, but that had been to protect himself. He wasn't a soldier, though he realized that if they were going to move forward, John had to turn himself into a soldier. And if possible, he needed to turn Ashley into one as well.

So they started making stops, usually out in the middle of nowhere off one highway or another where the horizon stretched endlessly. John hadn't known much about guns himself, but he was a fast learner, and everything he had learned he taught Ashley. How to assemble a gun. How to load it. How to shoot it. How to eject the magazine and insert another.

He'd set up empty soda cans fifty feet away and both he and Ashley would do their best to knock those cans down. John was a fast learner, sure, but it seemed Ashley had a true talent for target practice. The first couple of times she was nervous and the shots went wide, but after a while, once she started becoming more comfortable, her grip became steady, her stance loose, and she knocked down every can that John put up.

Of course, shooting empty soda cans out in the middle of nowhere wasn't the same as shooting another person. Ashley knew this because she'd shot that state trooper, had killed him. It had been in self-defense, sure, but still that didn't stop the guilt. There were even some nights when she murmured in her sleep, in the throes of a nightmare, and John wasn't sure whether or not he should wake her. The last thing he wanted was to be a dark shadow leaning over her when she opened her eyes.

After the first month—having checked out three of the storage units—John finally decided it was time to start checking out the other addresses in the journal Eli had left behind. What these addresses were, exactly, neither of them could guess, but they assumed it had to do with the people hunting them.

And that was the thing—how did you fight an army that was invisible? An army that the rest of the world didn't even know existed. From what John and Ashley had experienced, these people blended into the background of everyday life. They worked jobs just like everybody else. Which meant anybody could be part of the Legion—the guy behind the cash register at the gas station, or the waitress at the diner, or the police officers who entered the diner while John and Ashley sat in a booth near the back, both of them tightly gripping guns underneath their table and prepared to kill the cops if need be.

The first location they checked was just outside of Albuquerque, New Mexico. What appeared to be an industrial dry cleaners.

They found a secluded spot a quarter mile away to watch the building with a pair of binoculars. They watched trucks come in and go out. They watched employees come and go. For two straight days, they surveilled the dry cleaners, not quite sure what they were looking for but trusting that Eli had had reason to add the address to his notebook, even if there was the slimmest chance that it was somehow hiding the Legion's secrets.

In the end, it turned out to be a bust. They'd waited well past midnight to make their approach. The security system wasn't quite state of the art, and they managed to slip inside and search the entire place top to bottom. Ashley had suggested that there was a secret door that led to a basement which would be the real operation, but after an hour they couldn't find any secret doors, and besides, the more time they spent there, the more chance that they would get caught, so they chalked it up to a loss and hurried the hell out of there.

The second place they tried—a regional furniture office

sitting fifteen miles south of Colorado Springs—immediately sent up a red flag.

On the outside, the place looked normal enough—a tan brick building, its employee parking lot moderately full during the day—but when Ashley checked the website (using a disposable phone and a VPN to mask their location), the thing was chock-full of stock photos and gibberish about the corporation that any regular joe browsing the site might take to be blandly normal but which John and Ashley both agreed was most likely a cover.

After all, nowadays if your business had a physical location, it was expected to have a virtual location too. Plus, from what they could tell, the corporate office in West Virginia also seemed to be a front, so they figured they had hit jackpot.

After three days of surveillance—a number that would eventually decrease once they both became more confident and understood that depending on what was at the locations it could literally cost people their lives—they made their move at one o'clock in the morning when a white van pulled around to the back.

They surprised the two men from the van, and two men inside the building—shooting all four of them dead with sound-suppressed pistols, an act that may have seemed a bit too irrational except when you realized that both drivers were packing and when they heard John approaching one of them reached for his gun before taking a bullet to the head—and then they searched the building, every single room, but the entire first floor was empty.

The basement—which was in fact accessed by a secret door —was far from empty.

They found children, just like at the site back in Maryland, as well as two more adults who worked for the Legion. One of these was killed by Ashley, the other John wounded so that they could try to get some answers. But after an hour or so it became clear that no answers would be forthcoming, so John shot the man twice in the chest and then helped Ashley take the four children up to the first floor and load them into the white van.

They took every computer they could find below, too, as well as any paper file that they could access. It wasn't until two hours later, after they'd ditched the van and were on the road heading to St. Nicholas Home for Children, that Ashley cursed under her breath.

"What's wrong?" John asked.

"I should have taken pictures. Should have taken video. Anything that could be used to document what that place was."

They had the kids, of course, but like last time the kids wouldn't be able to tell them much. The best bet was to get them to Sister Sara and the rest of the nuns to take care of them.

Ultimately, they weren't able to access the computers, but some of the paper files were interesting. A few even had other addresses, all of which they eventually visited, and the more locations they visited, the more confident they became, and the more luck they started to have.

Ashley began taking photos and video, documenting anything she could. Before killing the members of the Legion at each location, they forced a few to access the computers—many of the computers were unlocked by fingerprint scan—so they were able to get to some of those records as well.

After almost two years, Ashley felt that she'd found enough information to expose the Legion—more than enough photos and video, plus the documents from the computers—and she contacted Tom Fisher, her old boss at the *Post*, who was naturally shocked to hear from her but who said that he was interested in hearing her story.

They communicated via an encrypted messaging app, and Ashley sent him some of the pictures and video, telling him everything that they'd managed to undercover, including the story that Eli Craig and Marta had told John and Ashley about the Legion program. Tom said that this was all promising but suggested they go to the *New York Times* with it and said that he would reach out to one of his contacts over there. And that was the last Ashley heard from him.

It wasn't until several days later that Ashley saw the news article about how Tom Fisher had hanged himself in his condo overlooking Central Park. The reporter at the *Times* which Tom had suggested they take the story to had also died, though apparently he'd slipped on the subway platform and fallen in the path of an approaching train.

When John read about that, he murmured, "Same old fucking tricks."

Still, Ashley was determined to bring the story to light. But she knew they needed to be careful. That they had to do it right so that nobody else died.

Over the next year they kept moving, never staying in one place more than a few nights, and they went from one location to another, checking them out and, if they determined that those locations were in fact targets, they made their attack. A few times they weren't successful, as obviously the Legion was on high alert for John Smith and Ashley Walker, and one time Ashley had gotten shot in the leg, though it was more a graze than anything else, and another time John had gotten stabbed in his side and shot in his shoulder.

Still, it didn't stop them, once they managed to rest up, and they kept shutting down those locations, saving children and sometimes adults who were at those locations, and obtaining more and more photos and videos and files—including technology that didn't make any sense, at least from what they knew of the Legion.

In one location they found eyeglasses that appeared to have cameras embedded in the frames. They found contact lenses with ultra-tiny cameras embedded in them too. They found syringes that they eventually realized contained injectable GPS trackers. They found all different types of cameras, including drones of all different sizes (one was the size of a quarter and was capable of streaming video in high def), as well as many other items, including high-tech thermal blankets, one of which John would eventually use in Addison, South Carolina.

Then, one day two years ago, a story hit the Internet. The story wasn't there very long—the Legion managed to scrub it pretty fast—but it was about a man who woke up one morning in a motel three thousand miles from home, and suddenly a large missing piece in the puzzle dropped into place.

Before, they'd been searching the message boards all over the Internet trying to find more information about the Legion, but now they expanded that search to include these games. That put them in contact with several different people, but John and Ashley knew they needed to be careful, needed to be fucking cautious, because there was very little doubt that the Legion would be monitoring these message boards.

That was how they eventually came in contact with Titus. Titus who, like them, was cautious not to say too much, and who they eventually started communicating with via an encrypted messaging app, and who—after several long months, once they had each determined the other was in fact real and was in fact not the enemy—let it drop that he knew the Kid.

Yes, *that* Kid—the one from the story of the Man of Wax —and John and Ashley immediately asked that they be put in contact with the hacker so that they could be put in contact with Carver Ellison, who based on Ben Anderson's story, was a kindred spirit and somebody who could help them go up against the Legion and the Inner Circle and apparently a man who called himself Caesar.

But while Titus said that he'd floated the idea across to the

Kid, the Kid had immediately shut him down, saying that it was best for Titus to stay as far away from that shit as possible.

John and Ashley encouraged Titus to send along some of the photographs and videos they'd found.

Titus said he tried but that the Kid refused to listen.

John had become absolutely livid, vowing to kick the hacker's ass if and when they ever met, but eventually he agreed with Ashley that if the roles were reversed they probably wouldn't want to deal with anybody else, what with the ghosts of several different reporters haunting Ashley.

Months after the deaths of Tom Fisher and the *Times* reporter, she attempted to reach out to other reporters. Some never responded to her. Of those who did, a few wrote her off as a nut job, but a few others were clearly interested.

Each and every one of them, once they started their own reporting based on the information Ashley had provided, ended up dead.

John and Ashley had contacted people at several federal agencies, thinking maybe that would be a better route, but again, either they never received a reply or if they did it was to tell them to stop wasting their time.

Only somebody from the CIA seemed to express real interest, and like the reporters before her, she had died in a car accident. Apparently her brakes had failed and she crashed into a highway median.

And so they kept doing what they did best—tracking down different locations, attacking the men and women who worked there, saving any children or adults who were imprisoned by the Legion, stealing any and all computers or other tech that they found—knowing that one day Ashley would have more than enough information to expose the Legion and the Inner Circle and Caesar to the entire world.

Then, two days ago, Titus contacted them out of the blue. He said that the Manhattan Blackout had to do with the Inner

Circle. That the Kid and Carver Ellison and a bunch of other people were dead. But that Ben Anderson and a few others were still alive, and that Titus had tried telling Ben about John and Ashley but that Ben, like the Kid, hadn't wanted to bring any new faces into the mix, which Titus said he guessed he understood but that things were getting out of hand and that there was a very good chance John and Ashley would be needed where Ben and the others were headed.

"Where are they headed?" John said.

To which Titus answered, "Addison, South Carolina."

THIRTY-EIGHT

The motel room was cramped with all of us squeezed in tight, Ronny and Drew and Ho Sook sitting on one bed, John Smith and Ashley Walker sitting on the other bed. Chin stood by the bathroom door, leaning against the wall, while Mason stayed by the room door.

He was quietly bouncing back and forth on the balls of his feet, anxious to get back to his wife who was currently being looked after by Beverly in the next room.

Graham was in the room, too, sitting at the small wooden table in the corner, the same table that had the Dell opened and Titus on the screen via secure video chat.

I stood in front of all of them, my back to the cheap TV, and looked around at each face staring back at me, including Titus'.

"So now we know what the Pax Romana is. And based on what we observed at that building, it's scary as fuck. We took the syringe and four vials with us, mostly because we didn't want to leave them behind, but in retrospect I now question if that was the right thing to do. Any one of those vials could go missing, or break somewhere, and that virus could start to spread. In many ways, there's a chance *we* could be the ones to cause the end of the world, and I don't know about you guys, but the idea freaks me out."

Everybody glanced over at the mini-fridge Drew had purchased at Walmart and which now contained the syringe and four vials of the Pax Romana. It sat right next to the cheap TV. Right next to me.

Graham shifted on the chair by the table, his cane between his legs.

"I still don't understand why you don't just take that stuff straight to the CDC."

Ashley answered before I could.

"In theory taking this to the Centers for Disease Control and Prevention would be the right move. But if Caesar and his people are as powerful as we believe—and thus far they've proven that they are—the CDC is compromised, just as is every other major organization in this country, and maybe around the world. Again, we've tried contacting these organizations before. The FBI, CIA, DHS, even the IRS. Nothing ever comes of it. Every time it looks like we have interest, our contact 'accidentally' passes away, usually in some freak disaster like a car accident or house fire or they all of a sudden decide to kill themselves."

Her anguish was clear in her voice, just as it was clear on her face. No doubt she was thinking about her contact from the *Post* and the reporter from the *Times* as the first ones to suffer an abrupt death. On the drive back from South Carolina, John Smith had done much of the talking, mostly because it seemed reliving those events had drained Ashley. Every time they went to seek help, it caused somebody innocent to die, so it made sense why they would eventually stop trying.

There was a beat of silence, where everybody digested this latest piece of info, and then I cleared my throat.

"We got lucky down in South Carolina. Very lucky. Part of

that has to do with our new friends. And based on what John told us, these people working for Caesar—they're not just normal people like the rest of us. They're ..."

John saw I was struggling to find the right words, and added his own.

"Lab experiments."

Nobody said anything to that.

John pushed up from the bed, came to stand beside me to address the rest of the room.

"In the end, that's basically the truth. For the longest time I had trouble accepting it, but that's what it is. At the very least, now you know that these people don't experience fear, not like the rest of you do. And they've been trained from the start to believe in whatever crazy shit Caesar has been selling. They don't just work for him; they *believe* it. And they've infiltrated places all over the country. Hell, I always suspected this thing had global reach, and now that I've heard what Ho Sook and Chin told me, I guess it's true that they're worldwide. It's fucking terrifying."

I nodded and leaned back against the nightstand, crossing my arms.

"Like I said, we got lucky down in South Carolina. Each of us managed to get out of there alive. Part of me thinks we should just quit while we're ahead—that we make everything Ashley has documented over the past couple of years known, and drop those vials off at the CDC—but another part of me..."

I let it trail off, like before, only this time I wasn't struggling to find the right words. I just didn't want to say it.

Still, the rest of them knew what I meant, especially Ronny.

He said, "The other part of you wants to end this once and for all."

I looked at him and nodded, then glanced around the room once again. Paused a beat to take a deep breath.

"I have an idea. Something that might help us learn the location of the place these people call Rome. Something that might even get us there. But there's no guarantee that Caesar will be there, or that if we even manage to find it and somehow destroy the place, that will end this. In fact, there's a chance that not all of us will be as lucky this time around. If we do this, we have to act fast. John and I have already worked out some of the logistics with Titus. He can get John to one of his storage units up north to get the tech we need. Then he can meet the rest of us in D.C. That's where Caesar's sister currently is. Tomorrow is Monday, and Congress is still holding emergency hearings. So far she's been making an appearance every day. The hope is she's there tomorrow. But if she is, she'll most likely be heavily guarded. And not with Capitol Police or any other kind of government protection. These will be part of the Legion."

Drew grinned.

"The strike team was most likely part of the Legion, too, and we managed to handle them just fine."

"That's a good point," I said. "John, if the Legion are the super soldiers you make them out to be …"

I wasn't sure how to say the rest, but John knew what I meant.

He said, "Over the past several years I've come to realize something about the Legion. They've been taught from the beginning that they're practically indestructible, and that causes them to build a level of arrogance I've used to my advantage. Despite all their training, they almost never have to actually use it, at least when it comes to something like what happened back at that site. They usually just move among the shadows, manipulate things behind the scenes."

"Exactly," I said. "And last night, we got lucky because they didn't expect us. They will this time. They might not know we're targeting Congresswoman Houser, but they know we'll be targeting something, and they'll be on high alert."

Graham said, "Even assuming you manage to get to the congresswoman, do you honestly believe she'll tell you where to find her brother?"

"Not at all. But the plan doesn't call for her to tell us his location. We have another idea in mind for that."

I told them the plan, ran through it quickly but with as much detail as I could, and then I let several seconds of silence pass before clearing my throat again.

"Like I said, it's no guarantee. The first part of the plan might not even get us to the second part. And even if it does, I'm not sure how effective we'll be. Not counting Titus, there are only eight of us. They have an army. Most likely we'll be walking into a slaughter."

Now there was a heavy silence, enough so that we could hear a couple outside arguing in the parking lot. I looked around the room again, but most people had diverted their eyes to the floor or their laps, taking in what I just said. Even Titus, secure in his trailer with Hercules in his pen outside, glanced away from the camera in his computer.

Mason, too, had stopped bouncing back and forth on the balls of his feet. He'd gone completely still in the past couple of minutes. He was staring across the room, at what looked to be nothing, and then he blinked and looked at me.

"Ben?"

"Yeah, Mason."

"That part about how we don't have an army? I might be able to help with that."

THIRTY-NINE

I stood at the railing overlooking the parking lot and lit a cigarette. I watched as Drew and Ronny helped Mason's wife down the stairs and into the car. Beverly was with them, carrying the bag of supplies she would need to keep care of her on the trip.

Behind me, a door opened and Mason stepped out.

He placed his large hand on my shoulder, gave it a slight squeeze, and said, "Good luck."

I turned to him, and nodded.

"Good luck to you too."

"I'll call as soon as I have an answer. Just"—he paused, searching for the right word, and then grinned—"don't get yourself killed."

I nodded again and watched him head down the steps to the parking lot. He shook Ronny's and Drew's hands, then climbed into the car behind the steering wheel. His wife and Beverly were in the back. He waved up to me one last time, and then drove away.

I tapped ash off the railing, watched as Ronny and Drew

got into another car. They were going to drive to the motel three miles away where they'd been staying to get their things.

Behind me, the door next to Mason's room opened. I expected John Smith to step out, but it was Graham.

He shuffled up beside me, set his cane aside, and gripped the railing with both hands as he stared down at the deserted parking lot.

After all, it was almost midnight. The rest of us would be leaving soon.

Graham said, "Now that Mason can't go to D.C. with you, you're down one person."

I took one final drag of the cigarette, flicked the butt over the railing.

"We'll manage."

"Let me come with you."

"Graham—"

"I mean it, Ben. Let me do something. I feel useless."

"You're not useless."

"Then name one thing I'm doing right now."

"To start, you're getting on my nerves."

I grinned when I said this, but it was clear by Graham's expression he wasn't in the joking mood. He just stared back at me.

I let out a breath.

"Graham, I appreciate the fact you want to help, but—"

"I was a detective, Ben."

"I know you were. But this situation doesn't call for the police."

"Based on what you explained, you're going to need all the help you can get. There's no reason you shouldn't want me to come along."

I opened my mouth, but he shook his head and held up his cane.

"Is it this? Do you think this will slow me down? I won't be running a mile, Ben. Stick me in a car. Make me a lookout. *Something*."

I heard the quiver in his voice, noticed his bottom lip trembling, and realized something. It hit me hard, the notion I hadn't seen it before, and I shook my head.

"Graham, it's not your fault what happened to Carver. Had you been there with the rest of them, you would have been killed too."

His eyes had started to tear up. He looked away, stared a beat, and then wiped at his face.

"I was only a couple of miles away. I was *asleep* when it happened. I—"

"Again, Graham, there was nothing you could have done. You would have just been one more body to bury."

"He was my son, Ben. My wife may not have given birth to Carver, but we raised him like our own. And now … now he's dead."

More tears were falling down his face, and I didn't know what else to do so I stepped forward and held him in a hug. Everything in the past two weeks had been happening so fast none of us had really had a chance to mourn. In fact, my mourning for Maya presented itself more like guilt with the knowledge that my wife and daughter were still alive— assuming Augustus hadn't had them killed by now.

Graham and his wife had never had kids. They'd adopted Carver because he was a scared little boy who had done a brave thing and would have suffered great consequences if the truth ever got out. They had given Carver another chance, and then, years later, when Carver came to Graham for help, for a place to stay, Graham had helped him without question. Graham had helped all of us, and what had he gotten for it? His farmhouse was destroyed, along with all his bees, and the one person he'd thought of as a son was now dead.

"Okay."

I said it so quietly I wasn't even sure I had said it at all, and then I said it again, leaning back to look at Graham.

"Okay, you can come with us. You can be a lookout. But any sign of danger, you get the fuck of there. You hear me?"

He wiped again at his eyes, nodding.

I said, "Then go pack what you need. We leave soon."

Graham grabbed his cane and turned back to the room. Just as he went to open the door, the door opened and John Smith was there, blocking the way. He stepped back, holding the door for Graham, and then he stepped out onto the walkway.

I offered him the pack of cigarettes, and he waved it away.

"Don't smoke. Never have."

"Good for you," I said, and lit a new cigarette.

We stood there for a beat, silent, watching the empty parking lot, and then John spoke quietly.

"Are you sure bringing him along is a good idea?"

"He won't be in any danger."

"We're all in danger."

"I'll put him in charge of the first part. He'll be fine."

John stared at me, studying my face, and then asked, "Do you think they're still alive?"

He meant my wife and daughter.

"I don't know. I hope so. But Augustus could have had them killed the moment his people killed Carver and the Kid and everybody else."

"Even if they are still alive, there's no guarantee they'll be at this place."

"I know."

"They could be hidden in one of the numerous sites they have around the country. Or hell, they might be in another country. They might not even be on this continent."

"I *know.*"

"I'm not trying to upset you, Ben. I just want you to be realistic."

I was inhaling when he said this, and snorted smoke out of my nose.

"You don't think I'm being realistic?"

"No, I think you are. But I think you're also holding out hope for something that might not happen."

The cigarette was almost finished. I took one last puff and flicked the butt over the railing so it could join its mate down in the scattered trash in the parking lot.

"As much as I do hope to see my wife and daughter again, that's not my main focus right now. The Pax Romana is, and making sure it never infects another human being."

John nodded, and glanced at the closed motel room door behind him. When he spoke next, his voice was almost a whisper.

"She's pregnant."

"Ashley?"

He nodded again, though he was still watching the door.

"I'd be lying if I said the first time I saw her I didn't think she was attractive. She walked into the bookstore with this other guy—another reporter from the paper, the one who was killed soon after—and I just ... it sounds cheesy, but for a moment I couldn't breathe. It was like she took my breath away. But then she started asking me about my sister and I immediately got pissed off and told the two of them to leave. And then ... then that guy showed up to kill me, and soon after Ashley had come back into the store, and then we ended up in that SUV with the guy I had always thought of as my father, and ... Ashley and I have kept running ever since. Every day that went by we were together, so of course we started having feelings for one another. I was always a loner most of my life. Never really cared about anybody else. And these past five years ... I've come to care about that woman a great deal."

"How long has she been pregnant?"

"Only three months. About three years ago she'd gotten pregnant too. That one lasted longer. We ... we had actually discussed the idea of her getting an abortion. We had been so careful making sure she wouldn't get pregnant, but sometimes shit happens. And we knew if she did have the baby, that would change everything. We could no longer work like we had at trying to stop the Legion. It's always been our dream, I guess, us bringing down this vast evil empire, and that was what drove us, what kept us going every day. But then Ashley got pregnant, and more months went by, and we discussed having an abortion, and then ... nature sort of gave us an out."

"She had a miscarriage."

John Smith nodded slowly. He was still watching the closed door, but I could see the emotion crossing over the side of his face.

"She took it hard. So did I. But we knew it was for the best, and we just kept working, gathering all that evidence, trying to find the different locations all over the country, and then ... she got pregnant again."

He paused, and took a breath.

"I guess the reason I'm telling you this now is because I wasn't entirely truthful with you when you asked for every detail after we first left that orphanage. This ... this was too personal, especially to tell strangers, and besides, I know how much it worries Ashley."

"You love her," I said. "I get that. And I get that you want to protect her."

He blinked and looked at me, and his eyes were intense.

"You're goddamned right I love her. And we made a decision on what we plan to do this time. Which is why I don't let her be on the front line anymore. She stays back until it's safe, just like back in South Carolina. I'm sorry, but that's how it has to be."

"Again, John, I get it. Believe me, I do."

He was quiet for another beat, and then he glanced up at the sky.

"In the story you wrote, you said you went out every night and looked up at the sky and asked if the sheep had eaten the flower or not. Did you really do that?"

I smiled, because there was no other way for me to respond just then, and then I nodded.

"Yeah, I did for a bit. But then … I stopped. It just didn't seem to matter anymore. Especially when they made me think that my family was in fact dead."

John stared up at the sky for a long moment, and then looked at me again.

"We're going to win."

"How do you know?"

"Because if we don't then a lot of people will die. And that's just not something I can live with."

"I hope you're right."

"I am. Plus, I don't know you well, but I get the sense you're a good father. So I'm going to need a lot of advice pretty soon."

"We make it out of this alive, I'll give you all the advice you want, much of which I'm sure you'll find unhelpful."

He grinned, and held out his hand. I shook it. Then he stepped back into the room to get Ashley and Graham as we needed to leave.

I stayed where I was. I thought about lighting another cigarette but instead stared up at the dark sky and all the stars.

I whispered, "Has the sheep eaten the flower or not?"

Then I closed my eyes and listened.

FORTY

Jake Tapper stared into the camera, impeccably dressed as always in a shirt and tie and jacket, his grayish dark hair swept to the side, and spoke in his direct, no-nonsense manner.

"Joining us now to discuss the Manhattan Blackout is the ranking member on the U.S. House Committee on Homeland Security, Congresswoman Francis Houser of North Carolina. Congresswoman Houser, thanks for joining us. What can you tell us about the emergency hearings that have been occurring behind closed doors on the Hill?"

The picture cut to her sitting in what looked to be another studio, but which was really a room in her house set up for TV spots such as this. A green screen towered behind her, so all the viewers saw were the graphics CNN wanted to display; in this case a blue background and the logo for *State of the Union*.

She wore her white blouse and dark jacket, and her makeup was just subtle enough to look natural. She opened her mouth to respond, but that was all Frank saw before she paused the video on the tablet.

She squinted, inspecting the lines on her face that had been spotlighted by the bright lights set up behind the camera.

Frank often enjoyed watching clips of herself the next day, seeing what worked and what didn't, what she could do differently next time.

Mostly, though, she wanted to make sure she didn't look weak. That she looked in control of herself and the situation. That, above all else, she looked like a leader.

And it wasn't just for the cable news viewers, or the pundits, or even her constituents back home. Instead, it was because she knew her brother often watched these clips, and whenever she misspoke or looked uncertain, he would be sure to say something to her, either on the phone or by text through an encrypted messaging app.

Of course, she always preferred to be in studio whenever she could, but due to the recent security concerns her brother had forbidden it, directing her to use the tiny studio he'd had constructed in her home so she wouldn't have to leave the house.

Like she was a fucking prisoner or something.

Frank tossed the tablet on her bed, not wanting to bother overthinking things today. All last week had been hellish on the Hill because of what happened in New York, and this week would be no exception.

Already showered and dressed, she stood in front of the wall-length mirror to make sure she looked presentable and then she grabbed her phone off the bedside table and headed downstairs.

"Good morning, Congresswoman."

Gabi, the old Honduran woman who worked as both her cook and housekeeper, already had her hazelnut coffee waiting in a to-go cup.

"Thank you, Gabi."

"Will it be another late night, ma'am?"

Meaning should she bother staying to make dinner tonight.

"Hopefully not, Gabi, but don't worry about staying late. Go home and see your grandchildren."

Gabi's smile was so bright Frank might have needed sunglasses. The old woman practically bowed as she thanked her.

Frank, cell phone in one hand and coffee in another, headed for the front door. Through the glass panes she saw Travis was already waiting outside. With his dark suit and sunglasses, he looked like Secret Service, but maybe that was just because it was Georgetown and practically anybody wearing a dark suit and sunglasses looked like they were Secret Service.

She didn't get her own security detail, but Travis was her bodyguard of sorts. He was part of the Legion program, just as was her driver Stefan. The only person who wasn't part of the Legion—who wasn't anything, at least in terms of the Inner Circle—was Gabi.

Her brother had insisted on assigning one of his people to be her cook and housekeeper, but she had adamantly refused, and as a cook and housekeeper didn't really involve security, her brother relented.

Frank had quietly taken that as a win.

It was her father, so many years ago, who had nicknamed her Frank. At the time it was because he'd joked that she was like a tomboy—always climbing trees and scraping her knees and getting into fights—but later she understood it was because her father had really wanted a son. And he'd had a son, though it had been in secret, something that her mother didn't learn about right away, though when she did her mother didn't react the way Frank had imagined she would. If her mother was angry, she barely showed it, simply remarking that she would refuse to see the boy and then never talking about him again.

Frank opened the door and stepped out into the early morning sunlight and scanned the street.

Travis said, "Good morning, Congresswoman."

She ignored him as she focused on the black Range Rover parked up the block. She could see two men inside, both wearing sunglasses.

Travis spoke again, though his voice had ticked down a notch.

"They're with us."

She started down the stone steps, slowly, taking a sip of her coffee and then frowning at Travis.

"Why?"

He opened the backdoor of the Town Car, said, "I'll explain on the way."

She glanced again at the Range Rover before climbing into the back of the Town Car.

Stefan already had the engine running and offered up a quiet good morning. Then Travis dropped down into the passenger seat, and Stefan slid away from the curb.

Frank stared out the window at the scrolling neighborhood. It was much too expensive for her, and every once in a while there would be editorials complaining about wasted taxpayer dollars, but the truth was her husband had been very wealthy, and when he passed away he left all his money to her, including the house which he'd owned before they were married, and so she just continued living in it when Congress was in session.

When Travis didn't immediately speak, she said, "What happened?"

He shifted uncomfortably in his seat, and cleared his throat.

"He didn't tell you?"

"My brother? No, he didn't tell me anything. What happened?"

"One of the Pax Romana sites was attacked."

"What do you mean, *attacked*?"

"Late Friday night, early Saturday morning, the site in

Addison was hit by intruders. Everybody inside was killed. As was the strike team that first showed up on scene."

Despite the warmth of the coffee cup in her hand, Frank's blood suddenly ran cold.

"It's been two days. Why am I just hearing about this now?"

"I don't know, ma'am."

"Who attacked the site?"

Travis didn't answer.

"Tell me," she said.

Travis cleared his throat again.

"From what I understand, it was Ben Anderson as well as a man named John Smith. Now, I don't know if you know about John Smith, but—"

"I am very well aware of John Smith. He and his siblings were part of the Legion program. Eli Craig and a woman named Marta smuggled one of the subjects out before she could give birth. Yes, Travis, I know all about John Smith. I also know about Ben Anderson. I was under the impression Carver Ellison and his team were killed."

She had watched the video sent to her and the rest of the Council of what happened in the hacker's basement.

"Yes, ma'am, it's true that Carver Ellison was killed. As was the hacker and another man. But not Ben Anderson and the others."

Stefan turned onto Pennsylvania Avenue, and for several seconds nobody spoke. Frank was taking in all this new information. She wasn't surprised that she was hearing it from Travis. If what he said was true, her brother wouldn't want her to know. It made him look weak. Foolish. The very thing that their father would shake his head at in disgust.

Then something else occurred to her, and once again her entire body went cold.

"How did Ben Anderson and John Smith find the Addison site?"

Before Travis could answer, his phone beeped. He placed it to his ear, listened, and then said, "Shit."

She twisted in her seat to glance back out the rear window at the Range Rover two car lengths behind them.

"What is it? What's wrong?"

"A car just exploded a block away from the White House."

Travis listened to the phone for another couple of seconds, then said, "Another car exploded down near the Mall. A third"—he listened some more—"a third exploded near the Capitol Building. All within the past minute."

Her first thought was a terrorist attack, the three explosions orchestrated at specific places around the city, and she wondered if this was maybe in response to the blackout in New York, if some terrorists had seen that as a green light to try their hand at continuing the mayhem.

But then Travis said, "That's weird."

"What's weird?"

"It seems all the traffic lights are malfunctioning. The lights going into the city are stuck on red, and all those going out are stuck on green. When the cars exploded, the city blocks were practically deserted."

"It's them."

He turned suddenly in his seat to look back at her.

"Ma'am?"

"Ben Anderson. John Smith. Whoever else there is. I guarantee you it's them."

"Ma'am, there's no way to know if—"

Stefan slammed on the brakes as the traffic light changed to red without warning. They nearly clipped the car in front of them. The driver of a Mercedes behind them wasn't paying attention and struck their rear bumper.

"We can't pull over," Travis said. "Not while this attack is going on."

"I can't be party to a hit and run."

"We didn't hit anybody. They hit us. If anything, they're lucky if we don't make a big deal out of it."

"We're stuck here as it is. Just go make sure they're okay."

Travis set his jaw. He didn't like it, and he didn't like being told what to do by an old woman, but the old woman in question was a Council member so he had no choice but to do as he was told.

He got out and headed to the back of the Town Car. The driver of the Mercedes—a younger woman, maybe thirty-five years old—was already inspecting the damage. The moment she saw Travis, she started apologizing.

"I am so sorry. I don't know what happened. Is everybody okay in there?"

Behind the steering wheel, Stefan said, "What the fuck?"

Frank redirected her focus, away from the woman and Travis to the intersection. Which was empty.

"What's happening?"

"Not sure," Stefan said. "Looks like every light is currently red."

That was when Frank heard the oncoming whine of a motorcycle. Despite all the stopped traffic, the noise was getting closer.

She turned in her seat again and watched the motorcycle cutting between the motionless vehicles.

The rider suddenly stopped and pulled out a gun and shot Travis in the head.

The driver of the Mercedes screamed.

Stefan punched the gas and jerked the wheel and suddenly they were bouncing up onto the sidewalk.

He cut across the still empty intersection.

Frank glanced back out through the rear window.

The motorcycle was still giving chase.

A couple car lengths back, the Range Rover had also driven over the sidewalk and was now passing through the same empty intersection. It was gaining ground on the motorcycle when the SUV exploded.

"Christ!"

Stefan shouted the curse as he swerved around the stopped traffic, bouncing up onto the sidewalk again. He had no choice but to take a side street, which was almost as congested, and still the motorcycle was directly behind them.

Frank dropped her coffee to pull her phone from her pocket. She opened the encrypted messaging app, typed out a hurried text.

THEY'RE COMING FOR ME. HELP!

That was when the truck came out of nowhere, just as they crossed over to the next street. Almost like it was waiting for them. It came from the left and hit the driver's side with enough force to flip the Town Car onto its roof.

The cell phone fell from her hand. The hazelnut coffee went everywhere.

Her head smacked against something. Not hard enough to knock her out but still hard enough to fill her vision with stars.

She was briefly aware of a vehicle pulling up outside. She was briefly aware of somebody shooting Stefan in the head, then of hands reaching through the broken glass to make sure she was still alive. The back door opened, and somebody undid her seat belt. Then she was being pulled from the car and placed into a trunk. Duct tape was pressed against her lips and a black cloth bag was pulled down over her head so that all she saw was darkness.

FORTY-ONE

Congresswoman Francis Houser sat on the metal folding chair, her ankles bound to the chair legs, her arms tied behind her back.

A black cloth bag covered her head.

I sat across from her, only a few feet away.

John Smith stood off to the side, his arms crossed, leaning against the cinderblock wall.

I checked my watch, then leaned forward and pulled the black cloth bag off the congresswoman's head.

Her hair stuck up in every direction, and her mascara had run in the past hour, which surprised me, because I'd thought she would be too proud to cry.

The same strip of duct tape we'd put on her mouth before shoving her into the trunk was still in place.

Her eyes shifted around the room but there wasn't much to see. We were in the basement of an empty construction site. Apparently the workers had gone on strike, so the company had temporarily shut down business while both sides negotiated.

All that surrounded us was cinderblock and metal pilings.

One of the construction lights was situated beside me, shining brightly at the congresswoman.

After she'd quickly scanned the room to find it was only the three of us, her heavy glare bored into me.

I smiled, leaned back, and crossed my ankle over my knee.

"Good morning, Congresswoman. We need to stop running into each other like this."

She said nothing. Which was to be expected. One doesn't usually say much with duct tape over one's mouth.

I tossed the cloth bag aside, reached down and picked up her cell phone.

"We had to turn this off just to be safe. We were hoping it could be unlocked with your thumb, which would have been extremely convenient on our end, but of course that didn't work. The same with flashing the phone at your face. That didn't work either. It appears the only way to access your phone is with a passcode. So ... you wouldn't want to help us out and give us that passcode, would you?"

Congresswoman Houser continued to glare back at me.

"Oh, right, I forgot. There's duct tape over your mouth."

I leaned forward again, reached out, but then paused.

"Now, if I take this off, you aren't going to start screaming, are you? I mean, you can, but we're far enough away from the general population that nobody will hear you if you do scream. Got it?"

She just kept glaring back at me.

I asked John, "Do you think she understands?"

He shifted away from the cinderblock wall, offered up an exaggerated shrug.

"She could just be scared. This is a traumatic experience."

I regarded the congresswoman again, and frowned.

"He's right. You have been through a traumatic experience. Do you want to talk about it, Congresswoman?"

Still with the glare.

I issued a heavy sigh, said, "All right, all right," and grabbed the loose end of the duct tape and peeled it off her lips.

She immediately said, "You will die."

"We all die, Congresswoman. That's just the way of life."

"While you two simpletons play your little games, my brother and his people are looking for me."

"Oh no," I said flatly, and glanced at John Smith. "Her brother and his people are looking for her."

John widened his eyes and placed a hand in front of his mouth.

"Oh no, I'm so scared."

"Congresswoman, if we ask nicely, do you think your brother will go easy on us?"

She just kept glaring back at me, though there was a touch of confusion in her face, like she wasn't sure just what our game was.

I reached into my pocket, pulled out one of the glass vials we'd taken from the building disguised as Harris World Industries. I held the vial in the palm of my hand for a beat, then held it up for her to see.

"Recognize this?"

She did, though she tried everything she could to make her face impassive.

"What's the plan, Congresswoman? The guy we spoke to at the lab told us what it does, but he didn't know much more than that. It was below his pay grade, as he kept telling me. You're going to use it to kill a shitload of people, aren't you?"

For several seconds she made no expression, just kept glaring back at me, and then little by little the corners of her mouth curled up into a smile.

"Of course we are."

"How many?"

"We're estimating at least two billion. Maybe three."

"You're fucking insane."

"Am I?" she said. "When God saw that his creation had gotten out of hand, he sent a flood to destroy every living creature. Left behind a handful of survivors to try it again."

"Are you comparing your brother to God?"

At this she actually laughed.

"Oh, heavens no. Not in the slightest. Besides, the Council made that decision."

I frowned at John, then said to the congresswoman, "What's the Council?"

"Think of it as a board of directors. We oversee everything. Augustus is merely a figurehead."

"So, what, did you guys get together one day over cocktails and hold a formal vote to kill billions of people?"

She smiled, and shook her head.

"Things have gotten too far out of hand. Do you think democracy is going to save the world? I've worked in Congress for the past twenty-five years. We can barely get a post office named, let alone try to come up with a way to solve all the world's problems."

"So your solution is to kill everybody."

"Again, not everybody. Only a couple billion people. Enough to create a hard reset, if you will."

"When is it set to be released?"

Her lips twisted in a sneer, and she shook her head.

"It should have been released long ago. But my brother keeps insisting it needs to be perfected first. The Council is growing impatient with him. I am too. We've invested billions of dollars to create the Pax Romana, and we're ready to cash in on our investment."

"I would call you insane, but part of me suspects you'd take that as a compliment."

"I don't expect the likes of Benjamin Anderson and John Smith to understand the complexity of what's at stake."

John said, "Hey, I understand complexity. I beat the first

ten levels of Candy Crush with no sweat. I probably could have kept going, but then I forgot my password."

"Speaking of which"—holding up the congresswoman's phone with my other hand—"would you be so kind as to provide us with your passcode?"

She just kept glaring, silent, until finally she released a breath.

"Why do you want to get into my phone?"

"John wants to know what Candy Crush level you're on."

John said, "I'm also curious to see if she's an Angry Birds fan. She strikes me as somebody who likes slingshotting birds at green pigs."

Congresswoman Houser didn't look amused. Her nostrils flared.

"Fine," she said. "If I give you the code, will you two idiots shut up?"

I looked at John. John looked at me.

He said, "Rude."

I said, "It's a little uncalled for, Congresswoman, but sure, give us the code."

She did. It was six digits long. I turned the phone on, entered the code, and the main screen came up.

After several seconds, the phone began pinging with emails and text messages.

"Those are undoubtedly my aides," she said. "They must be worried about me, what with all the explosions that occurred around the city. That was you, I surmise."

I scrolled through the emails and text messages.

"You would be surmising correctly. Snatching a sitting congresswoman off the street isn't an easy task. We needed to distract law enforcement."

"Did you really need to kill my men?"

I looked up from the phone to give her a blank stare.

"You and your brother are planning to kill billions of people."

"Yes, and? They deserve it."

"And why do they deserve it?"

"Because they aren't contributing anything to this planet. They're simply sponging off it, using up all its precious resources. Don't you get it, Ben? If we don't do something soon, *everybody* will die."

I opened an encrypted messaging app, saw that the congresswoman had sent a message right before we grabbed her.

THEY'RE COMING FOR ME. HELP!

Below, three messages had come through.

WHAT'S HAPPENED?

WHERE ARE YOU?

ANSWER ME!!

I said, "This is from your brother, isn't it?"

"So what if it is?"

"You have him listed here as Augustus. As you're his sister, I'd assumed you would have him listed under his real name."

"That is his real name."

"You're joking."

"I am not. It was our father who taught us about the Roman Empire. He was fascinated by it. Told us all the different things that occurred during that time, and how its government was much more efficient than the U.S Senate. I often believe the reason he became a senator was due to his fascination with the Roman Senate."

"Your brother told me about what you did in college. How you kidnapped that girl to get those frat guys in trouble."

Her eyes widened slightly, and I smiled.

"I think your brother wanted to brag about it. To be fair, he expected me to die soon after he told me the story. Something tells me he doesn't get a chance to tell that story much, does he?"

She didn't answer.

"Where is your brother?"

Still no answer.

"Where is Rome?"

Nothing.

I still had the vial in my other hand, and I held it up again.

"Don't make me infect you with this."

The spot near her left eye twitched, and when she spoke, her voice was low and tremulous.

"You wouldn't dare."

"Oh, I would dare. I'm sick and tired of you and your brother and everyone else in the Inner Circle. How about you, John? You sick of them?"

John was leaning against the cinderblock wall again, his arms crossed.

"Very," he said.

Congresswoman Houser said, "You realize what will happen if you infect me with that, don't you? This isn't a secure lab. The Pax Romana will get out."

"Isn't that what you assholes want, for this thing to spread?"

She didn't answer. Of course she didn't. The answer was yes, but not through her.

The encrypted messaging app also allowed users to make phone calls. I clicked on the phone icon under her brother's name, and placed the phone to my ear.

It rang twice before it was answered.

"Frank? My God, Frank, where have you been?"

"It's not Frank, Augustus."

There was a heavy beat of silence.

He said, "What have you done with her, Ben?"

"Nothing yet. But I have a vial of the Pax Romana here

with me. Was thinking about injecting your sister with some. Any thoughts on that?"

Another beat of silence.

"What do you want?"

"I think you know exactly what I want."

"Your wife and daughter for my sister? Fine, I can make that happen. Just don't do anything rash."

This made me laugh out loud, much like the congress-woman had done earlier.

"Don't fucking test me, Augustus."

"Where do you want us to bring them? We can drop them off wherever you want. Just don't hurt my sister."

"The Lincoln Park Zoo in Chicago. Drop them off at the entrance in twelve hours."

"Done. But I need your word that my sister will be safe."

"Twelve hours."

I disconnected the call, tossed the phone aside, then held out my hand. John Smith moved away from the wall, reaching into his pocket to withdraw the syringe.

"You see, Congresswoman, I didn't bring John along just for his Candy Crush skills. I brought him along as my assistant."

I unscrewed the cap on the vial, then took the syringe from John and inserted the needle into the top of the vial.

Her eyes wide again, the congresswoman started bucking on the metal folding chair.

"What are you doing? *What are you doing?*"

"What does it look like? I'm infecting you with the Pax Romana."

"No! But you can't! Your wife and daughter! Don't you want to save your wife and daughter?"

"At this point, I figure my wife and daughter are dead. Your brother probably had them killed the moment he killed Carver and the Kid."

"You don't know that! They could still be alive!"

I filled the syringe with the liquid, then tapped the side so the air bubbles would float to the top before spritzing a little bit out.

"You stupid fool! You're going to get us all killed!"

I held the syringe for a moment and looked at her closely, then shrugged.

"You're probably right. But at this point, I don't give a shit. How about you, John? You give a shit?"

"No shits to give on my end."

I handed him the syringe, and he stepped close to the congresswoman, who started bucking even more violently on the chair, screaming for him to stop.

John paused to glance up at me.

"Mind giving me a hand?"

"Don't mind if I do."

I stood up and crossed over to the congresswoman and placed both hands on her shoulders to hold her in place while John inserted the needle into her arm.

She screamed again and started crying, and then John and I backed away from her, cautiously, the empty syringe in John's hand.

Congresswoman Houser glared up at me again. Tears were in her eyes, and her voice trembled.

"You have no idea what you've done."

"Probably. Because I'm a simpleton, right?"

John said, "Hey, don't sell yourself short. I'm a simpleton too."

I clapped him on the shoulder, was about to say something else, when Titus spoke for the first time from the tiny earpieces in both of our ears.

"Caesar's people are five minutes away."

FORTY-TWO

The construction site sat just south of Alexandria, Virginia, about two miles from Route 1.

It was to one day become a ten-floor building, but only the skeleton had been erected so far. There were construction trucks and equipment everywhere, including a crane.

Titus kept the drone hovering just above the crane, at an angle that gave him a good sightline of the majority of the construction site but not high enough that it might catch the eye of one of Caesar's people as they made their approach.

Despite sitting in the comfort of his trailer just over one thousand miles away, Titus felt on edge. He knew what had happened to the Kid, and the Kid had always been cautious, making sure to cover his digital tracks.

There was a chance Caesar's people could be heading in his direction too. If that were the case, there was nothing Titus could do to defend himself. Ben had left behind a pistol, but Titus didn't know the first thing about using one outside of video games. Point and shoot was easy in theory, but when it came right down to it and somebody—an actual living, breathing body—was standing right in front of him ... no,

Titus just didn't see himself being the kind of person who could pull the trigger.

Of course, it wasn't just himself that he needed to worry about. There was Hercules to take into account, and he would be damned if he let anybody hurt his raccoon.

Every display in front of him was alive with motion. He'd been monitoring the traffic cams within a five-mile radius, so when he saw the three black SUVs moving in a tight formation down the highway, he knew it had to be the strike team.

The construction site was surrounded by a chain-link fence with only one entrance facing north that was locked with a chain that had been replaced after Ben and the others broke through.

It was this same entrance that the three SUVs barreled toward a minute later.

Titus wore his HyperX Cloud Revolver S headset, which he'd been using all morning to communicate with the team. They all weren't linked into each other unless one of them requested, but all of them could speak to Titus, who could then toggle them in between channels.

He felt a stab of loss remembering that he had always worn the same headset when he played video games with the Kid. His only close friend in the world, and he had never actually met the guy in person, which was a sad but sobering testament to how things worked in today's digital age.

He shifted the joystick in his hand just a bit, and one thousand miles away the drone hovering over the crane turned and focused on the approaching SUVs.

They would strike the locked gate within seconds.

Toggling the radio to all channels, he said, "Looks to be three SUVs, coming at you right now."

As the first SUV crashed through the gate and sped past several trailers, Titus maneuvered the drone to take in the rest of the construction site.

By that point, Ben and John were hustling Congresswoman Houser up the concrete steps to the first floor and toward the sedan they'd parked beside the structure. Only her hands were still bound behind her back, and as they tried pushing her into the back of the sedan, the congresswoman shoved the two men away and started running toward the SUVs.

Titus watched as John started to give chase, his gun now in hand. But the first SUV skidded to a halt, and the doors opened and men popped out with assault rifles.

They opened fire, and both Ben and John scattered for cover, Ben crouching behind the sedan while John dove behind one of the empty dump trucks. Ben had his gun in hand now too, and he waited for a pause in the volley of gunfire before peeking up over the car and returning fire.

Four men had gotten out of the first SUV, counting the driver. Congresswoman Houser was already climbing into the back of the second SUV, which then spun out in the dirt as it headed back toward the entrance.

The third SUV had stopped, and more men piled out, armed with assault rifles.

Eight in total, and so far it looked like they had Ben and John cornered.

Through the headset, Titus heard Ben shouting.

"Drew, light 'em up!"

Drew was already piped in through this channel. He was stationed on the third floor of the building with his sniper rifle, just waiting for Ben's go ahead, and once Ben gave it, Drew started taking out the strike team, one head shot after another. He'd dropped three of them before the others determined his location and started returning fire, and that was when Titus toggled to a different channel and issued the simple command.

"Now!"

Chin and Ho Sook popped out of one of the trailers near

the entrance, assault rifles of their own in hand, and opened up on the strike team.

It took less than thirty seconds when all was said and done.

Titus sat there, silent, rapt in fascination. It was like watching a video game, only it was real life. He briefly wondered if this was how drone pilots felt, and realized that it probably was and that was why many became numb to watching such action. It was almost like none of it seemed real, so bombing somebody out of existence was just like killing somebody's avatar in a video game.

He noticed movement near the side of the building. John was hurrying over to the sedan. Ben was climbing in behind the steering wheel, and seconds later they were peeling out toward the entrance.

Ben's voice came through the headset again.

"Where are they, Titus?"

Titus checked the traffic cams, spotting the fleeing SUV as it tore through an intersection.

"They just got on Route 1, headed north. They look to be going about sixty, so if you can do ninety, you'll reach them in no time."

FORTY-THREE

The windshield was spiderwebbed from the shootout. Even the side windows had shattered, and pieces of glass were everywhere.

We swerved through traffic, the speedometer going from fifty to sixty to seventy, blowing through one traffic light and then another, a chorus of blaring horns and screeching tires left in our wake, John beside me steely-eyed, his focus on the road as he loaded his pistol, and then we were on the expressway and the speedometer hit ninety.

We caught up with the SUV two minutes later. By then they'd just merged onto the Capital Beltway, headed across the Potomac River.

When we were fifty yards away, John leaned out the window, ignoring the ragged shards of glass, and let off three rounds at the back of the SUV.

The SUV started swerving, from one lane to the next, and the rear window was kicked open and one of the men was there with a rifle, firing back at us.

"Hold on!"

I jerked the wheel, almost sideswiped a minivan in the next

lane, but the driver stomped on its brakes, just like many of the other vehicles we'd passed so far.

Some bullets tore into the front of the sedan, and I jerked the wheel again, trying my best not to get us killed, but John yelled, "Get me closer!" and I thought fuck it and squeezed the steering wheel even tighter as I pressed my foot harder against the gas pedal.

That was when, through the spiderwebbed windshield, I saw the approaching helicopter.

It looked to be a Black Hawk, and it reached us in no time, a gunner already positioned to open fire as soon as it came into range.

A second before, though, John had shot the shooter in the back of the SUV in the head.

The SUV sped up, passing a tractor-trailer, and then suddenly swerved into its lane.

The tractor-trailer's driver, slamming on its own brakes, lost control of the vehicle, and within seconds it was clear that the thing was going to jackknife.

My foot still against the gas pedal, I angled the car toward the median and managed to squeak by right before the trailer went over.

The Black Hawk circled overhead, the gunner laying down more fire, and then the chopper landed two hundred yards away, meeting the SUV as it screeched to a halt.

I applied pressure to the sedan's brakes. Only a few other vehicles were between us and the SUV and Black Hawk. It was clear the plan now was to grab the congresswoman and then take off again.

We couldn't have planned it any better.

Even before the sedan came to a complete stop, John had his door open and jumped out. I pulled the lever for the trunk, and he was there a second later, grabbing the RPG-7 missile launcher.

I grabbed an FN 15 SRP Tactical rifle from the backseat and jumped out of the sedan, intent to provide cover fire.

But John already had the missile launcher on his shoulder, his aim directed at the SUV.

He squeezed the trigger, and a second later the missile had struck the back of the SUV—which exploded with enough force to tip it over onto its hood in a brilliant bloom of fire.

But Congresswoman Houser had already made it to the Black Hawk. She'd just been helped up inside, and the chopper was starting to take off.

As John hurried back to the trunk to load another missile, I fired up at the Black Hawk, but the rounds came nowhere close to hitting it.

The gunner, in return, opened fire.

I had to dive behind another car for cover, regretting that I was putting the driver of that car in mortal danger, but once I was out of sight the gunner didn't see any further need to keep firing.

After all, they'd succeeded in their mission, which was rescuing the congresswoman. The police still hadn't shown up, even though somebody was no doubt already posting video of the incident to social media.

But that didn't mean John Smith was done.

He had the RPG-7 loaded once again. He stood there, the launcher on his shoulder, and tracked the Black Hawk as it rose into the air.

He squeezed the trigger again.

The missile flew just underneath the chopper and continued out until it disappeared into the river.

I shouted, "Let's go!"

We were back in the sedan seconds later, maneuvering past the stopped vehicles and what was left of the flaming SUV.

In our ears, Titus asked, "You guys okay?"

I glanced at John, who nodded at me.

"Yeah, we're good. How long on emergency personnel?"

"They're headed right to your location as we speak. But you should be fine. Take the first exit and ditch the car at the National Harbor. Ronny and Graham are headed there now."

"Thanks, Titus."

For the next thirty seconds John and I were silent, watching the highway, keeping an eye out for anything unexpected, and then John grinned at me.

"That worked out better than expected."

I nodded, my focus still on the highway.

"I just hope Mason is able to follow through on his end."

John glanced at his watch and said, "Speaking of which, we should have an answer soon. Based on his time zone, he should have already made contact by now."

FORTY-FOUR

Bakersfield, California.

A place Mason had once lived with his wife and son—a place in which they rented a home which had a backyard with scraggly grass and a rusted swing set and shed whose door never properly shut, no matter how many times he oiled it—but a place that never felt like home.

In reality, Mason had never lived in a place that felt like home. Not even after he had gotten out of prison and they moved three states away from Bakersfield. Their new home had been theirs, yes, but for some reason it just didn't feel like *theirs*.

Like many kids he knew growing up, he'd been a mistake. His mom had been dating a guy off and on for a year or so, and she managed to get herself pregnant—a woman who didn't have a single maternal bone in her body—and it wasn't until he was six years old that Child Services finally had enough of making their weekly visits and just decided to take him from the home.

His father—whom Mason had seen only two or three times in passing, and even then the man had barely looked him in the eye—wasn't going to take custody, and there were no other family members who were able to take him, and so he went into foster care.

Had Mason known Carver Ellison for more than only a few days, maybe he would have learned that they shared a similar history, at least in terms of coming up through the system. Though this probably wouldn't have happened, as Carver hadn't been someone who liked talking about his past, just as Mason was someone who barely even liked thinking about his past.

Gloria knew he'd come up through the system because it was mentioned once or twice when they first started dating and she had asked about his parents, but she immediately sensed he didn't like talking about it and so she never asked again, didn't even hint at it, which was one of the things that Mason would later realize made him fall in love with her.

He'd promised himself that he wasn't going to be a dead-beat father like his old man. That he would never once be put in a position where Child Services knocked at the front door. He wanted the very best for his son, and while neither he nor Gloria had made much money, they'd still made due, making sure that Anthony always had nice clothes and the video games he wanted and every parental support that Mason had been denied when he was a child, and Mason believed that his son had been happy and felt loved.

Of course, his son was now dead, wrapped in plastic and buried in the Kid's backyard, along now with the Kid himself and the Kid's mother and, Christ, just so many other people.

"I believe this is him."

Mason blinked at the sound of Beverly's voice. Realizing that he'd been stuck in the past—was it called brooding?—and that it probably had to do with the fact that he hadn't gotten much sleep in the past couple of days, even when they were on the private jet the little man had secured for them.

He sat in the driver's seat, stuffed in behind the steering wheel, and he glanced over his shoulder at his wife and Beverly sitting in the back.

Gloria was awake, her eyes alert, and she had evidently tapped Beverly on the leg and pointed to get her attention, and so Beverly was simply translating for her because apparently this was now their fucking life thanks to Caesar and all his asshole minions.

That was when Mason heard the oncoming angry growling of the motorcycles, and he tilted his face and focused on the three riders coming down the highway.

They were parked in an abandoned self-serve car wash. Mason had remembered driving past it numerous times back when they lived in Bakersfield.

Every Monday morning the MC had their weekly meetings at a warehouse a mile away from here. Mason had never been in attendance—because he had never been a member—but he knew the location and he knew the time and he knew that if he was going to do what he planned to do then the best place to do it was in front of the entire club.

Sure, he could have driven straight to his brother-in-law's, knocked on the door, told him what he needed to tell him, but Mason knew Adam was different when he was at home, not the same Adam when he was around everybody at the MC.

At home, Adam was simply a husband and father. At the MC, Adam was a leader.

Or at least he had been years ago when Mason and his wife and son lived in town. Before they'd packed up their things and Gloria cut ties with her brother, blaming him for Mason's incarceration.

Now Mason watched as his brother-in-law and two other men zoomed past, each of them wearing helmets and sunglasses, and Mason waited a full sixty seconds before starting up the car and placing it in drive.

On the outside, the warehouse looked abandoned, but it really wasn't. On paper, it was owned by a businessman from Los Angeles who for years had planned to do something with it, but if anybody was inclined to do some digging they'd learn that the businessman didn't exist and the entire thing was a shell organization for the MC, whose bread and butter was dealing guns and drugs.

When Mason pulled into the deserted parking lot—everybody already parked inside—two men were standing out front, smoking cigarettes.

They watched him, silent, as he parked several yards away and cut the engine. Mason knew both were armed but so far neither had reached for his weapon.

He didn't recognize either man. They were prospects, new to the club, so they were doing the grunt work and keeping an eye out for law enforcement or any potential trouble.

Both of the men wore sunglasses. One was heavyset, the other skinny.

It was Heavyset who spoke when Mason climbed out of the car.

"Hey, pal, you can't park there."

Mason approached them slowly, his empty hands held out at his sides to show that he wasn't armed.

"I need to talk to Adam."

Skinny shook his head, flicked his cigarette away.

"Can't help you, bud. No Adam here."

"I saw him ride in here not too long ago."

Neither man said a word.

"Tell Adam that his sister and her husband need to see him as soon as possible. It's important."

Still neither man spoke. But Heavyset adjusted his posture, pushed back his shoulders. Skinny started massaging his hands, as if he were preparing for fisticuffs.

Mason took a deliberate step forward, decreasing the space between them by almost five feet.

"I need to see Adam and the other guys. Right now."

The men may have been prospects, but they weren't stupid. They understood what was in Mason's tone. Neither man reached for his weapon, but each of their bodies went as tense as a live wire.

Heavyset flicked his cigarette away, kept his gaze steady with Mason's.

"I don't know who the fuck you think you are, but if I were you, I'd get back in your car and drive out of here and never let me see your fucking face ever again."

When Mason didn't move, Skinny was the one who decided to be the hero. He reached for the piece he had secured in the waistband of his jeans, and it was as he stepped forward that Mason brought up his fist and connected it with the man's Adam's apple, not hard but just hard enough to stun him. As soon as Mason made that move, Heavyset made his, rushing toward Mason, also reaching for his gun, and Mason turned and held out his arm and clotheslined the man so that Heavyset fell off his feet and Mason took hold of his chest and slammed him down on the ground.

Within seconds, Mason had both men's pieces. He held a pistol in each hand, one aimed at Skinny, the other aimed at Heavyset.

"Listen, guys, no hard feelings, but if I told you what the fuck's going on here, you wouldn't believe me, so I'm not even gonna try. I'm only gonna tell the story once, and that's gonna be for Adam and the others. So you're gonna lead me to them, okay?"

Skinny glared back at him. So did Heavyset, still on the ground.

Mason motioned at Heavyset with the man's own pistol.

"Get back on your fucking feet and head inside. And either of you shouts a warning, I'll put a bullet in your kneecap."

Mason glanced one last time toward the car, at his wife and Beverly, and nodded once, letting them know the plan was still a go, and then he followed Heavyset and Skinny inside.

He could hear voices down the hallway, in the main room where the club was meeting, but blood was pounding in his ears so he couldn't make out much of what was being said, though he did recognize his brother-in-law's voice.

Inside the warehouse space, a good portion of the bikers were sitting on metal folding chairs while Adam and another man were standing at the front, and it was Adam who spotted him first, his expression at first blank before settling into confusion.

"Mason?"

That was when everybody else turned in their seats to see who had just walked in on their meeting. They saw Heavyset and Skinny, and they saw Mason, standing behind them with a pistol in each hand, and several of the men jumped to their feet, reaching for their own guns.

Adam shouted, "Wait, wait, wait! Everybody, fucking chill for a second!"

It took longer than a second, but everybody did chill, at least in terms of not reaching for their weapons. Those who had jumped up from their seats stayed standing, their hands hovering over their guns.

Adam looked over the members, made sure none of them were going to do anything stupid, and then focused on Mason.

"Mason, what the fuck are you doing?"

"I'm not here to hurt anybody. I know it's been years since I saw you last, Adam, but the fact is I don't have any place else to go. I need a favor. And it's a big one—believe me, I know it— but the thing is if you and the club don't help me, there's a good chance all of us are going to die."

Adam, standing tall in his MC vest with all its patches, stared hard at Mason.

"What the fuck are you talking about? You're not making any sense."

That was when Beverly, who had been waiting out in the hallway, helped Gloria into the room.

The hardness in Adam's eyes faded. He started toward his sister, relief washing the anger from his face.

Adam took Gloria into an embrace—but immediately sensed something was wrong. He took a step back, looking at her as if for the first time, looking her up and down, and that was when Gloria, tears in her eyes, opened her mouth to show him what was missing.

Adam turned away, glared back at Mason.

"What the fuck? What the *fuck*?"

He grabbed his holstered piece, aimed it at Mason, but Gloria shook her head and reached out, pushing his gun away.

"I didn't do that to her," Mason said, and he felt his voice starting to tremble. "*They* did it to her."

Adam's face was contorted with fury.

"Who the fuck is *they*?"

"The same fuckers who killed my boy."

He waited a beat to watch the understanding flash through Adam's eyes, and nodded.

"That's right, Adam. You need to listen to me, because what I'm going to tell you is true, every single word, even though you're gonna think I'm crazy. But look at Gloria, Adam. Look in her eyes. You can see right there that it's true."

He waited another beat, letting his words take hold.

Adam said, "What the fuck are you talking about?"

Mason answered as simply as he could.

"The end of the fucking world."

PART III

WHILE ROME BURNS

FORTY-FIVE

Augustus had always been fascinated by silence.

Not just *normal* silence—the kind one associates with being alone in their house late at night—but true actual silence. The kind of silence that happens in a vacuum. Or in space.

Unlike many boys growing up, Augustus had never had much interest in going to space. Floating over two hundred miles above Earth? Not really his cup of tea. The same with bouncing around on the surface of the moon. Both were certainly ambitious goals for any young boy, but Augustus never saw the point. Just so that you can proudly say you were one of the few who had accomplished such a task? There was certainly merit in that. But overall, space seemed to lack a certain form of power that was missing from what happened right here on the earth.

Earth was where people lived, after all. It was where they went to school and where they went to work and where they bought houses and where they got married and fucked and had children and eventually grew old. Billions of people on earth, and yet at any given time only a handful of people in space.

Power, Augustus learned at an early age, was only truly worth it on earth.

But silence was always something he'd appreciated. He knew why. He didn't need a therapist to explain to him his fascination with silence.

When he was just a boy—not the age yet when he would spy on those high schoolers and learn the ways of the world—his mother often dated bad men whom she would bring home and they would yell and fight and have sex and then yell and fight some more.

The affair with Augustus' father—the sitting U.S. senator whom he sometimes saw in pictures in the newspaper—had been a fluke, he eventually came to realize. His father had been out looking for somebody to sleep with, and his mother just happened to be there. And so that was the way things sometimes happened in life. There was no order, no design. It was simply chaos. Had his mother not been in that bar that night, the senator would have found somebody else to take back to his hotel. Maybe that woman never would have gotten pregnant. Maybe she would have. Either way, the main thing was that Augustus never would have been born.

A few minutes of passion, two bodies of cells merging, and then nine months later Augustus came along.

And so, eventually, did the Council and the Inner Circle and the rest decades later.

But silence—when his mother brought those men back to their apartment and they started to get loud, he would clamp his hands over his ears to try to drown out the shouting as much as he could. Sometimes he used his pillow. Both helped muffle the noise, but it was never true silence, not the kind that one finds in a vacuum or space, and Augustus found himself yearning for true silence more and more.

To experience true silence was a sort of Zen. A way to clear your mind and be alone with the universe.

Locking yourself away in a room and putting on noise-canceling headphones? That was cheating, Augustus thought. You could experience silence from that, yes, but it wasn't *true* silence. Not the kind in nature. The kind that actually allowed you to get one step closer to being at peace with the universe.

When he was in Rome, he sometimes slipped out of his residence late at night and walked through the empty streets. He'd ignore the sidewalk and stroll directly down the middle of the street, passing the diner and the bank and the movie theater and the grocery store, all the way to the center of town.

A single traffic light hung by wires in the middle of the intersection. For as long as Augustus had been visiting this place, the traffic light never worked. There was no need for it; not in a town like Rome.

Augustus didn't even know if the traffic light had a functioning lightbulb.

Tonight he stood directly underneath the traffic light, right in the middle of the intersection, and closed his eyes and listened to the silence.

It was deep, almost true, but not quite there.

A light breeze was pushing through town, so faint it could have been the passing of a ghost, but it was enough to shatter the illusion of true silence.

Which was just as well. Augustus didn't think he could truly appreciate the silence right now. Not after everything that had happened the past week and a half. Not after everything that had happened in the past twenty-four hours.

He couldn't sleep, couldn't settle his mind long enough to get some rest, and so he'd dressed in slacks and an undershirt and slipped out of his residence because he knew if he stayed in his bedroom he might go mad.

Footsteps behind him, soft but distinct. The pace hurried but not quite a run.

Augustus opened his eyes and turned to find Zach

cautiously approaching him. The sky was clear and the moon was bright so Augustus could read the worry across the man's face.

"Sir, are you all right?"

Part of him wanted to snap *Do I fucking look all right?* but he knew snapping out like that—showing emotion of any kind —was a sign of weakness. His father had once taught him that. Staying in control of your emotions, never letting people see you tremble or hear the quaver in your voice, was what made a great leader.

"How is she?" he said.

"I stopped by the residence but you weren't there. I had security check the cameras to locate you. Sir, are you sure you're all right?"

Once again Augustus felt the rising urge to snap at the man. Too much had happened too quickly, and in his seventy-odd years of life, never once had he felt so helpless and out of control.

But no—he needed to stay in control. Couldn't let his people see him fazed by what had happened. The recent attacks and all the other shit that Ben Anderson and John Smith and the others had caused.

He stared back at Zach and suppressed a yawn.

"How is she?" he said again.

Zach said, "That's why I came to find you. It would be best if you saw for yourself."

FORTY-SIX

Zach led the way.

Up Main Street and past the dark movie theater and bank to the grocery store where Zach turned at the corner and walked directly to a side door.

He inputted his code on the panel beside the door, put his thumb against the scanner, and a second later the door clicked open.

Zach held the door, and Augustus stepped through the doorway and went directly to the elevator in the bright corridor. He had his own code, and could access anything in Rome with his thumbprint, but he waited for Zach to step around him to input his code again and press his thumb against the scanner, and then the elevator door opened.

Thirty seconds later they were under the town, stepping into another bright corridor, and Zach once again led the way.

Augustus was becoming irritated with the man. Based on how Zach had handled himself at the Coliseum, Augustus had decided to give him a chance, though in retrospect maybe that was simply because all his trusted men had died in the explosion and so he didn't have anyone else. He knew Zach's history, and that the man was a good soldier. But he didn't like being kept in the dark. He supposed if his sister was dead, Zach would have said as much, and the simple fact that he hadn't meant ... well, what did it mean?

Zach held another door open for him, and Augustus stepped into the laboratory.

It was an expansive space with all the state-of-the-art technology one could wish for. It was the place where the idea of the Pax Romana was initially created, and where it eventually evolved to the virus it was today. The other labs were simply used for running tests on live subjects. In the past year or so, since they'd more or less perfected the virus, this lab hadn't seen much use.

That was until yesterday afternoon, when Augustus' sister was flown in from D.C. and immediately put in quarantine where she had been ever since. Their top scientist had been called in—the man having worked his way up to the very top of the CDC—and he'd made sure to inject Frank with the vaccine but, as Augustus was told, it would take at least twelve hours before it started working its way through her system, and the entire time he'd been a mess of nerves, both from the attack but also from the fact that his sister—the only person in the world whom he was close to—might die a horrible death.

The scientist was already in the lab, a thin, baldheaded man with a gray beard and glasses, and he nodded solemnly at Augustus as he crossed over to the one-way mirror to check in on his sister.

She lay on a hospital bed, hooked up to several different machines to monitor her vitals. When she'd first arrived, she had looked awful—her pale face drenched with sweat—and he'd feared that the virus had somehow skipped the twelve-hour incubation period, and Augustus' first thought was that the virus hadn't been perfected after all.

Now, however, his sister looked restful. She even appeared

to be asleep, her mouth slightly open and her chest moving up and down with her breaths.

Feeling his fingernails digging into his skin, Augustus said, "Well, what is it? What was so urgent you made me come down here at this time in the morning?"

The scientist stepped forward and cleared his throat.

"I'm sorry to have woken you, sir, but there seems to be a bit of confusion."

"What confusion?"

"Well, your sister"—he paused, and cleared his throat again—"I analyzed her blood and she doesn't appear to have been infected with the Pax Romana at all."

Augustus glanced into the quarantine area, at his sister asleep on the hospital bed, and then turned back to the scientist.

"Say that again?"

The man froze, his expression creeping on panic, and it was Zach who spoke up.

"He's saying there isn't a drop of the Pax Romana in the congresswoman's system."

Augustus stared in at his sister again, started to shake his head.

"That ... that's not possible. She said she recognized the vial. It was the Pax Romana. Christ, five vials were stolen from the Addison site. How is it possible they didn't infect her?"

Zach shot a hesitant glance toward the scientist, as if expecting the man to speak up again, but when it became clear the scientist didn't want to clarify, he continued.

"Once it was determined that she wasn't contagious, I put on a hazmat suit for precaution and scanned her entire body."

"What do you mean, *scanned her entire body*?"

"I was immediately put in mind of something that happened years ago, back when I was dealing with Eli Craig. We had captured him and taken him to a site in Maryland, which was the closest location to Dr. Matheson, and then later John Smith—"

"Yes, I know all about what happened. John Smith's presence ultimately cost us that facility, let alone the lives of several of our people. What does that have to do with this?"

"Well, sir, when I scanned her, I was alerted to the fact that she's been sending out a signal."

"Sending out a signal? What the hell does that—"

But Augustus stopped himself, suddenly putting all the pieces of the puzzle together.

"Injectable GPS," he whispered, staring again into the room at his sister.

Zach said, "That's right, sir. I'm almost one hundred percent positive it's our technology. And as you well know, over the past several years John Smith has been attacking several of our facilities, and he's stolen much of our tech, which—"

Augustus cut him off.

"How long has it been transmitting?"

"No idea, sir. But if I had to guess, I'd say it's been transmitting since the moment they injected her, which means—"

This time it was the radio on Zach's belt that cut him off. One of the security men was hailing him.

"Sir?"

Zach placed the radio to his mouth.

"This better be important."

"It is, sir. We just spotted somebody coming up the road leading into town."

Zach shot Augustus a hesitant glance, then said into the radio, "Can you make out who it is?"

"Yes, sir. It appears to be the Man of Wax."

FORTY-SEVEN

The town sat about two miles down a long road from the main highway.

It was just a narrow two-lane road, and it was at just past four o'clock that morning, halfway up the road, when they came for me.

I'd been walking the entire time at a leisurely stroll. Not too fast. Not too slow. The kind of walk one does in the middle of the night when they're outside trying to clear their head.

I wasn't armed, because I knew the first thing they would do when they arrived would be to search me for weapons.

Which was exactly what they did—the second the SUV screeched to a halt, all four doors opened and men stepped out aiming assault rifles at me. One of the men told me to put my hands on the back of my head and lower myself to my knees. I did as instructed, and that was when two of the men advanced and one covered me while the other searched me.

I said, "Easy, fella. Buy a guy dinner first, huh?"

It was clear they expected to find a gun, or a knife, or *something*, based on the man's confused expression once he stepped back and shook his head at the driver.

"In all seriousness," I said, "my car broke down about a mile or two away. Think it has something to do with the alternator or the flux capacitor or something with the engine. I'm not really a car guy, you know?"

No answer.

"Are any of you guys mechanics? Maybe you can take a look. At the very least, is there a rental place nearby? Like a Hertz or an Enterprise or a—"

The guy who'd searched me used the stock of his M4 to hit me in the face. It was a solid hit, the guy having put some momentum into it, and I knew if I survived the next couple of hours, my jaw would be swollen by the afternoon.

I spat blood out on the road, then squinted up at the man.

"So is that a yes or a no on the car rental place?"

The man stepped forward to hit me again, but the driver stopped him.

"Enough," he said. "Man of Wax, give us one good reason why we shouldn't put a bullet in your head in the next ten seconds."

"Because I'm pretty sure Augustus Caesar would like to see me."

"He doesn't."

"Maybe his sister, then. Hopefully she's feeling a bit better than the last time I saw her."

Another hit to the face, though this one wasn't nearly as powerful. Maybe the guy's heart just wasn't in it.

I spat more blood out on the road—the spatter of blood looking pitch-black in the moonlight—and then said, "If you guys are car rental employees, I've got to say the customer service here is pretty shitty. You know, I'm a Yelp reviewer, and so far I'm leaning toward giving you guys one-star."

The driver said, "Kill him."

"Wait!" I shouted. "Before you do that, at least pass along a message to Augustus."

The driver glanced at the man standing behind me, who no doubt had his rifle aimed at the back of my head, and then he shifted his focus back to me.

"What message?"

"That I know his secret."

There was a heavy beat of silence. Except for a soft breeze blowing across the field, stirring up some of the tall grass. It stretched out on both sides of the roadway, an endless field of grass. No trees for at least a quarter mile. This part of the state was mostly just rolling fields, hardly any people at all.

The driver touched his right ear. Presumably that was where his comms link was located. A tiny earpiece, just like the three other men wore. To keep them in communication with the base.

Or, in this case, the boss.

I knew very well that Augustus was watching me right now. Maybe a drone was hovering soundlessly above us, feeding live video back to town. Or maybe one of the men had a body-cam on him that I couldn't see. Whatever the case, I knew Augustus was watching, and I knew he would want to see me.

Well, I was pretty sure he would.

"Roger that, sir," the driver said, and he was most certainly not talking to me. Then he addressed the three other men: "Secure him and load him in the SUV. Caesar wants us to bring him back to town."

FORTY-EIGHT

Zach turned away from the monitor and said, "How many men do we have here right now?"

The question was directed to the two security men standing behind them. Augustus knew the men were intimidated by his presence, as he had never been in this room before. When he was in town, he usually spent his time in his residence … except for the mornings when he would walk down Main Street and listen to the silence.

The one security man said, "Counting the four just outside of town, there are a dozen."

"Counting me?" Zach asked.

"No, sir. Not counting you."

Zach turned back to the monitor. It showed an aerial view of the road from one of the drones they'd dispatched. Like the drone that had been dispatched back at the site in Addison, it was highly advanced and could detect heat signatures, and so far the only heat signature it had detected (besides the men they'd sent out there) was Ben Anderson's.

Assuming those on Ben's team weren't hiding themselves under more thermal blankets.

"Using our own tech against us," Zach whispered.

Augustus said, "What was that?"

"Nothing, sir." Zach turned back to the two security men. "Do we have people nearby?"

The other man said, "A half hour away, yes."

"How many?"

"I believe the team consists of six men."

"Get them here ASAP. The same with the next closest team." Zach turned to Augustus. "Can I speak to you out in the corridor, sir?"

Once they were alone in the corridor, Augustus spoke right before Zach could open his mouth.

"I'm beginning to lose confidence in you, Zach."

Zach was quiet for a beat. Then he said, "Sir, I think it's best we move you to another location."

"This is our base of operations. If we're not safe at our base of operations, then we might as well give up."

"You don't understand, sir. It's not just Ben Anderson. If he found this place, that means the rest of his team is out there too. And if they're out there—"

"Are you honestly afraid of a handful of men and women?"

"They're more skilled than we initially gave them credit for. I'd rather be safe than sorry."

Yes, Augustus thought, and he'd rather know what it was Ben Anderson had to say to him. Ben claimed to know Augustus' secret, and he was very curious to hear what that secret was.

Zach said, "Sir?"

Augustus blinked. He stared at him for a beat, thinking, and then said, "Where is the best place I can speak with Mr. Anderson?"

"Sir, I'd advise against that."

"I'm sure you would. But you're not the one who's in charge. So tell me: Where is the best place I can speak with him?"

"We don't have a place for interrogations, sir."

"How can that be possible?"

"When you took over this installation, everything was modified. We can certainly find a room—maybe under the movie theater—to place him. But again, I strongly advise—"

"My residence," Augustus said. "Bring him to my study."

"Sir—"

"Do as I say."

Augustus started to turn away but paused, noting the worry on Zach's face.

"He has no weapons on him, correct? His wrists, I presume, will be secured behind his back. And you'll be there the entire time, with a gun held against his head if you so choose. Trust me: Ben Anderson does not have control of this situation. He never has, and he never will."

FORTY-NINE

They bound my wrists and forced me into the SUV, cramming me in the back between two of the men who held pistols against my sides.

Any quick movement, and they would shoot me dead. Then again, if one of them sneezed there was a chance they would shoot me dead because all it would take was a slight squeeze of the trigger and then it was lights out—though, judging by the close quarters, the one on the other side would probably get shot too.

"Do me a favor, fellas, and don't sneeze, okay?"

Neither man answered me, which was just as well.

The driver and passenger didn't answer either. The driver had maneuvered a three-point turn and was speeding up the road toward town.

It was still dark, but the sky was clear and the moon was bright enough to see the town as we crested a small rise.

The town didn't look very large at all. A cluster of buildings in the heart, with a few other buildings spread out around it. No more than a dozen buildings in total. Off to the side was an empty field where two helicopters sat.

All said and done, it was pretty unimpressive.

I said, "I expected more."

No answer.

The road led straight into what was clearly marked Main Street. But the street wasn't much of a street at all. It was narrow and wasn't very long. There was what looked to be a movie theater and a grocery store and a bank and a hardware store and a diner.

Except for a handful of lights scattered about, the town was dark and quiet.

"What's playing at the theater?" I asked. "You guys have the new Marvel movie?"

Again, no answer. Not even a chuckle.

We came to the end of the street and the SUV eased to a stop in front of a small, two-story house. A white picket fence ran the length of the yard. A few lights were on inside.

The SUV's doors opened and the men piled out and I was pulled out along with them. Suddenly another man appeared. He wore khakis and a black polo shirt, and there was something official in his look, like he was in charge.

"Hold him steady," the man said.

The man had a device in his hand and scanned my entire body, from head to toe, and then he motioned at the house.

"Take him inside."

The other men marched me through the gate and up the brick walkway to the porch. They didn't pause to knock or ring the doorbell. Instead, they opened the door and pushed me through, down a short hallway and then to an open doorway.

I'd caught glimpses of a living room and dining room but couldn't make out much. A few photos on the walls, a few paintings, a few knickknacks spotting the tables and bookcases, but that was it.

This room was clearly a study. A large oak desk sat near the far wall. Bookcases stood tall behind the desk, each filled with numerous leather-bound volumes. A Queen Anne globe took up one corner of the room. A large TV sat in the other corner.

In front of the desk were two chairs. I was pushed down into one of the chairs and then the men left. I just stared ahead, at the empty leather chair behind the desk.

I waited maybe ten seconds before the door opened and heard the soft shuffle of footsteps behind me. There was something calm in the shuffle, something not so official, so I wasn't surprised when Augustus stepped into view.

"Are you the guy who runs this place?" I asked. "Because I have to say your employees are a bit rude. Terrible customer service, if I'm being honest."

He lowered himself down onto the leather chair, pulled it forward a bit so he was sitting directly behind the desk. Both hands clasped in front of him, like he was ready to say a prayer.

The last time I'd seen him in person was at the Coliseum, not even two weeks ago. He'd been clean-shaven then, immaculately put together despite the fact he wore a Bauta mask most of the night. Now he had some scruff on his cheeks and his chin. His dark blue eyes stared at me from across the desk, and there was something tired in them, something exhausted.

When he didn't speak, I said, "I see you've got a lot of books. You actually read all of them, or you just like having them there to feel special?"

Augustus still didn't say anything. He shifted his gaze at something behind me, and that was when I realized somebody had been standing behind me the whole time. Somebody that I didn't hear enter the room.

"Let me see those," Augustus said, and gestured at my face.

The man from outside—the boss who had scanned my body—stepped up beside me. He pulled the glasses off my face and handed them across the desk to Augustus.

Augustus began inspecting the glasses, turning them back and forth in the light of his desk lamp.

"Doesn't appear to be one of ours. Who made it?"

I decided enough of being a smart-ass. I stared hard at the old man and answered simply.

"A friend."

"Your hacker friend, I assume? The one who had an unfortunate end in his very own basement?"

There was a smile in his eyes when he said this, and it took everything I had not to pop up from the chair and launch myself over the desk at him. Mostly because, well, my wrists were bound behind my back, and I knew the moment I moved, the man standing next to me would most likely place a bullet in my head.

"No," I said, my voice steady. "It was another friend. The same one who predicted that your base of operations was in this part of the country."

Augustus snapped the frames in half at the bridge. A thin wire was inside, the width of tooth floss, and he snapped that too.

"Whoops," he said. "I guess that takes the camera offline, doesn't it?"

"My friend isn't going to be very happy. He spent a lot of time making those."

"What is the name of this friend of yours?"

I said nothing.

Augustus squinted at the side of the frames, where the tiny camera was located. So minuscule you could barely tell there was anything there at all. He then twisted that part of the frame enough to snap it in half too, and then tossed the discarded pieces onto his desk.

Leaning back in his chair, he said, "How did he know that this was our base of operations?"

"He mapped out a good majority of the games in the United States. From where they originated and where the players ended up going and where the games ended. There was no activity in this part of the country. Which I guess makes sense. You don't shit where you eat, or however the saying goes."

Augustus said nothing and merely smiled.

I glanced around the room and said, "Nice digs. You live here all year round or is this like your summer home?"

"Most of the time this is my home. This desk? It used to be my father's. The same with that globe over there."

"Speaking of your daddy issues, how's your sister doing?"

"From what I'm told, she doesn't have the Pax Romana in her system."

"No, I don't imagine she would. Not unless somebody injected her with that stuff."

"You injected her with a GPS tracking device instead."

"Guilty as charged."

"One of our technologies, I believe."

"Yeah, it seems like your people make impressive stuff."

"You planned for my people to rescue her. You knew the moment you turned on her phone, we would find it."

"Again, guilty as charged."

"Your plan was for her to be rescued all along."

"Uh-huh."

"My sister believed she managed to escape, but that's what you wanted her to believe."

"Can I get an amen?"

"My men were surprised the RPG missed them on the bridge, but it was supposed to miss them."

I shrugged, said, "Had to make it look convincing."

"All of that work, and for ... what? To bring you here? Alone?"

Augustus paused a beat, and smiled.

"Of course, we know that you aren't here alone. The others are with you too, however many of them there are left. Can't be many, I don't think. Only a handful. Though, I can't begin to imagine what it matters. Do you honestly believe your people will be able to attack this place? We're out in the middle of nowhere. All my men are on alert. More are coming as we speak."

"What is this place, anyway? You just built a town out in the middle of nowhere and called it Rome for the hell of it?"

"Back in World War Two this place was built as a covert military installation. The military wanted a private place to do whatever it is they did, and then for decades they just left it empty until one day it happened to become available to us. Every building you saw on the way in is functional—the movie theater even has a film projector—but it's all cover. Most of the operation happens underneath the surface. Such as our lab, the place we first created the Pax Romana. In fact, come to think of it, that's where your family has been for most of the past two years."

My heart skipped as my body stiffened, but I did everything I could not to show emotion.

I didn't do enough.

Augustus saw the flicker of hope flare in my eyes, and he chuckled.

"Yes, Ben, your wife and daughter are still alive. Would you care to see them before we kill you? I believe Simon gave you a choice once. To pick one to die and one to live. Maybe I'll give you that choice again."

"Besides the lab," I said, still managing to keep my voice steady, "what else do you have here?"

Augustus had clearly been wanting a reaction from me, and the fact that I hadn't given him one was disappointing. He stared for a moment, and then shrugged.

"What do you care, Ben? You'll be dead within the next hour."

"I'm a curious human being. It always annoyed my mom when I would ask her a thousand questions. She was my mom, so she loved me and tried to answer as many questions as she could, but I could always tell I was getting on her nerves."

"You have a knack for that."

"Gee, thanks. So what about the server farm?"

The smile from the old man's eyes faded.

"What about the server farm?"

"The tech back at your lab in South Carolina mentioned it. His name was Eric. Seemed like an okay guy. Shame we had to kill him."

Augustus shifted his gaze to the man standing behind me. It was clear he'd been caught off guard by the question, and wasn't quite sure how to regain control.

"So we have a server farm," he said. "So what?"

"I'm just surprised. Figured a big organization like this would use the cloud or whatever you want to call it."

"Even cloud-based data needs a server farm."

"Does it? If you say so. But still, curious what you would keep on it. Everything, I imagine. Every game ever played. Every name of every member of the Inner Circle. Even every member of the Council, which your sister happened to tell us about. Probably every name of everybody who came up through the Legion program too."

Mention of the Council and Legion program caught him off guard again. Another hesitant glance at the man standing behind me, and then Augustus cleared his throat as he leaned forward.

"What is my secret?"

"Say what now?"

"You're testing my patience. One simple nod from me, and Zach will shoot you in the head."

"And splatter blood all over your study? I don't think so."

Augustus spread his hands, and smiled.

"You're right. We'll have you taken out of here first. Then Zach will shoot you in the head."

I twisted slowly in my seat to glance up at the man.

"So your name is Zach? I'm Ben. Nice to meet you."

The man said nothing.

Turning back to Augustus, I said, "Are you sure you want Zach to hear your secret?"

Augustus stared back at me, again emotionless.

"Zach is my first in command. Whatever you say to me, you might as well say to him."

I glanced up again at Zach, then shrugged at Augustus.

"All right, then. If that's what you want. But let me just warn you. This secret of yours? Part of it has to do with the Pax Romana."

Still Augustus just stared back at me, his face blank.

"The other part? That has to do with what you did to those assholes in the fraternity. You know, the ones you got arrested after you kidnapped that girl."

And there it was, just like that, a spark of panic flashing in the old man's eyes. He stared for a beat, just stared at me, and then he cleared his throat.

"Leave us."

He was staring at me when he said it but was clearly speaking to his right-hand man.

Zach said, "Sir?"

"Leave us for now. Close the door behind you and wait out in the hallway. This won't take long, I'm sure. Once I call you back in, you'll take Mr. Anderson out of here and shoot him in the head as promised."

FIFTY

Once Zach had closed the door—after a lengthy moment of silence where he didn't move, no doubt wanting to argue the point with his boss—Augustus leaned forward again and dropped his voice.

"You don't know anything."

I shrugged.

"Don't I? Okay, if you say so."

Augustus said, "I have no secrets."

"We all have secrets. That was something Simon taught me during my first game."

He stared at me, his brow creased, and then held out his hands again.

"Fine," he said. "Tell me what my secret is."

"On second thought, it might be easier if you just told me. Would save time."

His eyes narrowed but he didn't answer.

I waited a beat, drawing it out, and then said, "You're a phony."

He just stared back at me. Didn't even blink.

"A phony. A con man. Whatever you want to call it. You're not a true believer, not like the rest of these assholes."

Still nothing.

"You said as much when you told me that story about growing up. How you learned that the trick to gaining power was to tell people what they wanted to hear. That, when you're really skilled, it's making people believe what you tell them is what they've believed all along. It came natural to you, you said."

Augustus didn't answer.

"It wasn't until I learned about the Pax Romana and how it had been perfected for nearly a year that I started to suspect the truth. The lab tech, Eric, he didn't know everything that was going on, but he said that they'd been testing the same stuff for months, and that everybody was getting restless. But it was your sister who really tipped me off. When she mentioned how the Pax Romana should have been released long ago but that you kept insisting that it needed to be perfected first, and that the Council was getting impatient with you. If I'm being honest, Augustus, your sister sounded pretty disgusted about it. That woman, she's pure evil. But not like you. You may be a twisted piece of shit, but you're not evil. Killing a few hundred people here and there? Sure. But mass genocide? You just don't have it in you."

He kept staring back at me, his expression hard, and then, bit by bit, the sternness cracked like a sheet of ice. He glanced past me, at the closed door, and then lowered his voice to a whisper.

"What do you want me to say? That these people are fucking crazy? Okay, fine: They're fucking crazy. You wouldn't even believe half the shit they've wanted to do over the years. I had to keep coming up with excuses why we couldn't, like the logistics wouldn't work. And then, to get them to focus on something else, I'd suggest something even crazier, thinking that they wouldn't want to go that far, but of course then they did, each and every one of them."

"Do you mean the Council?"

"That's right. We're talking about the most powerful men and women in the world. People who own more than half the wealth in their respective countries. They can't take it with them when they die, and they don't want to give it away, so they're happy to invest it in whatever crazy cause they come up with."

"Like killing billions of people?"

Augustus nearly barked out a laugh as he shook his head, but he managed to keep his voice down.

"If they had it their way, practically the entire *world* would be decimated. Start from scratch, is what they wanted to do. I had to talk them out of it, and it took a lot of work for me even to accomplish that much. Think about that: the compromise was just killing off a few billion people instead of nearly everyone."

Augustus shook his head again, balling his hands into fists.

"It started when I was twenty-two. My old man would keep talking about the Roman Empire, how things were so perfect back then, and so I played along, telling him it would be great if we formed a group that continued the tradition. A secret group, I told him, one that worked in the shadows. He fucking ate it up. So did a lot of his close friends. That first group we assembled included a handful of senators and governors and congressmen. Even a retired U.S. president. It was mostly an excuse to get together once a month, smoke cigars and drink expensive whiskey, but you could tell they were starting to get restless, so I suggested that we add some games like they did back in the Roman Empire. I was mostly joking, but everybody thought it was a great idea, especially my father. And so what was I supposed to say then? That I was joking and that they were batshit crazy? I made it happen. Found two homeless men nobody cared about and put them in a dark room with some swords and maces—the kind that had spikes sticking out of them—and told the homeless men that whoever killed the other would get ten thousand dollars. All of my father's friends were there, smoking their cigars and drinking their whiskey, and I honestly didn't think they would let it happen. I figured hell, I would call their bluff, but they immediately started cheering on the two men. It took less than five minutes before one of the men killed the other. He bashed the man's head in with a mace. I watched, dumbfounded, not believing it actually happened, but my father's friends were cheering like it was the fucking last inning of the fucking last game of the fucking World Series. I actually intended on paying the homeless man who won and send him on his way—I was too flabbergasted to think straight, like how he was now a witness to everything—but my father told me I couldn't do that, that I had to eliminate the man just like the other one."

"Did you kill him?"

Augustus just stared back at me, and I read the truth on his face. The homeless man had died, but of course Augustus hadn't killed the man himself. He'd probably never killed anyone himself. Always had others do it for him.

I said, "So then what happened?"

"They wanted more games. And I ... provided more games. Made my father proud, it did, and I have to admit, it felt good making him proud of me. It was around that time I brought in my sister. I figured she'd balk, but she barely even blinked when I told her about the two homeless men."

Pure evil, I thought.

Augustus said, "Things progressed from there. We started hosting more and more games. The group started expanding. But they weren't happy with just games. Oh, no, they wanted so much more. My father had always talked about a new Roman Empire, and so I started theorizing that we could make that happen, and the entire group fell in line. They offered up as much money as I needed. And that's when I started suggesting off the wall ideas, like creating our own army, a group raised from birth to fight for our cause and which we could place inside the government and business world to keep an eye on things. I thought it was a ridiculous idea, but they loved it. One of them even knew of a scientist they thought could make this happen. They brought him into the group, and that's how we started the Legion program."

He paused again, shaking his head at the memory, and then fixed his gaze on me.

"So is that my secret? I guess it is. My sister has always been the true believer, the one who has wanted to continue our father's legacy. She suspects I'm weak, and maybe she's right. Killing off billions of people? It's fucking insane. But I can't put it off much longer. The Council has been demanding it for months. Word has trickled down to the Inner Circle, and even they're starting to get impatient."

"That's why you hosted the Coliseum. Not just so you could kill Carver. That was the cherry on top. The whole point was to reveal the Pax Romana."

Augustus was nodding, his jaw tight.

"And I was hoping there would be pushback from the Inner Circle. Enough so that it would force the Council to reconsider. But then ... everything went to shit. Your people attacked us, and it caused the Council—those who are still alive—to dig in even harder. Even those still alive in the Inner Circle have been braying for blood."

"Fuck you," I said. "Are you honestly trying to blame all of this on us?"

"I'm not blaming you. I'm simply stating a fact. Your actions have caused the timeline to accelerate."

"If you really didn't want to proceed, you wouldn't have

gone to all the trouble of tracking down Carver and the Kid and killing them. At least they posed a threat to your cause."

"You're damned right they did. Which was why the Council demanded I track them down."

"You could have refused."

"I'm not your friend here. I wasn't Mr. Ellison's friend or your hacker friend's friend either. They were the enemy, and so they needed to be eliminated. When they were alive, did their mere existence give me reason to be extra cautious and create excuses to keep putting off certain things? Yes, it did. I used your antagonism to my advantage as long as I could. Unfortunately, I have no other excuses left."

"You could let me go."

The corners of Augustus' lips twisted up into a tight smile.

"Don't be delusional. Not in the final minutes of your life. I don't exactly know what your game is here, but whatever it is, you've failed. Just count yourself lucky that you won't have to experience the world once the Pax Romana is unleashed."

"Two billion people," I said.

"Thereabouts, yes."

"You're going to kill two billion people, and for what? A bunch of rich assholes who only care about themselves?"

"It's the way of the world. Money talks. Money controls every facet of life. Normal people like you don't count. You're just fodder for the games."

"I guess I was wrong, after all. You may not be a true believer, but you are an evil piece of shit."

Augustus started to shake his head, started to open his mouth to say something else, but that was when the door flew open.

I expected it to be Zach, but it was Congresswoman Houser who hurried forward. Her hair was a mess, her face red. She paused beside me, glared down, and spat at my face.

I said, "Good to see you too, Congresswoman."

She stepped away, the thin fabric of her hospital scrubs whispering in the sudden silence, and redirected her glare toward her brother.

"I heard Ben Anderson had shown up in town—that he was meeting with you here in your fucking house—and I had to see it for myself."

"He's not *meeting* with me."

"Oh really? Then explain exactly what it is the two of you are doing. Zach told me that you'd asked him to leave."

There was a knock at the door, a sudden, solid knock, and then the door opened again. This time it was Zach.

"Sir, I'm sorry to interrupt, but I need to speak to you immediately."

Congresswoman Houser said, "What is it?"

"We just got word two of the Pax Romana locations were hit in the past few minutes."

Augustus' jaw went tight again.

"What?"

"The McLaughlin site, and the Silver City site. The others—"

I cut him off.

"The others are being attacked as we speak. It's just that the staff at those facilities haven't had a chance to notify you yet."

Now Augustus' face filled with color, much like his sister's. He rose behind the oak desk, and his hands were visibly shaking.

"It's not possible. They barely have a team."

Zach said, "The reports we received is that they're being attacked by an army of bikers."

"Weird," I said. "I thought normal people like me don't count. We're just fodder for the games, right?"

Zach said, "And that isn't all, sir. We've also received reports of news outlets airing information about the Inner Circle and the games. Videos, photographs, documents—everything has been uploaded online."

"How?" Congresswoman Houser asked. "We *control* the media."

"Not all of it," Zach said. "Once one outlet went live with it, the others knew they had no choice but to go live too."

Augustus said, "How is this even possible?"

I smiled.

"Does the name Ashley Walker ring a bell? I guess your people had to deal with her a few years ago. She's been collecting information from day one. She'd approached a few reporters about you assholes over the years, but you always managed to shut it down. Then we realized ... why not just send it to everyone at the same time? And not just news outlets, but every single law enforcement too. Those Pax Romana sites? Local news should be there soon, if they're not there already. The same with local law enforcement. In fact ... turn on the TV. It should be on the air by now."

Both Augustus and his sister stood silent. Both looked too furious to speak. They look panicked too. All their work, all their planning, was crashing down around them, and they didn't know what to do.

Zach stepped over to the TV and turned it on. It was already tuned to CNN. BREAKING NEWS flashed across the screen. A chyron informed viewers that mass documents had just been dumped onto the Internet about a secret organization. And already streaming on the screen was Augustus, though the network thoughtfully censored out his curses:

"What do you want me to say? That these people are [beep] crazy? Okay, fine: They're [beep] crazy. You wouldn't even believe half the [beep] they've wanted to do over the years. I had to keep coming up with excuses why we couldn't, like—"

Zach muted the TV. Slowly turned to face me. The video

of Augustus had been coming from directly across the desk. Right where I was sitting.

Augustus managed to say, "How did he—"

"Video contact lenses," Zach said quietly. "Our own fucking tech."

I smiled again.

"Surprise. When you scanned me with your little device, I was wearing those glasses. Which we knew you'd find. We wanted you to find them. So then that way … well, now here we are."

Congresswoman Houser spoke between clenched teeth, her voice shaking.

"Bring his wife and daughter here right now. I want Mr. Anderson to watch them die before we kill him."

Zach pulled a radio from his belt. He relayed the congresswoman's request, then asked, "Anything else, ma'am?"

Her dark gaze remained steady on me.

"Yes," she said. "Make sure they bring tools. Pliers, wire cutters, bone saws—I want them to bring everything they have."

Zach put the radio back up to his lips. But before he could speak, the first explosion went off outside.

FIFTY-ONE

Every screen was lit up on Titus' workstation. He even had two tablets set up because there just wasn't enough room on each screen.

Two of the screens were split in two with video.

One of the screens showed the site in Silver City, Arizona, which was being led by Ronny.

The site in Lawen, Oregon, was being led by Drew.

The site in Mt. Pleasant, Michigan, was being led by Chin.

The McLaughlin, South Dakota, site was being led by Mason.

And the Woodbury, Vermont, site was being led by Ho Sook.

Along with hundreds of bikers, all that they could amass across the country in the short amount of time.

They'd anticipated higher levels of security at each site, especially after what happened days ago at the Addison site, but they had the element of surprise on their side, or so they hoped.

Titus had provided drones to each team, and while those were now flying above each site and the live feeds were transmitting to his monitor, he wasn't the one operating them and he certainly wasn't the one closely monitoring each. That was being done on the ground, either by the team leaders or somebody they put in charge.

Right now Titus was focused on the drones he had flying above the town called Rome.

Four drones in total, and he'd started them high enough that they wouldn't be detected by the drones the security detail would send out once Ben was captured.

All four drones were transmitting live video back to Titus, but that wasn't all.

Each drone was also decked out with C-4. Not a lot, as the drones needed to be light enough to fly and maneuver, but still enough that if need be they could cause quite a blast.

It was with one of these drones that Titus flew toward the two helicopters in the open field. He'd been watching the main monitor closely, the one that was transmitting live video from Ben's contact lenses. He'd already started uploading the video to sites all over the Internet, as well as to all the major news organizations, and a few of them had already started to take them live, which was great but which also put them in a bind, because the sooner the video started to broadcast, the sooner Ben would be exposed.

So when the congresswoman appeared, and when the other guy with the gun rushed in and turned on the TV, Titus knew he had no choice.

He flew the closest drone under one of the helicopters, and hit the button on his keyboard to set off the charge.

At once, the feed from one of his monitors went dead, but he saw from two of the other drones nearby that the explosion was quite large. Larger than expected, to be honest.

Titus hit the button so that his voice would transmit to Ashley and Graham.

"Are you both ready?"

Ashley came back with: "Yes."

Graham replied: "I am."

Titus said, "Hold steady."

Then he toggled to a different channel, to John Smith who was currently more than thirty thousand feet in the air.

"Go," Titus said.

FIFTY-TWO

Five seconds before John Smith stepped out of the cargo jet that Titus had hired to circle above Rome—high enough that it wouldn't be detected by the town's radar, if they had such a thing—he thought about his old roommate Duncan.

Duncan, who had taken John in when he had nobody else, who maybe had used him to take care of the apartment, but that was okay because John had nowhere else to go and nobody else to call a friend.

Duncan, who had told John he had a death wish from all the crazy things he wanted to do, like skydiving and bungee jumping and getting into a shark cage.

What's your point? he'd asked, and Duncan had said, *My point is you've always been living on the edge, man, always staring death in the face. I'd hate to see you finally embrace it.*

Duncan had said it moments before he was killed by one of the Legion, and at the time John hadn't had any answer for him on why he wasn't afraid.

Even now, standing at the rear of the cargo jet, the air so thin he needed an oxygen mask to breathe, suited up with a parachute and helmet ready to do a HALO jump, he felt no fear.

At least, not for himself. If he felt any fear, it was for Ashley and their unborn child and the idea that he might fail and cause billions of people to die.

In his earpiece, Titus said, "Go," and like that, John jumped.

It took him a couple of seconds to gain control of his free fall, and then he was slicing through the air, his arms down at his sides, making himself as small as possible as he stared ahead at the ground.

He saw a fire down below, and then a second explosion of what he would soon learn was the second helicopter, and he made that his target, what he was aiming for, and so far ten seconds had passed and then twenty seconds had passed and little by little the earth below him was getting closer until the ground seemed to come up out of nowhere and he knew he had no choice but to deploy his chute.

John was already coming down fast, and he knew he wouldn't have much time to find the perfect landing spot. He also wouldn't have time to reach for a weapon if Caesar's men spotted him and opened fire. So when he did spot the two blazing helicopters—he could just make them out now—and saw the handful of men rushing over to see what had happened, he tugged on the cords to direct him to the area between the town and the men.

He landed harder than he would have cared for—his knees would be sore in the morning if he survived this, for sure—and a second later he'd shed the parachute and grabbed his holstered FNX-45 and opened up on the three men standing just outside the blast zone.

Two of them still had their backs to him, not having heard him land, but the third turned at the last second and raised his weapon, so John shot him first, two bullets to the head, and then killed the two other men as they turned, and then he rushed forward and grabbed two of their M4 rifles and shouldered one and took the other and hustled toward town.

Taking off his helmet and discharging his oxygen mask, he said, "How many?"

And Titus, who was watching from the drones hovering above the town, said, "At least eight more from what I can tell. And about half are headed to your location right now."

FIFTY-THREE

One second after the explosion, Congresswoman Houser said, "What the fuck was *that*?"

"That?" I said. "If I had to guess, I'd say that was one of your helicopters."

Five seconds later, another explosion, this one just as loud and nearby, and I couldn't help but smile.

"And if I was a betting man, I'd say that was your second helicopter. Those weren't too important to you, were they?"

The congresswoman's gaze sizzled with hate.

"Kill him!"

But Zach didn't. He was turning away toward the door.

"I need to see what's happening."

He was saying it more to Augustus, as way of excuse, but it was Congresswoman Houser who shouted after him.

"At least leave us your gun!"

Zach hesitated. Clearly he needed his pistol if he was going to run out into whatever the fuck was happening outside. Already we could hear gunfire, distant but distinct, and suddenly a siren started going off, a low and ongoing wail all over town.

At the sound of the siren, Zach started for the door, but the congresswoman shouted at him again.

"Your gun, you imbecile!"

He hesitated again. Then said, "I shouldn't leave you anyway."

"No," Augustus said. "We'll be fine. Go find out what's wrong."

Zach nodded. He started for the door but paused and handed his Glock to the congresswoman before sprinting out of the room.

Congresswoman Houser hefted the gun in her hand, a demented sort of glee in her eyes.

"Now," she said, pointing the gun at me, "does the smart-ass have any last words?"

The gunshot wasn't as loud as I expected, not in the tight space that was the study, but then again, the gun in Augustus' hand—the one he'd pulled from the top drawer in his desk—was a .38, so it didn't have much stopping power.

It was clear Augustus had never fired a gun before. He lacked a certain confidence in how he held it and how he squeezed the trigger that if he was aiming for his sister's chest, he missed by at least a foot, instead hitting her in the shoulder.

She spun away, crying out, and stared back at him in puzzled amazement.

"Augustus?"

He fired the gun again, only feet away from her, and one of the three shots hit her in the throat, which was enough to do the trick.

She fell to the floor, dropping the Glock as she reached for her throat and gurgled blood.

Then Augustus pivoted so he aimed the .38 directly at my face.

"You screwed me."

I swallowed and nodded, not sure what to say.

Augustus said, "The Council and the Inner Circle … they'll see what I said about them. I'm a dead man."

I didn't answer.

"Do you think you could stop the Pax Romana?"

"Yes."

He stared back at me for a beat, not speaking, not moving, not doing anything at all. Then finally he spoke.

"I'm probably going to hell, and I deserve it. My sister was right when she thought I was weak. But she's dead now, and I'm not."

I wasn't sure where he was going with this but nodded anyway.

Augustus reached into the drawer he'd taken the gun from and extracted a pair of scissors. Then he stepped around the desk, not even looking at his sister's dead body, and came up behind me and cut the binds keeping my wrists in place.

Stepping away, holding the pistol at me cautiously, he said, "I started this mess, so I might as well be the one to end it."

I stood slowly, rubbing at my wrists, and glanced around the room as that siren continued to wail.

"What do you have in mind?"

"I'll take you to the lab. I'll take you to the server farm. Hell, I'll take you to your family."

He set the .38 aside, bent down, and picked up the Glock. He hefted the pistol, much as his sister had done moments before she was killed, and then hesitantly handed it to me.

"But there's only one way I think this'll work."

FIFTY-FOUR

When she heard the first explosion, Jennifer thought it was part of her dream.

She'd continued having trouble sleeping the past several nights, dipping in and out of slumber, and she was still having that dream of the night they were taken, the one where she thought she heard something downstairs and Ben went to check but found nothing, and when Jennifer later stepped inside Casey's room she thought maybe she was stuck in the dream—because the moment she stepped into her daughter's room she was stepping back into the hallway, like she was in some twisted M.C. Escher painting.

That was when she heard the faint noise somewhere beyond the dream, something that was new and didn't quite mesh with the same nightmare she'd been having these past few nights.

Jennifer opened her eyes.

She was lying on the same bed she'd lain in since they came to this godforsaken place. She turned over and saw that Casey was in her bed too, and that her daughter appeared to be sound asleep.

Had she really heard anything at all? Maybe it was just part of the dream. Maybe—

She heard the noise again, a sudden but muffled blast coming from somewhere above them.

Her heart skipped. Maybe they were being rescued?

Then, just as suddenly, her heart stopped. Maybe this entire place was being demolished, with them inside it.

A siren started wailing, a siren she had never heard before, and Jennifer pushed the sheet off her and jumped out of bed and hurried over to Casey.

"Baby! Baby, wake up."

Her daughter stirred, still stuck in that realm between sleep and wakefulness, and Jennifer lightly shook her shoulder, like she did when she was trying to rouse Casey out of another nightmare. As the siren kept wailing, Jennifer shook her daughter even harder and practically shouted in her ear.

"Wake up!"

Casey's eyes snapped open. There was sleepiness there, and there was confusion at first, followed quickly by panic when she sensed the urgency in her mother's words and heard the siren.

"Mommy?"

"Get up. Put on your slippers."

"What's happening?"

"Do it now, Casey."

Jennifer stood from the bed and crossed over to the bathroom, noting the camera in the corner of the ceiling watching them but not caring at all, focused instead on the siren that kept wailing and waiting for the sound of another explosion.

She crouched down and reached behind the toilet, suddenly worried that the shank wouldn't be there. That the people who ran this place had been messing with her head this entire time. But the shank was right there where she'd left it, as solid and real and dangerous as it had been the last time she touched it, and she brought it out just as she heard the door to their room open.

Jennifer froze. Anybody could have just walked into the room right now. One guard, two guards, maybe a dozen. Her silly shank wasn't going to help her or Casey at all.

She stood up and crept over to the bathroom's open doorway. Peeked around the corner.

Two of the female guards had entered the room. They looked harried, their eyes wide, and one of them was already starting toward Casey while the other was heading toward the bathroom—the only place Jennifer could possibly be.

Jennifer said, "What's happening?"

Neither guard answered. At least not for a second or two. Then the one already coming in her direction spoke.

"Come out here."

Squeezing the shank in her hand, Jennifer said, "No."

A pause, but only a pause, the guard no doubt surprised Jennifer had told her no, especially now after two explosions had gone off, and Jennifer knew that her only chance—*their* only chance—was getting the guard to come into this bathroom.

She closed her eyes, said a small prayer—and then heard the same guard take a few more steps in her direction.

"Come out here right now."

Jennifer didn't answer. She stayed where she was by the toilet. The shank held tightly in her hand, her fingers practically white.

The guard stepped into the bathroom. She paused again for a beat when she saw that Jennifer was bent over the toilet, her back to the guard.

"What are you doing?" the guard growled, and used her free hand to grab Jennifer's arm.

And that was when Jennifer spun into her and drove the tip

of the shank—the thing that Jennifer had spent hours upon hours sharpening—into the side of the guard's throat.

Blood squirted out. Some of it hit her face, but Jennifer didn't pause, pulling the shank out and stabbing the guard's throat again, and again, and again. The guard started to gurgle, and gravity started to pull her body down to the floor, and Jennifer kept the shank in her throat and wrestled the pistol from the guard's grip just as the other guard rushed over to the bathroom.

The moment the second guard stepped into view, Jennifer shot at her head. The close distance—only a couple of feet—made it practically impossible for her to miss. The bullet tore apart half of the guard's face, and the guard hit the floor with a heavy thud.

Jennifer stepped into the main room, looking for more guards. She didn't see any, but she turned toward the camera in the corner of the ceiling—the thing that had looked over them all this time—and she fired two bullets at the thing, enough so that she was certain it had been destroyed, and then she turned back to her daughter.

At first Casey didn't do anything, just stood there staring at her. Then she screamed.

The pistol still in her hand, blood that wasn't her own all over her face and T-shirt, Jennifer hurried over to her daughter and crouched down in front of her.

"It's okay, baby. It's okay. Look at me, Casey. Look at me."

Her daughter quieted, and looked at her, and Jennifer saw fear in her eyes, not just at their whole situation but fear—however brief—at her own mother.

"We're getting out of here, okay? Look at me, Casey. We're getting out of here."

Her daughter nodded, silent, and Jennifer grabbed her daughter's hand and tugged her toward the open door.

FIFTY-FIVE

With Titus' drones in the air, pinpointing Caesar's men on the ground, John Smith was practically unstoppable.

He knew where men would be seconds before they arrived, what with Titus feeding him that information into his earpiece, and within a minute he'd eliminated six soldiers.

John would run at a slight crouch, staying low to the ground, keeping the assault rifle at the ready, and he would fire in three-round bursts, taking out one man after another, and if he was close enough he would finish them off with an extra head shot if need be, just to make sure they were in fact down for the count.

He'd been training for this moment his entire life, he realized.

"Head north," Titus said.

John didn't bother questioning the man. Titus saw all—not just from the drones but from the cameras in Ben's contact lenses—and so he went where Titus told him to go.

Up one block, then up another, taking out a few more men, taking cover when they fired back, and all around them a siren blared.

Then in his ear, Titus said, "There's a new development."

This made John pause.

"Say again?"

"I'll keep you posted. For now, four men are waiting at the end of town. Ashley and Graham are on their way. They could use some backup, I think."

On such short notice they hadn't been able to secure another tractor-trailer, not like in Addison, South Carolina. But they'd learned from that experience, especially with what had worked so well, and so now it was Graham behind the wheel of a 60,000-pound Mack dump truck, picking up speed as its diesel 455-horsepower engine barreled them down the single road leading into town.

Like back at Addison, they utilized a score of Kevlar vests, practically wrapping both Graham and Ashley in them. Only Ashley was in the bed of the dump truck, gripping an FNX-45 and waiting for the signal.

Graham's foot pressed hard against the gas pedal, and when he crested the small rise and saw the town spread out before him, his breath caught short because he wished Carver were here with him right now, that it was Carver sitting in the passenger seat beside him.

When he was only fifty yards away, the men stationed near the end of town opened fire.

Graham crouched low behind the wheel, trying to make himself as small a target as possible, and when the windshield spiderwebbed and then shattered he didn't slow, keeping his fingers tight on the steering wheel and his foot heavy on the gas pedal, and then the next thing he knew they'd reached town and he'd slammed into a man who hadn't been able to jump out of the way in time.

Once the truck slowed to a stop, Ashley—wearing a Kevlar

vest and dark baseball cap—climbed up over the edge of the bed and began firing down at the men. As John Smith had observed, she was a natural with a pistol, and she took out one man after another until suddenly one of the men stumbled forward from a shot to his back, and that was when Ashley saw John hurrying toward them.

She slid back down to the base of the bed, grabbed the two knapsacks, and then started toward the back.

John met her there, covering the rear of the truck, and she saw the concern in his eyes, the worry that the past several minutes might have somehow hurt their baby.

"I'm fine," she said, and she tossed him one of the knapsacks as she hefted the other and climbed down from the truck.

Graham opened his door as they approached but he didn't step down.

John said, "How are we doing, old timer?"

Graham waved them on.

"I'm fine. Go do what you need to do."

John nodded, and he and Ashley started up the street.

"Titus?" John said.

Titus said, "Keep going north. There's a house near the end of the street with a white picket fence."

At that same moment, Zach was standing in the security office underneath the grocery store.

Two other men were there, working the monitors.

From here they could view the entire town. What Zach saw now roiled his blood.

Dead bodies, all of them their own people, were splayed on the sidewalks and in the streets.

But that wasn't all.

A dump truck had arrived, and with it Ashley Walker.

Zach watched John Smith meet her. She handed him what

looked to be a knapsack. She shouldered another knapsack, and they started up the street.

Zach said, "How long before more men arrive?"

One of his men checked his tablet, and said, "An incoming Black Hawk is five minutes out."

Zach nodded, satisfied. Though what good more men would do right now he wasn't sure. They'd never placed too many men in town because there was never any need. Virtually nobody knew their location. Rome wasn't a place that needed protecting because as far as the rest of the world was concerned it didn't even exist. That was why they'd spread out their men to the other Pax Romana sites.

Only those facilities were being attacked right this instant. Ben Anderson was right: they'd received word from the other facilities that they, too, were under attack. Several strike teams had been automatically deployed, but from what Zach could ascertain, none of them was having any success.

Local law enforcement and news media had also shown up. It was pure chaos. The only thing that was now certain was that there would be no hiding the Pax Romana.

In the back of his mind, he remembered what he'd seen Caesar saying as the video was streamed on CNN.

What do you want me to say? That these people are [beep] crazy? Okay, fine: They're [beep] crazy.

Zach wasn't sure what to think of Caesar's appearance on TV, at least not yet. Eventually he would need to learn everything Caesar had told Ben, and why Caesar had asked Zach to step out of the room in the first place.

The other man in front of the monitors said, "Um, sir?"

Zach blinked. "What is it?"

"It's Caesar's residence, sir. You're going to want to see this."

FIFTY-SIX

As I had with Eric back at that first Pax Romana site, I used Augustus as a shield as I directed him outside.

Three men were lined up in the yard. Their backs were to us, so it was clear they had been tasked with guarding the house, but when one of them heard movement behind them, they spun around and aimed their rifles at us.

Clutching the back of Augustus' shirt in one hand, I held the Glock 17 with my other hand and kept the barrel pressed tight against the side of his head.

"If you don't want me to blow his brains out, drop your weapons!"

The trio did not comply.

Augustus shouted, his voice trembling, "Do what he says!"

One of the men said, "Sir, I'm sorry, but we can't do that."

I pushed Augustus a couple of feet forward, and the men moved a couple of feet back.

Augustus tried again, this time with even more panic in his voice.

"I order you to drop your weapons!"

The three men shot each other hesitant glances. Clearly

they wanted to listen to their boss, but they also didn't want to expose themselves if they didn't have to. Because then I would be the only one with a weapon.

The same man spoke again.

"I'm sorry, sir, but again, we can't—"

The back of his head burst open like a rotting watermelon.

The gunshot had originated from John Smith's gun, and as the two other men turned, John Smith and Ashley Walker dropped them within seconds.

"About fucking time," I said.

As John Smith covered the area, Ashley hurried over. She dropped the knapsack to the ground, dug around inside it, and came out with a familiar sunglasses case.

I released my grip on Augustus and secured the Glock in the waistband of my jeans. Then I immediately pinched out first one contact lens, then the other, and flicked them to the ground.

There goes a couple hundred thousand dollars, I thought, and opened the case and pulled out the pair of glasses that Titus had made for me—the pair I'd worn into town had been one of his first failed attempts; the camera didn't even work, and the lenses weren't my prescription. So this entire time I hadn't been able to see much at all, which was why I'd hoped the trio would drop their weapons, because I was sure my aim would have been shit. But now I could finally see, and with a working camera in the frames, Titus could see too.

Ashley dug out an extra earpiece, and I secured that in my ear and said, "Titus?"

A heavy sigh of relief came through on his end.

"Good to hear your voice, Ben."

"How's everybody at the other sites?"

"Overall, they're okay. Only a few casualties, but so far no fatalities. Drew took a bullet to the leg, but he tells me he's fine. Ho Sook was shot too, but she thankfully had her Kevlar on. Some local law enforcement is trying to arrest everybody because they don't know what else to do, but it looks like each facility has been secured."

I glanced at Ashley, asked, "How's Graham?"

In my ear, Graham said, "Graham is fine. Now hurry it up and get this over with."

John gestured at Augustus, who was just standing there beside us.

"This the guy?"

"It is."

"Titus says he flipped."

I glanced at Augustus, and shook my head.

"I wouldn't say flipped. But he is going to help us. Isn't that right, Augustus?"

The old man looked deeply ashamed to admit it, but he nodded his head without a word.

"Okay," John Smith said. "So where to next?"

Augustus said, "There's an entrance behind the bank. I suggest we enter through there."

"Bank?" John asked, shooting me a raised eyebrow.

"The town here is just cover," I said. "Most of the operation is located underneath us. That's where—"

But I cut myself off when I heard the noise. A faint, distant thudding in the predawn.

We moved several paces to the left, so that we could see the open field behind town. The direction was east, and some light was starting to materialize on the horizon, which made it easy to spot the approaching helicopter.

"That'll be the strike team," Augustus said. "Zach called for it as soon as you showed up."

I asked, "Is it the only one coming?"

"I don't know."

I glanced at John. "You didn't happen to bring your rocket launcher along, did you?"

He shook his head, watching the horizon. The chopper would reach us within a minute. There would be at least a half-dozen men onboard, and they would be heavily armed and ready to fight.

I glanced around the yard, at the dark buildings and the dead bodies, and was at a loss. We could hurry to the bank, head down to the lower level, but that wouldn't stop the chopper. Right now, nothing would stop the chopper as far as I could tell, which meant we might as well wait for it and open fire right as it started to land, otherwise—

"I have an idea," Titus said.

That was when I noticed one of the drones floating above the house, maybe one hundred yards in the air. It hovered there for a beat and then zoomed out into the field. Directly at the approaching helicopter.

Twenty seconds later, a touch more orange light in the purple sky, it was clear the approaching bird was a Black Hawk and that it was coming in fast.

Ten seconds after that, the drone must have made contact and Titus must have triggered the C-4, because the helicopter's tail rotor suddenly burst apart.

It was unclear if that was Titus' intention, but the majority of the chopper hadn't been hit. Still, without the tail rotor, everything was now fucked, and the Black Hawk started to spin as it dipped toward the ground.

We watched as a few of the men tried bailing before the crash, but it was no good. The moment the chopper touched down, the gasoline tank ruptured, and the entire thing exploded in a giant ball of fire.

"Holy shit," Titus said in our ears. Then: "Let me check to see if there are any survivors."

Another drone zoomed overhead, out toward the field. It was the last drone, by my count, which meant that we no longer had any eyes in the sky. Which meant that until the drone returned, we wouldn't know if any of the Legion was hiding around corners.

But we didn't have time to wait. Not if we wanted to finish this before another strike team arrived.

"Let's go," I said.

FIFTY-SEVEN

Zach stood on the edge of town, watching the aftermath of the explosion. The *third* explosion in the past fifteen minutes, and none of them were in their favor.

Movement in the sky caught his attention, and he saw a drone zip toward the wreckage. Probably headed to check to see if there were any survivors.

He grabbed the radio off his belt and placed it to his mouth.

"The Black Hawk's down. What's the ETA on the next strike team?"

There was a heavy beat of silence, and he was unsure if his transmission had gone through. Then one of the men answered.

"Half hour at the earliest, sir."

Fuck.

There was no telling what kind of damage the enemy could do in that amount of time. But their own resources were low—maybe three or four men still alive, by his latest count—and Zach wasn't sure he could trust any of them not to get themselves killed.

The radio crackled, and the same voice said, "It looks like they're headed to the bank."

Zach placed the radio to his mouth.

"Is Caesar with them?"

"Yes, sir. It appears … he's leading them there himself."

Zach turned back to town. It was a straight shot to reach the bank. He could make it there in less than thirty seconds. Caesar's residence was a bit of a detour, but he needed to see it for himself. Needed to confirm the worst possible scenario was true.

And so it was, forty-one seconds later, standing in the study he'd stood in less than a half hour ago, that Zach stared down at Congresswoman Houser's dead body. From how she had fallen, it was clear from which direction the shots had come.

He glanced down at the broken zip-ties on the carpet beside the chair Ben Anderson had been sitting in. It looked as if they'd been cut straight through.

Then he noticed the pair of scissors left on the edge of the oak desk.

He sprinted for the door, toggling the switch on his radio.

"Where are they now?"

The answer came back almost immediately.

"Almost ready to enter the bank."

"What's the status on the woman and child?"

"That team hasn't checked in yet."

Zach hurried past the three dead bodies in the yard and through the white picket fence, a pistol in one hand, the radio in the other.

"Repeat that again."

"The team dispatched to retrieve them hasn't returned and they aren't answering us. And the camera in their room has gone dead."

If Zach ran, he'd reach the bank in about twenty seconds. So he started sprinting as he shouted into the radio.

"Then you two need to get off your fucking asses and find them!"

FIFTY-EIGHT

I watched Augustus enter the six-digit code on the panel beside the door and press his thumb to the scanner beside the panel, and then watched the red light on the panel turn from red to green and heard the door go *thunk* as it unlocked.

Augustus opened the door, and motioned for us to enter.

"After you."

John Smith had been covering the rear while I covered the door, in case any of the Legion was waiting just inside ready to open fire.

"No way," John said. "We're not walking into a trap."

"I can assure you, it isn't a trap."

John glanced at me, and raised an eyebrow.

I said, "Get going, Augustus. Take us to the server farm."

"I still don't understand what it is you expect to find there."

"Everything," I said, and grabbed the door so that Augustus could head inside.

As he started to take a step forward, a single gunshot pierced the dawn and the bullet tore through his neck.

John Smith immediately returned fire, shooting toward the

other end of the street where a man was crouched behind a car. It took me a moment to recognize Zach.

I shouted, "Let's go!"

Ashley hurried inside, followed by John who walked backward as he continued to release suppression fire.

Augustus was still alive, though he wasn't going to be for long. I grabbed his arm and started tugging him through the door, and John shouted, "Leave him!" and I shouted back, "We still need him!" and John fired off a couple more rounds before grabbing the old man's other arm and yanking him inside.

The door closed with a heavy thud, and for a moment there was complete silence.

John let go of Augustus, and continued to cover the door. Ashley, meanwhile, covered the stairs leading down.

I crouched down in front of Augustus. He was losing a lot of blood. Like his sister, he was gurgling out the final moments of his life, his lips moving but making no sounds.

I stared at him, wanting to ask a thousand questions, but within seconds his lips stopped moving and the gurgling quieted and his eyes glazed over.

Staring at Augustus' pale, still face, I said, "Do either of you have a pair of wire cutters?"

Still covering the door, John said, "For what?"

"We need his thumb."

John pulled a switchblade from his pocket, flicked his wrist to pop the blade. He spun the knife with his fingers, so the handle was pointed toward me, and I took it.

Twenty seconds later, Augustus' severed thumb now in my possession, we continued down the steps into a brightly lit corridor. It looked to stretch for nearly fifty yards. A camera was positioned near one corner, and Ashley used black spray paint from her knapsack to cover the lens.

We went room to room, John and Ashley covering both sides of the corridor as I punched in the six-digit code I'd watched Augustus enter behind the bank and then pressed his thumb on the scanner. Then I kicked open the door and swept the room.

The first three rooms we tried were empty offices.

The fourth was a lab.

Like the one in Addison, the lab was brightly lit and packed full of equipment.

The moment we stepped inside, nothing happened. But then suddenly somebody popped up behind a table with a gun.

It was an older man, with a bald head and glasses dressed in a lab coat, and he barely got off a round before John placed two bullets in his face.

As the guy dropped to the ground, we spread out to sweep the room.

Ashley noted the door in the corner. It led into a walk-in fridge. Inside we found hundreds of vials marked as the vaccine to the Pax Romana. The hope was that the Pax Romana would never see the light of day, but if so, we were going to make sure the CDC received these vials as soon as possible.

As Ashley and I began loading the vials into cases, we heard distant gunfire.

I glanced at John, and John nodded.

"I'll check it out," he said, and headed for the door.

FIFTY-NINE

The siren was still wailing, and the steady noise was enough to drive Jennifer crazy.

But she tried to force it from her mind, tried to focus on the task at hand, which was getting them the fuck out of this place.

She had no idea where they were—no idea where they'd been kept this entire time—but she knew that there had to be a door somewhere that would lead them outside, and hopefully to freedom.

In the back of her mind, she knew that plan was all fantasy —that they were never going to leave, at least not alive—but still she pushed on, her hand tightly gripping her daughter's as Jennifer tugged her down the corridor, checking one door after another, but none of them would open, not without a code which Jennifer most certainly did not have.

Casey had finally stopped sobbing, but there were still tears in her eyes which she kept trying to wipe away, and Jennifer wanted more than anything to console her daughter but she couldn't stop, she needed to keep going, needed to keep moving, because if they slowed for even a second, they might die and Jennifer wasn't going to let that happen, *couldn't* let that happen, and so—

She heard footsteps around the corner, coming their way, and she immediately put a hand over Casey's mouth to keep her quiet.

Jennifer glanced over her shoulder, but it was several yards to the next hallway, and there was no way they would make it there in time. Then she glanced down at herself, at the guard's blood drying on her shirt and skin, and bent down and whispered to Casey to stay very still and very quiet and that she would be back, and when Casey nodded—her brave little girl who had never hurt a living thing a day in her life—Jennifer released her hand over her daughter's mouth, terrified that her daughter might start screaming, but Casey didn't, she stayed as quiet and still as instructed, and that was when Jennifer started screaming herself.

Leaving Casey where she was, Jennifer ran forward, toward those approaching footsteps, still screaming, concealing the gun behind her back as she turned the corner and saw two men approaching.

"They're dead, they're dead, they're dead!" she screamed, pointing with her free hand down the corridor, and the two men—dumbfounded for a second, unsure what to do—trained their weapons on her.

But when they took in the blood on her shirt and neck and face, they rushed forward, but in a cautious way as they neared the corner.

The moment they took their focus off her, Jennifer brought the pistol around and stepped close and shot the one guard in the stomach, then turned and shot the other guard in the chest, one shot to each, though once they were down Jennifer started firing at them again and again until the gun stopped kicking in her hand.

She looked up and saw Casey there, staring at her. Was that

the same fear she's glimpsed before in her daughter's face, fear at what her mother had become?

"It's okay, baby," Jennifer said, and she wasn't sure if she sounded like a mad woman in that instant. She was worried that Casey would take off running, afraid that her mother would do to do her what she'd done to those men, but Casey took one slow, hesitant step forward, then another, but that was when Jennifer heard more approaching footsteps—a single set this time—and motioned for Casey to stay where she was.

The pistol still in her hand, Jennifer turned to watch a man hurrying toward her. He was dressed differently than the other men. He wore a black jumpsuit and had a gun in his hand, much like Jennifer's, though Jennifer was sure that his was loaded while hers was not.

The man held up his other hand, trying to calm her, to keep her quiet, and he took in the two dead bodies at her feet before saying words that nearly broke her.

"You're Ben's wife, aren't you?"

SIXTY

Zach applied pressure to the wound on his shoulder. John Smith had managed to hit him there before they disappeared through the door behind the bank. Had Zach not been shot, he probably would have pursued them, but he wasn't going to go after them alone and wounded.

Besides, right now, he wasn't sure just how many of his men were still alive.

He ignored the radio on his belt and pulled his cell phone from his pocket. He stared at the screen for a beat, and then dialed a number he hadn't dialed in years.

A voice he hadn't heard in a long time answered.

"Is that you, Zach?"

"Tyson, I need your help."

"Sorry, but I'm dealing with a lot of other shit right now. Every single Pax Romana site is being attacked, and—"

"I know," Zach said. "I'm at Rome, and it's being attacked too."

There was a heavy silence as Tyson processed this.

"Why are you calling me?"

"Because everybody else in town is dead, as far as I can tell."

"Even Caesar?"

"Yes, even Caesar. They shot him dead. I saw it happen but couldn't get there fast enough to save him."

"I heard that footage of him is on the news. But people are saying it's a fake. That it's all fake."

"It is fake, Tyson. Which is why I need your help. Can you access Rome's security feed?"

Another beat of heavy silence, and then Tyson said, "Hold on."

It took nearly a minute, the siren continuing to swell all around him as his head pounded, and then Tyson came back on the line.

"Okay, I'm in. What am I looking for?"

"Can you access the lab?"

"I can. But … the cameras are all dark. They don't appear to be offline. Most likely somebody blackened the lenses."

Zach bit his lip, wincing against the pain as he kept the pressure against his shoulder. Taking care of the wound wasn't an option right now.

His options, to be honest, were pretty limited.

But at least he knew where Ben Anderson and John Smith and Ashley Walker were. They were down in the lab. There were only so many entrances and exits to the underground facility, only so many places to hide. They would need to come back out eventually. But where they would come out, and when, was the question. Until another strike team arrived, it was just Zach.

Besides the lab, what else do you have here?

Ben Anderson had asked that right before mentioning the server farm. Which had struck Zach as strange at the time.

"Tyson, can you access the server farm?"

"I can."

"Can you … take it offline?"

"The entire thing? No. Why are you asking?"

Zach wasn't quite sure. He had a hunch, but it was just a hunch.

"If you can't take the server farm offline, can you take … everything else offline?"

"What do you mean?"

"Jam cell reception. Internet. Whatever. Turn this place back into the stone age so that they can't communicate with anyone outside town."

"I could probably shut down several of the cell towers in the region. But it wouldn't just affect Rome. It would affect hundreds of thousands of people."

Rule of thumb had always been to stay so far under the radar that nobody knew they existed. It had worked that way for decades, but clearly everything had gotten fucked in the past hour, so what harm would affecting a few hundred thousand people do when it felt like the whole fucking world was on fire?

"Do it," Zach said.

He stepped out onto Main Street. The sky was starting to lighten more and more. Pretty soon the sun would rise, daylight would break, and then what? Practically everybody Zach knew was dead. Even Caesar, it turned out, had been a traitor. Zach didn't feel one iota of guilt at having placed a bullet in his neck. He'd thought it appropriate seeing as how that was where Augustus had shot his own sister.

He had been created to be a soldier in this army, but now what army was there? What were they fighting for, now that the Pax Romana locations had been found and it looked as if the entire organization had been exposed to the world?

Zach glanced up and down the street, spotting the dead bodies of his fellow Legion scattered about, and then his gaze settled on the dump truck parked toward the end of town.

"Tyson?"

"Yes."

"Can you shut off the fucking siren here in town? And can you feed me into the intercom system so I can talk to the enemy down below?"

"Sure thing."

"Actually," Zach said, "wait on that for a minute. Let me call you right back."

Keeping the phone in one hand, his pistol in another, Zach started down the street toward the dump truck.

SIXTY-ONE

"Hey, Ben? I think these are yours."

I turned at the sound of John Smith's voice, and my heart nearly stopped. Not just at the sight of my wife and daughter —my wife and daughter!—but at the blood splattered all over my wife's shirt and neck and face.

They both stood in the doorway to the lab, John behind them. They stared at me, and I stared back. I had the insane notion that if I blinked, if I breathed too hard, they would suddenly disappear. And so I just stood there, staring, until Casey uttered one trembling word.

"Daddy?"

That broke the trance.

I rushed forward, nearly tripping over a chair, and fell to my knees and pulled Jen and Casey into a tight hug, held them so tightly that I worried maybe I'd hurt them but that didn't stop me from holding them, trying to keep the tears back but doing a poor job of it, my body shaking and their bodies shaking and me saying their names and them saying my name and then I remembered the blood all over Jen and leaned away.

"Are you hurt?"

She shook her head, said that she wasn't, that it wasn't her blood, and when she reached for me I noticed her missing ring finger—just a stub among her other digits—and a rage I hadn't felt in a very long time coursed through me.

Jen saw it, and there was fear in eyes.

"Ben?"

I let the rage go, or at least I thought I did, and I hugged them again, but only for a moment, because I knew that we had to keep moving.

"I've missed you so much. Both of you. But we have to keep moving, okay?"

Ashley stepped out of the fridge unit, saying that she had what she needed, and then we were back in the corridor again, John covering the rear while I led everybody forward, checking one door after another using Augustus' thumb—I saw the revulsion pass over Jen's face at the sight—until we finally found the server farm.

The space was about the size of a small gymnasium. The ceiling wasn't quite as high but the space stretched out for nearly one hundred feet. And neatly lined up in racks that were about six feet tall, were server upon server upon server.

"Titus," I said. "Are you seeing this?"

In my earpiece, Titus said, "I am. Just trying to take it all in."

"What do you need me to do?"

"Go over to the rack to your left. Pull out one of the trays."

I did as instructed, Jen and Casey watching me as John and Ashley covered our position. Ashley looked up and down the large room while John kept one foot in the corridor. We'd covered every surveillance camera we'd gone past with black spray paint, but those had been lower because the ceilings weren't so high. Here the ceiling was much higher, and John and Ashley shot out the few cameras stationed about, causing Jen and Casey to jump each time they fired.

I set the knapsack on the floor and pulled out the small laptop that Ashley had brought along. Titus could see what I was doing, and he guided me, telling me which cord to insert into which port, and then what to type on the keyboard once the laptop was up and running.

I took my time, wanting to make sure to type exactly what Titus instructed, and I could sense the impatience on his end, that I wasn't moving nearly as fast as he would if he were here in my place.

After I hit ENTER and watched the screen cycle through a mishmash of letters and numbers and symbols, I asked, "Now what are you doing?"

Titus said, "Using a program to remotely gain access to the system."

"How long will that take?"

"Honestly, Ben? I'm not sure. It could take seconds. It could take minutes. It could take—yes!"

"What happened?"

"I'm in."

"The entire system?"

"From what I can tell, yes. Now I'm locating the information you requested and … Okay, here we go."

I wanted to look away, to check on Jen and Casey, but I knew that what I saw Titus saw and that right now what he needed to see was the laptop screen. So I stayed where I was, staring at those random letters and number and symbols as they streamed across the screen, and then Titus spoke again in my ear.

"Starting the download now."

"How long will that take?"

"Hopefully not too long. A minute or two at least."

"You're downloading it all?"

"I am. The information is compressed. It makes it faster. Plus, it's straight-up personal data."

Right now Titus was downloading the entire list of every member of the Inner Circle and the Council and whoever may have had contact with the group, including everybody in the Legion program and where they had been assigned in the U.S. government and all over the world.

Essentially we were going to dox them, which was a term Titus had explained, meaning that we were going to publish their private information on the Internet for the entire world to see.

Information overload, sure, but this kind of thing couldn't be dripped out over time. It needed to come out all at once. We needed to strike while the iron was hot.

"Titus, can you also access the Pax Romana files?"

"I can."

"Download all the research that was done. Especially on the vaccine. Send it all to the CDC."

"Will do. You want me to start the virus now, or wait?"

"Can you do both?"

Titus was quiet for a beat, thinking about it, and then he said, "I'm almost done here. As soon as everything is downloaded, I'll start to upload the virus."

The plan was to corrupt the entire server farm. The majority of these servers housed thousands and thousands of the games from all over the world. My game and Carver's game and Ronny's game and Drew's game and the games of every single person who had suffered in the name of entertainment. We'd debated whether or not we should leave those servers as evidence, but we didn't like the idea of law enforcement or whoever poring over countless hours of people's misery, especially when Titus pointed out that there was a chance that stuff would get stored on other servers that could potentially be hacked so that somebody else could leak it out into the world.

We all agreed that those who had played Simon's game— those who had lost their loved ones before undoubtedly losing their own lives—deserved better than that, and so Titus said he had a virus that would spread like wildfire and corrupt all the servers, essentially permanently deleting those games.

"Titus?"

"Yeah, Ben."

"Before you upload the virus, can you tell if there's a file containing the names of every player of every game, whoever was taken?"

There was a beat of hesitation on Titus' end.

"I thought we were going to destroy all of that stuff."

"The videos themselves, yes. But I think records of who was taken and who was killed should be out there too. A lot of people have gone missing over the years. A lot of families have been holding out hope. I think they all deserve closure."

"I can do that."

In my ear then, just as in John's and Ashley's ears, a new voice spoke.

"Oh shit," Graham said. "I think they—"

There was shouting, and the sound of a struggle, and then nothing as Graham's earpiece was either turned off or smashed to pieces.

Then, suddenly, the siren stopped, though it continued to echo in my ears.

Several seconds later, a voice came over the intercom. A voice that I last heard back in Augustus' study.

"John? Ben? I know you can hear me, so listen carefully."

I had no choice but to look away from the laptop. I glanced back at John, who was still standing with one foot in the corridor. We stared at each other for a moment, neither one of us breathing, and then Zach spoke again.

"I don't know what it is you think you're doing down there, but if you don't want your friend to die, you both need to come up top right now. In fact, bring Ashley Walker with you. I haven't seen her in years."

We could hear Graham shouting, telling us not to worry about him, to just do what we needed to do, and then we heard the wind get knocked out of him.

On the laptop in front of me, the letters and numbers and symbols had disappeared and now there appeared a progress bar. Five percent of the virus had been loaded so far.

"By the way," Zach said. "All radio communication is going to cease in the next minute. Admittedly that puts my people and me at a disadvantage, but we believe the same applies to you. Use the stairs outside the lab. It'll bring you out through the hardware store. You now have one minute to come up here to save your friend."

On the laptop, the progress bar had reached ten percent. It was working its way up to fifteen percent before the screen flickered and then the progress bar paused.

"Titus?" I said.

Nothing.

I turned away from the computer.

Jen stood there holding Casey in front of her. Both of them looked terrified.

John Smith still had one foot in the corridor, looking back at me.

Ashley Walker stood somewhere between them, her face ashen, her hand unconsciously touching her belly.

"What do we do?" she asked.

I thought about it for a moment, and then I looked at my wife.

"I have an idea."

SIXTY-TWO

The stairwell outside the lab led up to the hardware store, just as Zach had said.

We went up cautiously, guns in hand, and I opened the door while John stepped out and surveyed the empty hardware store, sweeping his pistol back and forth, until he nodded that the coast was clear and we continued toward the front of the store.

By then, the sun had started to rise, faint golden light slanting through the dust-covered windows.

John went to the door, gripping his pistol with both hands, and surveyed the street before nodding to us again.

He opened the door, and a tiny bell hanging above it jingled softly.

Zach was standing at the far end of the street, by the dump truck. He held Graham in front of him. One hand on Graham's shoulder to keep him steady, his other hand gripping a pistol aimed at Graham's head.

We were maybe one hundred feet away. The three of us stepped out of the hardware store and spread out along the street.

"That took longer than a minute," Zach said. "You should be happy I'm a patient man."

We said nothing.

"You don't remember me, do you, Ashley?"

Her dark baseball cap tilted down, and she spoke quietly, one simple word.

"No."

"Five years ago, I was tasked with drawing out Eli Craig. You got involved, and we ended up taking you to your parents' place in Martha's Vineyard, myself and somebody else. His name was Hogan. He ended up becoming a Simon. He was your Simon, Ben. Carver Ellison killed him, if I'm not mistaken."

"That's right," I said. "Carver shot him in the face."

Zach smiled, and shook his head.

"All those years ago, who would have thought we'd end up right here together like this?"

John said, "Do you want us to get into a circle and sing 'Kumbaya'?"

The smile dropped from Zach's face, and his eyes darkened.

"No, I want to see how far your loyalties lie. Who's willing to give up their life for their friend's?"

Graham shouted, "Don't worry about me! Just kill this son of a—"

Zach slammed his pistol into the back of Graham's head, told him to shut up. Then he smiled at us again.

"Who is this old man, anyway? How the fuck did he get involved with you guys?"

Despite being hit with the pistol, Graham wasn't deterred and growled back at him.

"Carver was my son."

Zach seemed to find this hilarious, and barked out a laugh.

"Your son? Hate to break it to you, old man, but you're white, and Carver wasn't."

"My wife and I—"

Zach pistol-whipped him again, and said, "I don't give a shit." Then to the rest of us: "So what's it going to be? Who wants to give their life for this old fuck?"

We didn't say anything.

"Fine," Zach said. "I'm not going to wait forever. You have five seconds to make a decision."

The street was quiet. Graham tried wiggling out of Zach's grip, but Zach kept him in place without much effort, the barrel of his gun still pressed against the side of his head.

I called up the street, "Your friend Hogan—he was my Simon, huh?"

Zach grinned, clearly amused by this fact.

"That he was."

"I have to admit, he taught me something very important. Though, in the end, it led to his downfall."

The grin started to slip from Zach's face.

"What the fuck are you talking about?"

"Do you know how he died? How we managed to make it back to the Paradise Motel without notice so Carver could shoot your friend in the face?"

Now the grin had vanished completely.

"Misdirection," I said, and that was when Ashley Walker—not standing between John and me, but having exited behind the bank and crept all the way down to the end of town behind the buildings so that she could come up on Zach and Graham from behind—fired a single shot at an angle so that it wouldn't hit Graham, and suddenly half of Zach's head disappeared in a burst of red spray.

John moved instantly, toward Zach's falling body to secure Graham, and I turned to Jen, who had swapped out her clothes with Ashley's, including the baseball cap. Her entire body was trembling, and when she realized she no longer needed the gun, she let it fall from her grasp where it clattered to the pavement.

I took her into an embrace, telling her that she'd done great, that everything was okay now, and she was openly sobbing, still scared out of her mind, and I kissed her tears and then directed her back toward the hardware store where Casey had been hiding behind the counter the entire time.

I didn't want to leave them but knew I had no choice, so I said, "I'll be right back," and hustled down the street.

John had already searched Zach. He came away with a cell phone, but shook his head at me, indicating that it didn't have a signal.

"The fucker wasn't lying. This entire area has been jammed."

Ashley had approached and crouched down next to Graham who was on his knees. She whispered, "Jesus Christ. When were you hit?"

It was then I noticed the blood soaking Graham's side. From the distance, it had been shadowed by the rising sun, but now it was clearly coming through, and it was still fresh.

Graham grimaced in pain as he held his side. His face, I saw, was very pale.

"When we … drove in," he said, his voice soft. "Guess the Kevlar … wasn't wrapped as tight … as I thought it was."

"Why didn't you say something earlier?" John asked.

Graham squinted up him. "My role in this … is quite minor. I didn't want to slow … any of you … down."

"It doesn't matter anyway," I said. "Titus managed to download several of the files we needed, but he wasn't able to upload the virus in time."

"What does … that mean?"

John said, "It means all those games are still there on the servers."

Graham winced again, holding his side.

"Carver's … game?" he asked, his voice even softer.

I nodded. "Everybody's games, most likely. All we can hope now is that law enforcement makes it here first before any of Augustus' people."

"You know … what law enforcement … is going to do … with that stuff. We had … this conversation."

"Yeah, well, at this point we've run out of options. We need to get out of here ASAP. And we need to get you to a hospital."

Graham's face seemed to have paled even more in the past minute. He slowly shook his head.

"You brought … explosives … didn't you? Why not … just blow up … the whole thing?"

"Because," I said, "without a cell signal, there's no way we can remotely detonate it."

"Who says … it has to be … done remotely?"

It hit me then, what he meant. I think it hit John and Ashley at the same time too. We just stood there for a moment, stunned silent, letting his words sink in, and I shook my head.

"No fucking way."

Graham just stared up at me, and nodded slowly.

"This is why … I came. It's time … for me … to see my wife … again. And to see … Carver."

SIXTY-THREE

In the end, when it was clear that they had no other choice, and while Ashley took Ben's wife and daughter to find them a vehicle in which to escape, Ben and John carried him down the street and through the empty hardware store and down the steps and through the corridor to the room with the computer servers, and Graham was carefully placed on the floor while Ben and John hurried around the room, placing the blocks of C-4 throughout, making sure that each of them was connected, and it was a minute or two or three—Graham was beginning to lose sense of time, his head too light, his vision starting to blur—when he sensed them in front of him, talking to him, and he opened his eyes and nodded at what they were saying but he couldn't really hear them, not anymore, but he did understand their meaning, what with the detonator that John Smith placed in his hand, and the two of them lingered for what felt like a very long time, just staring down at him, and he saw tears in Ben's eyes and wanted to tell Ben that it was okay, that Ben had finally found his wife and daughter so he no longer had anything to fear anymore, and then he felt Ben's hand on his shoulder for a moment before Ben and John hustled out of the room, and Graham started counting in his head, started counting from one and kept going up and up, though his vision was going in and out and his breathing was becoming even shallower, and he reached maybe one hundred —or was it one hundred fifty?—before he realized the darkness was about to swallow him and he pushed down on the plunger.

SIXTY-FOUR

Titus had never felt this much panic in his life. Not even when he was a boy on the schoolyard and the bullies surrounded him, tripping him and pushing his face into the ground and threatening to force him to eat worms.

He sat in his chair, his entire body tense, and stared at the monitors.

On one of them he had CNN and Fox News and MSNBC and BBC all playing in different boxes, and while some of them were giving the Pax Romana raids and all the information that had come to light in the past hour more attention than others, he was still glad that each network was covering it in their own way. Plus, it was early morning, most of the country just starting to wake up, and this would be the lead story all day and hopefully all week and maybe even longer.

But what had happened to his friends? What had happened to Ben and John and Ashley and Graham? The last thing he'd heard was that one of the bad guys had captured Graham, and then there was nothing.

He'd been in communication with the others—Ronny and

Drew and Mason and Ho Sook and Chin—and each had already left their respective sites, along with most of the bikers.

Titus had searched for news from the section of the country Rome was in, thinking he might find something there, something to tell him what had happened, and he'd found that there were reports of cell and Internet reception having gone out for hundreds of thousands of people in the past half hour. It seemed to have affected several counties, and right now nobody knew what had happened or why, though Titus suspected he knew. Hadn't the bad guy said as much?

So he was sitting there, still tense, when Ben's voice suddenly came over the radio.

"Titus? Can you hear me?"

He nearly sprang out of his chair in his excitement. He grabbed his headset and put it on and toggled the switch to respond.

"Ben? Ben, is that you?"

"Thank God. We've been trying to reach you for the past ten minutes."

"Where are you?"

"About ten miles outside Rome at this point."

"What happened to Graham? The last thing I heard was—"

"Graham didn't make it. Look, Titus, I'll explain more later, but I just wanted to touch base and see how everybody else is doing."

Titus felt his heart sink at the news of Graham's death. He hardly knew the man, hadn't even once spoken to him directly, but still Graham was a member of the team, which meant he was a friend, and for Titus—somebody who didn't have any friends at all—he took the news hard.

"Titus?"

He blinked, and said, "Everybody seemed to have made it out for the most part. Law enforcement attempted to arrest some of them, but Ronny and Mason and the others made it out okay. They just don't know where to go to next."

"John suggested a place," Ben said. "It's a place everybody can stay for a couple of days. I'll text you the address."

"My virus never—"

"I know. But the server farm's been destroyed."

"But how did—"

"I'll explain more later. Thank you, Titus, for everything. I think you would have made the Kid proud."

Titus felt his eyes starting to water. He said he'd send out the address to the team once he received it, and then he set the headset aside and dropped down from his chair and went into the kitchen. He opened the fridge and pulled out a fresh pack of Kraft American cheese and he opened the pack and took it outside.

The sun had been up for almost an hour now, and most of the sky was a deep blue, and he heard the usual birds all around him singing their usual morning chorus, and he couldn't contain himself any longer.

"We did it!"

None of the birds quieted down at his outburst. None of them seemed to care. Which was just as well. Most of the world wouldn't even know what they'd done, but that didn't matter.

"Hercules!" he shouted, peeling one of the slices of cheese from its cellophane.

The raccoon poked his head out of his home. He looked around, his snout in the air, and once he smelled the cheese he ventured out and approached Titus, eager for a treat.

Titus rolled up some of the cheese and pushed it through the chicken wire to Hercules.

"We did it, boy," Titus whispered, fresh tears in his eyes. "We won."

EPILOGUE

It was almost midnight by the time we turned off the secondary road onto the long drive, our headlights flashing on the stone sign by the entrance announcing ST. NICHOLAS HOME FOR CHILDREN.

A half mile up the drive, the mansion stood on a slight hill. Three stories tall, over fifty rooms, made completely of stone, John had told us, and now here it was, a beacon of sanctuary in the dark night.

We'd driven straight through the day—stopping only for gas, John and I switching off driving every couple of hours to give each other breaks—and Ronny and Beverly were already there, as were Mason and his wife and Chin. Ho Sook and Drew would arrive in the morning, we were told by Sister Sara, who met us just inside the entrance doors.

She was an older woman, with an angular nose and her white hair pulled up into a bun, and it was clear that she didn't like the idea of all these strangers showing up all of a sudden, but at the same time she seemed to understand.

"Your aunt asked to be notified once you arrived," she said quietly to John.

"It's too late. Let her sleep."

But a woman appeared through a doorway, and hurried down the hall. Tears were in her eyes, and she hugged John tightly.

"I saw the news," she said. "Does this mean the bad people—"

John nodded, a somber smile on his lips, and said, "Yes."

We were taken to a wing on the far side of the mansion. John and Ashley were shown to a room, and Jen and Casey and I were shown to another. It was a tight space, only two twin-sized beds and a wooden table and lamp. A painting of Jesus hung on the wall, looking down on us. Once the nun left, and it was just the three of us alone for the first time in over two years, in the sudden silence we stared at each other, like we weren't sure what to do next, and then I stepped forward and kissed Jen on the lips and kissed Casey on her forehead, and we held each other as we cried.

As promised, Drew and Ho Sook arrived in the morning. Drew's leg was wrapped, and he needed the use of crutches to walk.

We had breakfast in the dining room. About fifty children were in the dining room too, children that John and Ashley had saved over the years or those still in the system who hadn't found any foster homes yet. Sister Sara had announced that we were friends visiting for a few days and then left it at that, and while some of the kids threw us curious glances, most of them busied themselves with their meals as they talked and laughed amongst themselves.

Casey sat between Jen and me, and we noticed how she watched the children interact, and it broke my heart to realize that my daughter probably hadn't seen another girl or boy her age in almost two years.

Mason was the one who talked most during breakfast. With a hushed voice he told us about what happened at the site in McLaughlin, and how they'd managed to secure the facility before the local cops even showed up, and there was a touch of pride in his voice that didn't quite match the sorrow in his face, and then he paused halfway through and wiped at his eyes.

"I just miss Anthony so goddamned much," he whispered. Then, remembering that children were nearby, as well as nuns, he looked around quickly and said: "Whoops."

Nobody else wanted to talk much about their experience at the sites. It was clear that everybody was just happy it was all over. They'd all heard about Graham, and what he'd done, and Ronny had made a comment about him being a hero, and nobody disputed this.

Afterward, when we cleared our trays and headed back to our rooms, Sister Sara pulled me aside.

"If you don't mind, I would like Sister Jessica to meet with your wife and daughter sometime today." She noted the question in my face, and quickly added, "She works as a therapist with the children here."

I nodded numbly. Of course Jen and Casey would need therapy. I wanted to kick myself for not thinking of it sooner. It certainly made sense, especially based on what had happened last night. We'd pushed the twin beds together, so we could all be in the same bed, Jen on one side, me on the other, with Casey between us, and most of the night I hadn't slept, afraid that this was some dream and that the moment I fell asleep I'd wake from that dream and they'd be gone, and at least twice I needed to wake Casey from what appeared to be a nightmare as she kept trembling and whispering in her sleep.

"Would that be okay?" Sister Sara asked.

"Yes," I said. "Of course."

But then later in our room, when I broached the subject with Jen, she became angry.

"Absolutely not. I don't need to talk to any therapist. Neither does Casey."

"Jen—"

"You had no right to make that decision without me. No right whatsoever."

"Jen, please—"

"I said no!"

We'd been whispering back and forth, but this was enough to draw Casey's attention. She looked up at Jen.

"Mommy?"

I wasn't sure why Jen was giving me so much pushback. She'd dealt with depression and anxiety during her teenage years. She'd seen a psychiatrist. She'd gone to therapy. She'd always made it sound like it helped, but now when she and our daughter needed this kind of support the most, she was refusing.

Jen crouched down and took Casey into an embrace, and for the first time in the past forty-eight hours I just stood there and didn't feel compelled to join them. I felt like a stranger, an outsider, somebody who didn't belong here with the two people I loved more than anything else in the world, because for two years we'd been separated and tortured in our own different ways, and there was a chance we would never get back to a place where we stood on the same ground.

Finally Jen told Casey they would go for a walk, and she stood back up, wiping at her eyes.

"Okay," she whispered. "Fine. We'll see the therapist."

"Are you sure?"

She gave me a piercing look, like I was somebody she'd never met before and had no right to question her.

"God, Ben. Yes. Isn't that what I just said?"

And she walked out of the room, practically slamming the door behind her.

"It's going to take time," John Smith said.

"I know."

"It's going to take a lot of time."

"I know."

"I wish there was something more I could help you with, but …"

We were sitting on a bench out by the lake, watching a cluster of ducks float on the placid surface. The property took up about twenty acres, and much of it was pine trees. Some of the children were playing in a field, monitored by a few of the nuns. I'd considered getting Casey to see if she wanted to play with the children too—she'd looked too scared to approach any of them during breakfast—but I didn't want to risk Jen blowing up at me again.

I asked, "How long can we stay here?"

"The truth? I have no clue. Sister Sara can be generous and patient, but she's not that generous and patient."

"I spoke to Mason earlier. He said he and his wife plan to leave soon. They want to go back home. Which makes sense, I guess. They haven't been gone that long. It probably won't raise too many questions when they show back up. Except for what happened to Gloria's tongue. And for what happened to their son."

I shook my head slowly, still not being able to comprehend just how much anguish the two of them must still be going through. For two years I'd felt the loss of my family, but that loss wasn't quite the same as it must have been for Mason when he buried his own son.

"Titus will help where he can," John said. "He told me if

need be he can get new IDs, new social security numbers, new credit histories, whatever. His thinking is that most of you have been gone from your previous lives for years, and it's not like you can just show up now out of the blue, so it might be better to start over someplace else. He even said he'll throw in as much money as you need to get you started with your new lives."

"He's pretty amazing, isn't he?"

"That he is. In the next couple of days Ashley and I plan to drop off the Pax Romana vaccine at the CDC in Atlanta, and we figured what the hell, we'll go down to Florida to finally meet him in person."

"I think he'd like that."

We were quiet then for the next several minutes, just watching the ducks out on the lake, and then John shifted on the bench beside me.

"Were you scared right before your daughter was born?"

"I was terrified."

"Good. So that means I'm not the only one."

John smiled, but then the smile slipped off his face.

"I keep thinking that it's not really over. We may have stopped the Pax Romana, and we may have exposed the whole operation to the world, but the Legion ... some of them are still out there."

"I know. But there's always been bad people in the world. The only bright side—the only reason we shouldn't worry too much—is that there are way more good people."

The next day Mason and his wife headed out, and an hour later Ronny and Beverly announced that they planned to leave too. Where would they go? Neither of them quite knew, but Titus was providing them with new identifications, as promised, as well as some seed money, and they planned to stake out a home in a new part of the country.

Ho Sook and Chin had discussed about returning to South Korea, but there was nothing there for them there anymore, what with Chin's family having been killed in that automobile accident and Ho Sook ... well, with her father having been killed, she didn't have anybody either.

As for Drew, he wasn't sure what he would do next, he told me. He said he noticed that the nuns could use some help around the place and said he might talk to Sister Sara about staying to be a janitor or a maintenance man or somebody who took care of the grounds and everything else.

"Heck, I used to be a plumber," he said as we stood out near the trees behind the mansion, furtively smoking cigarettes. "This is what I do."

Yes, but he had also become an exceptional sniper, who had killed his fair share of bad guys, so I was pretty sure he could excel at whatever he put his mind to, but I didn't want to argue the point. Whatever made him happy.

He asked, "So did you start writing it yet?"

I frowned. "Did I start writing what?"

"The rest of the story. You know, so everybody will know the truth about what happened. How we"—he paused, and for the first time in a long while a smile touched his lips—"saved the world."

Honestly, I had zero interest in telling the rest of the story. Two years ago, I'd written about my game and how we'd beaten Simon because I'd just needed to get the story out. It had been therapeutic, I had come to understand, my way of moving past the trauma of waking up in a strange place three thousand miles from home with my wife and daughter missing, but now I had my family back ... or at least Jen and Casey were here with me, and we were together, though we weren't the same and probably never would be.

So why did I finally decide to sit down and write this? I guess because it's good to remember. It's good to know that Edmund Burke was right, and that the only thing necessary for the triumph of evil is for good men to do nothing.

Good men—and women—did something here, and because of that, we managed to beat that evil.

But that's not the only reason.

We've been here now for two weeks. Jen and Casey have met with Sister Jessica every day. Sister Jessica has also met with me, and she's explained how it's going to take a long time for Jen and Casey to heal, which I knew was the case but I guess it was good to hear it from somebody who knew what they were talking about.

Sister Jessica has been doing art therapy with Casey, providing her with blank pieces of paper and markers to express how she's feeling. My daughter was once the most talented little girl I had ever known, and the pictures she drew —often of characters from *The Little Prince*—were amazing. But Jen has since told me that Casey was denied paper and markers while they were being held captive, and in that time my daughter had lost that spark of imagination. She becomes easily frustrated now when she makes mistakes, and she'll take the paper and rip it up and throw the pieces on the floor.

She's done this at least three times, from what I've been told, and each time Sister Jessica calmly sits there, waiting for my daughter to tire from her temper tantrum, and then she'll lay another blank piece of paper down in front of her and tell her to try again.

You see, Augustus was both right and wrong when he said that in life there is no restart. Yes, it's true that if you die, you don't come back to life like characters do in a video game. But if you don't die, if you manage to stay alive long enough to see the next day, then in a way you've experienced a restart. No matter what mistakes you made the day before, no matter how badly you screwed up, you get another chance to change all of that for the better.

It's something that Casey is being taught, and in a way, it's something that both Jen and I are being taught too.

Eventually we're going to leave here, Jen and Casey and myself. We're going to find a new town to live in. We're going to start Casey in a new school, and Jen and I are going to find new jobs, and we're going to build a new life.

It won't happen overnight, and that's okay. At least we'll be together. We'll heal together. We'll manage to get through it together.

And, I guess, that's ultimately the reason I've written this story. Not just to tell about what a ragtag group of ordinary people managed to accomplish, especially those who've died over the years—Carver and the Kid and Graham and Jesse and Maya and Larry and Bronson and David and Vanessa and Seung and Bae—but that it's okay to feel defeated and depressed. To get angry at ourselves. To get angry at other people.

We all get countless restarts, though some of us get more than others.

It all comes down to how we use the restart. Whether we stand as still as statues and watch the world pass us by, or whether we ultimately take a step forward and do something.

Sister Sara says that it's God who gives us this chance, and maybe it is, or maybe it's just the human spirit within each of us.

That lets the sun rise every morning on a new day.

So that one of these days maybe, just maybe, we'll get it right.

ABOUT THE AUTHOR

Robert Swartwood is the *USA Today* bestselling author of *The Serial Killer's Wife*, *No Shelter*, *Man of Wax*, and several other novels. He created the term "hint fiction" and is the editor of *Hint Fiction: An Anthology of Stories in 25 Words or Fewer*. He lives with his wife in Pennsylvania.

www.ingramcontent.com/pod-product-compliance
Lightning Source LLC
Chambersburg PA
CBHW030555020726
47494CB00005B/1616